Blessed Are Those Who Mourn

By Kristi Belcamino

BLESSED ARE THE DEAD
BLESSED ARE THE MEEK
BLESSED ARE THOSE WHO WEEP
BLESSED ARE THOSE WHO MOURN

Blessed Are Those Who Mourn

A Gabriella Giovanni Mystery

KRISTI BELCAMINO

WITNESS IMPULSE
An Imprint of HarperCollinsPublishers

This is a work of fiction. Names, characters, places, and incidents are products of the author's imagination or are used fictitiously and are not to be construed as real. Any resemblance to actual events, locales, organizations, or persons, living or dead, is entirely coincidental.

BLESSED ARE THOSE WHO MOURN. Copyright © 2015 by Kristi Belcamino. All rights reserved under International and Pan-American Copyright Conventions. By payment of the required fees, you have been granted the nonexclusive, nontransferable right to access and read the text of this e-book on screen. No part of this text may be reproduced, transmitted, downloaded, decompiled, reverse-engineered, or stored in or introduced into any information storage and retrieval system, in any form or by any means, whether electronic or mechanical, now known or hereafter invented, without the express written permission of HarperCollins e-books.

EPub Edition SEPTEMBER 2015 ISBN: 9780062389428
Print Edition ISBN: 9780062389411

10 9 8 7 6 5 4 3 2 1

This one's for Supergroup

Chapter 1

Saturday

THE SETTING SUN turns my family into dark silhouettes as I step onto the warm sand. The beach is nearly deserted, except for a lone figure walking north of us along the sand where the waves are crashing in from the Pacific Ocean.

A cool breeze makes me glad I trekked to the car to retrieve my daughter's little lavender parka. We promised her we'd stay until the sun set.

Donovan's back is turned, phone held to his ear. He's pacing in his bare feet, his jeans rolled up, a scowl on his face from what he's hearing. A murder. Every once in a while he glances back at Grace kneeling in the sand, playing.

Grace has dug deep channels with a small red shovel, chatting to herself, weaving tales about mermaids and sea creatures and fairies. She bounces a plastic dinosaur along the sand, a prize won in kindergarten for reading two books in one week.

Everything I've ever wanted is on that beach—Donovan and our daughter, Grace. My own little family. My life.

I'm still far away, closer to the parking lot, when I see the figure walking along the shore growing closer. It's a man. His shadow, with its elongated arms and legs, stretches across the beach until it seems to take on a life of its own. Something about the way he moves seems frenetic and sets off small alarms in my head. I walk faster, the sand seeming to reach up and grab at my ankles, slowing my progress.

Donovan's pacing takes him in the opposite direction, away from Grace. He's not paying attention to anything besides his phone call. The man is now closer to Grace, who seems alone on the beach, although Donovan is twenty feet away. Donovan squints up into the pink and orange clouds, raking a hand through his perpetually spiky hair.

The man's path takes him straight toward Grace. My heart races. I can't tell for sure, but it seems like he's looking right at her. He walks at a determined clip, covering ground much faster than me in my flat, strappy sandals. I lean over in midstride and rip a sandal from one foot without stopping. Then I scoop up the other in one fluid motion.

Still, each step feels like my bare feet are being sucked into quicksand. I hurry but feel like I'm moving in slow motion.

"Grace," I shout, but my words are carried away on the wind. I'm nearly breathless from fighting the sand tugging at my feet. The breeze, which has grown stronger in the past few minutes, whips my hair. Grace's brown ringlets bob as she hops her plastic dinosaur around, not noticing anything else.

Donovan isn't far from Grace, but now the man is closer.

At the same moment Donovan turns and sees the look on

my face, the man reaches Grace. His long shadow falls over her small figure. She looks up with a smile and starts chatting. He leans down. His hand reaches toward her, his fingers millimeters from her arm. A wave of dread ripples through me. My feet feel cemented into the sand. My mind screams, but no words come out of my open mouth. Inside, I'm flailing and thrashing to get to Grace, but on the outside, I'm struck immobile.

The man reaches down and grasps Grace's arm, turning her toward him, and the spell is broken. I'm on wet sand, running, the scream caught in my throat coming out as a birdlike garble. I scoop Grace up onto one hip and take a step back. I gasp for air. My heart is going to explode in my chest.

The man looks at me with surprise, and for a split second, there is something in his eyes that sends panic racing up into my throat, but then the look is gone, as if I imagined it.

"Gosh. I'm so stupid." His voice is nasally. He wipes his palms on the legs of his jeans, as if he is sweating even though the temperature is rapidly dipping along with the sun.

Donovan is at my side.

At first glance, the man seems boyish, with his bowl haircut, baggy jeans, and sneakers. Up close, a few crow's-feet shows he is older. Maybe even closer to my age—thirties. He has feminine pink lips and piercing blue eyes, the color of Arctic sea ice. The collar of his black jacket is pulled up. His smile is all "gee, golly, shucks," abashed and embarrassed, but it doesn't reach his eyes. He paws at his jeans with his palms. He's done that twice now. He's nervous.

When the man meets my eyes again, I realize that something about him seems off, something about his eyes, more than just their intense color. One eye is close to his nose, and the other is set far apart. It's jarring and somehow unsettling.

"I'm so sorry," he says in that same stuffed-up-sounding voice. "What a knuckleheaded move. I should know better than to walk up to someone else's kid like that."

Donovan grips my arm.

"Everything okay here?" His words are clipped.

I'm finally able to catch my breath. Still, the words will not come.

"Your kid is so darn cute." The man won't meet my eyes. "She looks just like my little sister used to look. I just wanted to say hi to her and didn't even think that was a total bonehead move to walk up to someone else's kid when her parents weren't around." He gives an odd smile as he says this, looking at Donovan.

"We were around," Donovan says in a monotone, staring the man down.

The man looks at the sand.

Grace is kicking and trying to get down. My knuckles are white gripping her.

"Ow, Mama, you're hurting me," she says and tosses her curls in irritation.

Donovan shoots a glance our way before turning his attention back to the man.

"You live around here?" Donovan asks, seemingly casual, but the muscle in his jaw is working hard. His dark eyes under thick eyebrows have narrowed and hold a glint of menace. In a second, it alters him from the man on the cover of the Sexiest Bay Area Cops calendar into something feral and dangerous.

The man meets Donovan's eyes, and for a second it looks like he is challenging Donovan to dispute his story, but then he looks down again and digs a sneakered toe into the sand.

"Marin. Meeting some friends here in the city for dinner. Was early, so I came here to kill some time. I didn't mean to cause any problems. I just wanted to say hi to her. Maybe you're overreacting a bit."

Donovan runs a hand through his hair. His posture relaxes. Instinctively—or luckily—this man has honed in on Donovan's Achilles' heel. We've talked at length about our tendency to be overprotective parents because of our jobs, me as a crime reporter, and him as a detective. Donovan has argued we can't let this affect Grace's childhood. We need to protect her but let her grow up carefree. I agree. But it's easier said than done.

We've also talked about my irrational fear that something will happen to Grace.

This man, whoever he is, may not realize it, but he's instantly off the hook with this one simple word—"overreacting."

"Why don't you continue on your way, buddy," Donovan says, dismissing him.

"My bad, really. Wasn't using my head. Have a nice night," the man says and turns to leave.

I set Grace down, and Donovan wraps his arm around me.

"You okay?"

"I don't know." I don't tell him that it felt like I was having a heart attack, that I couldn't breathe or move. A stranger walked up to my daughter and I stood there, weak, helpless, frozen.

Donovan gives me a look before we both turn and watch the man's figure growing smaller. We watch without saying a word. We stand there until the man turns and heads toward the wooden boardwalk bordering the road. He never looks back.

Chapter 2

"Wasn't there something you wanted to talk about before your phone rang?" I ask after the man leaves.

"Another time," Donovan says, looking away.

Earlier, he was acting odd: pulling me away from Grace, swallowing, shoving his hands in his jacket pockets, and not meeting my eyes. Then his partner Finn called. Nine times out of ten, that call meant they were up for a murder. As Donovan talked to Finn, I spotted goose bumps on Grace's bare arms. We'd promised her we wouldn't leave until the sun set, so I went to grab her jacket out of the car.

Now, with her wrapped in the jacket and snuggling close to me, my heart has returned to normal. I'm appalled at how my own body betrayed me by freezing when I needed to act. The man's "gee shucks" act didn't fool me. There was something about him that struck terror in my heart.

"Look, Mama," Grace says. The three of us turn toward the horizon as the last orange sliver of the sun slips into the dark water.

"No, green." The corners of Grace's little pink lips turn down in disappointment.

"Maybe next time," Donovan says, ruffling her curls with his hand. "If it happened every time the sun set, it wouldn't be magical, would it?"

Her face scrunches as she thinks about this. She takes his hand as we walk to the car.

We talked about the green flash on the drive here. How a vivid and intense green light could appear right as the sun disappears. How she had to keep her eyes open as the sun set, since the flash only lasted a second. Sitting in her little car seat on the drive to the beach, she practiced not blinking so she wouldn't miss it.

It's not until we are in the car and Grace has dozed off in her car seat that Donovan brings up what happened at the beach.

"Dude probably didn't mean anything. Unless you're a parent, you don't think of things like that, that coming up to someone else's kid is not cool."

It sounds like he's trying to convince himself.

"He *grabbed her arm.*"

"Come on, Ella. You know you and me got some baggage around strangers coming up to kids." He says this staring straight ahead out the windshield. When I don't answer he darts a glance my way, but I quickly turn my head and look out the window.

My sister's murder isn't *baggage*. But deep down inside I know what he means. We both have a tendency to be overprotective and sometimes over react.

Like last year when a man came up to Grace while she was playing in Washington Square Park. I was sitting nearby on a bench, drinking a cappuccino. My phone was ringing, and I was digging around in my big purse to find it. When I looked up, I couldn't see Grace. When I spotted her near the edge of the park, a man in a hat was leading her by the hand. I took off at a run.

When I reached them, I barked, "Let go of my daughter," and yanked the man's arm so hard he fell on his butt. To my horror, it was my grandfather's old friend Gino. I hadn't recognized him with a hat on.

Gino blinked up at me with a confused look. I apologized profusely and helped him up, feeling awful, especially when I saw his wife, Carmela, on a bench at the edge of the park. She watched us, horrified.

"I was just taking Grace over to say hello to Carmela," Gino said. "Carmela's knee is so bad, she can't walk on this uneven grass."

It was mortifying.

When I told Donovan about it, I cried, saying I would never be a normal mother. I would always be looking for danger around every corner.

But today is different.

I know what I saw on the beach. I know what I saw in that man's eyes. *Stay the fuck away from my kid.*

Donovan changes the subject.

"Finn says we caught a body in Suisun Bay," he says, looking in the rearview mirror at Grace. She's in a deep sleep, her mouth hanging open, softly snoring. It's past her bedtime.

"Floater?" I ask.

"You're going to want to be there."

Instead of taking the exit for Oakland, he keeps going. Without saying a word, it's agreed—we're dropping Grace at my mom's house in the East Bay.

Chapter 3

THE WAVES ARE gently lapping against the body lying on the banks of Roe Island in Suisun Bay. It's not the first time a dead body has been found near the entrance to the Delta, a waterway that stretches inland near Sacramento. Giant spotlights shine down on the sandy bank, covered in driftwood and seaweed. As darkness falls, shadows grow longer and anyone outside the circle of light is hard to see. I stand in the dark with a cluster of other reporters gathered on this tiny island, watching and waiting, shifting from foot to foot.

My stomach growls as I think about the leftover linguine with lobster sauce dinner waiting for me at home. I'm still uneasy about how I reacted at Ocean Beach. Aren't mothers supposed to have superhuman strength when their kids are in danger? My greatest fear is something bad happening to my daughter. But today, when I thought she was in danger, instead of springing to her rescue, I was frozen with fear. Another thing to bring up with my therapist next week. I've been seeing Marsha for seven years. I've made progress, but I'm still dealing with my sister's death and the knowledge that I've killed two men. The deaths were ruled self-defense. But in the darkest of night, my conscience whispers that no matter how it's dressed up, I'm a killer.

Now that I'm a mom, I wonder what this means for my daughter. How am I supposed to teach her right and wrong without sounding like a Class A hypocrite? What happens when she is old enough to find out what I have done?

Tonight, on this tiny island, I push down those worries and shift from Italian Mama into crime reporter mode. I'm peering through binoculars as I stand way back from the crime-scene tape. The dead woman has long blond hair. She seems thin in soggy jeans and a dirty white fisherman's sweater. One shoe is still on, a white Converse tennis shoe. She's sopping wet, but she's not bloated and discolored like a floater. If she'd been in the water, it hadn't been for long.

Donovan is crouched beside her, eyes narrowed.

"Wish they'd turn her over so I could see her face," the cameraman from Channel 5 says beside me. He hoists his heavy camera onto his shoulder for a second and then decides to put it back on its heavy-duty tripod.

"Not me," I say.

I ended up hitching a ride to the island with the Channel 5 news crew in a boat they rented. Donovan was escorted front and center in the sheriff's launch that ferried all the cops to the island, a half mile offshore. He waved and winked as I sat on the dock with the rest of the media. I was not amused.

I called my close friend and favorite photographer at our paper, Chris Lopez, on the drive in, but he was shooting a Giants game and said not to wait for him. He'd figure out his own ride onto the island.

Now, all the reporters huddle behind the crime-scene tape, trying to warm our cold hands while we wait for some official to come talk to us. All the TV camera guys have jockeyed for pole position and are lined up in a row facing the sandy bank.

I absentmindedly adjust my press pass, on a lanyard around my neck, identifies me as a reporter with the *Bay Herald*. In the distance, the fog parts, revealing the massive shapes of several dozen ships anchored in the middle of the water. They stand sentry against the remaining traces of light on the horizon. I point my binoculars toward the fleet.

Nicknamed both the "Phantom Fleet" and the "Mothball Fleet," the Suisun Bay Reserve Fleet is a ship graveyard that is home to dozens of U.S. Navy warships that are decommissioned or inactive and some old merchant ships, probably about seventy-five altogether.

A shiver trips down my spine as I look at the looming carcasses of once-great warships. I'm sure they must all be haunted by the souls of all the dead sailors who once lived there.

"Ever gone out there, Giovanni?" the cameraman asks, seeing where I'm looking.

"What? How?"

"They did a media tour back in 1990 for some big anniversary of one of the ships. Got to see inside. Trippy. Some of the cabins still have books and beds, perfectly preserved from the 1970s. It was like a ghost ship. I could almost hear eerie music filtering around and the cannons blasting."

I knew it.

"Must've been before my time at the paper," I say, returning my gaze to the beach behind the crime-scene tape. "Wish I would've been able to go."

He readjusts the tripod his heavy camera rests on and fiddles with some cables as he talks. "You could launch a rubber dinghy at the slough in between Coast Guard patrols. They are usually every half hour. See the station over there? They are supposed to guard the ship against squatters. You have to pull your boat up on the ship or you're busted."

"You did that?"

He chuckles and adjusts the focus on the camera lens he has pointing toward the dead body on the beach. "Nah, not me. I'm not that dumb. But I grew up in Benicia. This was our backyard. A kid I knew snuck onboard in high school. Claimed it was a cool place to party. There used to be more than three hundred ships here then, so it was easier to get away with. Plus it was before nine-eleven. There was only one old beat-up patrol boat, and the dude was probably drunk half the time anyway. You've got to go a few rows in, though, or they could see you from the Coast Guard station."

I study the dead woman's body through my binoculars again. I can't figure it out. She's not bloated and gruesome-looking like a drowning. She looks like she's resting from a swim. How did she wash up on this forgotten little island?

"Who found her?" I ask. A fisherman, most likely, since the channel nearby is a popular fishing spot. But even then, what were the odds someone spotted her on this shore?

"Tipster," the cameraman says.

I'm glad I decided to stand near this guy. He's obviously got some good insider information from a source. Crime scenes can be like happy hours. While reporters wait for an official to give us details, we gossip about off-the-record info we've heard. But never with the competing newspaper, only with the TV people, and never anything that is truly a scoop. I eye Andy Black, from the *San Francisco Tribune*. It looks like he's trying to charm information from the well-endowed Channel 4 reporter. Like always, he looks like a hair-and-makeup crew on a movie set just finished touching him up. Guess that's what you look like when you work for the biggest paper in town. I cringe thinking I ever found his preppy good looks attractive.

"What else did you hear?" I ask.

"Doesn't your cop husband give you the skinny?" the cameraman asks, squinting at me sideways.

"He's not my husband." I'm glad the dark hides the heat flaring across my cheeks.

"Well, then your baby daddy or whatever you call him?"

I'm opening my mouth to answer when the crowd clears and Rosarito Police Sergeant Beverly Anne Fazio heads our way in her navy blue police uniform, her sleek auburn bob ruffled by the wind. She sees me and offers a quick smile before growing serious and professional.

All the reporters stop talking and cluster around her. She stands so the orange skies of the Martinez refineries lit up in the dark are behind her, puffy clouds of refinery smoke billowing out at regular intervals.

"At eighteen hundred hours we received word that a body had been found at Preston Point on Roe Island," she says. "The Coast Guard and Solano County sheriff's water patrol units deployed boats to investigate. Upon arriving, officers found the deceased body of a woman in her twenties. The medical examiner's office will confirm identity and determine cause of death."

The island is in Solano County, but it still doesn't explain why Rosarito PD and Donovan, aka *my baby daddy,* were called out. I'm grumbling inside about the cameraman calling him that.

I know I'm extra sensitive because my entire Italian-American family is mortified I had a child out of wedlock, but I'm not getting married simply because they want me to. We keep talking about tying the knot, but who has time? With Donovan's schedule as a murder cop and my erratic schedule as a crime reporter, lately we're lucky if we're able to do what we did tonight—have a few hours with just the three of us together. Who says we need a piece of paper to prove it anyway? Oh yeah—according to my family, that would be the pope.

As soon as Beverly Anne finishes speaking, several reporters shoot questions at her all at once.

"How long has she been dead?"

"Is there any sign she drowned?"

"Are you investigating it as a homicide?"

Beverly Anne holds up her hand. "Come on, guys, you know the drill. Just because we're on a deserted island doesn't mean you should forget your manners. Okay, Mary Jo, you first. You asked whether it's a homicide. Right now, we are investigating it as a suspicious death."

More reporters throw questions out. Andy Black and I hang back, waiting, as we usually do, for the TV reporters to take a breath. I scoot as far away from him as possible.

At that moment, a small boat careens in near the shore where giant spotlights are set up to illuminate the crime scene. The cops use their hands to shield their eyes, squinting toward the noise. The boat's waves lap the shore, making the body bob where it rests at the edge of the water.

The cops scowl and shout at the boater. In the shadows of the boat, a figure holding a camera snaps off pictures. The engine on the small boat starts up again, and a familiar cackle drifts across the water. In the commotion, the press conference is forgotten. Who would have the balls to come in at the murder scene from the water? Lopez. He lives and breathes the crime beat. He's never without a small earbud headphone trailing down to the police scanner clipped to his belt.

Lopez was with me the night I hunted down and killed Jack Dean Johnson at the former Fort Ord military base after he kidnapped my niece. At the time I also thought he'd killed my sister.

As soon as everyone settles down, Beverly Anne turns back to us, and Black speaks up. He's so nonchalant that you wouldn't suspect what a lying snake he becomes just to get a story.

"Is it true that a tipster called in the body?" he asks.

Beverly Anne purses her red lips together for a second, thinking, and then decides it's okay to answer. "Yes."

My turn. The question I've been waiting to ask.

She sees my hand.

"Gabriella?"

"Do you have any way of tracing calls that come into your tip line?"

"I'm not at liberty to release that information," she says, shooting me a warning look. Beverly Anne and I have hung out at department picnics and are friends, but she's not going to play favorites. She's a real cop.

Plus, she's sharp. She knows my question was geared to find out if the tipster had called the Rosarito Police Department or a different cop shop. She just confirmed it. I've been wracking my brains trying to figure out why Donovan and the Rosarito Police Department are on this homicide if it's on some island in the Suisun Bay. Rosarito is around the peninsula from here. The closest Solano County city is Benicia. Both Benicia and Solano County investigators are here, but why is Rosarito involved? *Unless the tipster called their tip line.*

Chapter 4

AFTER THE PRESS conference ends, the TV crews hang around, waiting to go live on the ten o'clock news. I head for the east side of the island, waiting a few seconds until I see that Andy Black is deep in conversation with the Channel 4 reporter before I slip behind some brush. It won't take long for him to talk her into going back to his place. I know. I also know that he's ruthless and will sleep with anyone for a scoop.

Stickers and small branches tear at my bare legs as I tromp through the bushes. A small strip of beach lies between the shrubs and the water, so I make my way toward that, keeping to the sand bordering the water. The farther I get from the murder scene and the big spotlights, the darker it gets and the louder the crickets become. I unearth my small flashlight from my bag. The island can't be that big. I figure I will round it and meet up with someone at the south side, where I can hitch a ride back to the dock.

To the west, the fog has rolled in, erasing the orange skies of the Martinez refineries and the looming ships of the Phantom Fleet like they never existed. I pick my way along the shore, not sure what I'm looking for. Maybe the woman's handbag or something else that belongs to her has washed up nearby.

My focus is on the wet sand near the shore, so when my flashlight reveals deep footprints embedded in the sand, I know they are fresh. There are two sets of prints, coming and going. I follow them back toward the crime scene until they dead-end at a tall bank of tangled branches. What I see there makes me draw back.

Branches are broken in one spot, revealing a perfect glimpse of the detectives working on the crime scene more than thirty feet away. Someone was here. Watching. An icy chill races down my spine. I look behind me but see nothing. The fog has crept onto the island now and is making its way toward me. Without thinking, I shine my flashlight down on the receding footprints and follow them. I'm short of breath, and my heart is pounding when I round a corner and see something move.

In the fog, about ten feet away, a figure in a thick jacket and baseball cap pushes a small rubber boat away from the shore. His hat is pulled low over his face so I can't see his features. Before he leaps into the boat, the man turns, his arm swooping in a big arc as he tosses something onto the shore behind him. Then the fog swallows him and the boat into its midst.

My shout brings Donovan and several other cops running. It takes them nearly a minute to get to me since they have to take the same path I did inland and around the big thorny brush near the shore.

"A man took off in a boat right here. He threw this at me," I say when they finally arrive, pointing to the sand. "He was watching you guys through the bushes."

I spend the next ten minutes telling Donovan's partner, Finn, what I saw. Finn, balding, soft-spoken, and as tall and thin as a poplar, takes careful notes.

As soon as I'm done, the media is booted off the island. The TV reporters grumble. The entire island is now considered a crime scene. I watch as they bag the small white plastic square he threw at me. I don't say that I saw what it was. Before the police responded to my shout, I shined my light on it and memorized what it said.

All the journalists are crammed on one boat this time. The cops aren't messing around. They want us gone yesterday.

Somehow, Black worms his way over to where I sit in the small boat, trying not to get motion sick as the boat lurches and bucks in the waves.

"Nice going, Giovanni, ruined the live shot for the TV folks," Black says with a smirk. "What'd you see out there anyway?"

I shake my head and look away, glad the wind blows my hair across my face so he won't see me flushing red with anger and embarrassment. Black got the best of me once a long time ago. Never again.

The man in the boat had thrown a college ID from the University of California, Santa Cruz onto the sand. Agnes Clark. Twenty-two years old. Although I have no way of knowing for sure, my gut tells me it belongs to the dead woman on the beach. In the ID photo, the woman's blond hair is sleek, her smile brilliant, her eyes twinkling with mischief. With life. A friend. Daughter. Maybe sister. Dead now. The figure on the boat had wanted me to see it—had thrown it right at me. But why?

Chapter 5

THE NEWSROOM IS nearly empty when I rush in an hour before deadline.

A few reporters remain, pounding on their keyboards. The big-screen TV that takes up one whole wall of the newsroom blares highlights from the Oakland A's game. A few copy editors gather around the table where we put free food. Someone scored mini muffins from a local bakery, and people are popping them like pills. I throw my bag on my desk and head for the food, but when I show up, there is only a box with crumbs.

"I need food ASAP!" I shout to nobody in particular. "If I don't get something to eat soon, there's going to be another murder to write about around here."

Nobody looks at me.

The executive editor, Matt Kellogg, is squeezed into his cubicle, big belly indented where it is squished against his desk, knees crunched, brow furrowed in concentration. He refuses to move into a big corner office, claiming he wants to be on the newsroom floor with his "troops." I called him on the way in and gave him the gist of my story.

I pause beside him.

"How much room do I got?"

"Fifteen inches. Paper's tight tonight," he says, stroking his bushy beard without looking away from his screen.

"Got it."

"Hold up," he says when I start to walk away. He digs under a stack of today's newspapers and hands me a small pizza box. "I don't have space for another murder in the paper. Save it for tomorrow."

I sneak a peek inside the box on my way to my desk. Score! Two pieces of sausage and pepperoni pizza. Settling in at my desk, I wolf down one piece of the pizza, washing it down with an old bottle of water that tastes like dirt.

While I wait for my computer to boot up, I dig in my bag for my cell phone.

I'd called Donovan on the drive to the newsroom, but he couldn't talk. Probably worried someone would think he was giving me insider dirt on the murder. I wish. Or maybe he was going to warn me not to use what I saw on the ID.

I won't use her name, because the last thing in the world I want to do is have her family read about it in the newspaper before the cops do a death notification. But there are some details I'm going to include. For instance, that she was a twenty-two-year-old college student in Santa Cruz.

When I unearth my phone, I'm rewarded with a text from Donovan: *We need to talk. Call me after deadline.*

I won't see him tonight. It's the first twenty-four hours of a homicide investigation, so he'll work straight through the night. I think of the bottle of red wine I picked up earlier to have with our lobster linguine after Grace went to bed. So much for a romantic Saturday night together.

I'm logging onto my computer when the night cops reporter, May, slides into her seat. I give her a cursory hello. "Anything else going on besides my murder?"

She bends and buffs a scuff on her white Chanel flats as she speaks, her neat brown bob hiding her face. "Not really. They had a missing kid earlier today, but she ended up being at a park near her house."

Once upon a time, just the words "missing kid" would have sent me into a panic attack. Now I take it in stride. It's hard to believe it's been nearly thirty years since Caterina was kidnapped.

I punch out a quick story about the murder and scan the pictures Lopez e-mailed to me.

"Want to see the murder shots?" I ask May. Most of them are no good for the paper. We don't print pictures of dead bodies. But one picture is spectacular and will shoot my story right to the front page. The foreground of the pictures shows dark water leading to a shoreline where several cops, including Donovan, crouch in a half circle. The body in the foreground is blurry, so the paper will probably use it. The cops' faces are, however, in focus. Some of the men are smoking. All of them are frowning or have intense looks. Behind them, about ten feet back, stands a blurry line of journalists holding cameras and notepads. I'm grateful that I was somewhere in the back. Standing in front of the journalists, Sergeant Beverly Anne is in focus, turned halfway toward the camera, looking right into it. Her auburn hair is whipping in the wind, and she holds up a hand to shield her eyes, trying to figure out who is interrupting her press conference. C-Lo is brilliant at capturing the exact mood of a scene.

May avoids answering my question about seeing the photo, adjusting the silky scarf around her neck and changing the subject. "Anything on that Roe Island murder that needs following tonight?"

Questions like that are why I'm glad May's the night cops reporter even though we really don't like each other that much. I gather up my things but keep my computer on with the pictures of the murder scene, squinting to see if there was something there I missed.

"Sure. Make a call before you leave to see if there's anything new," I say. "There's a slight chance they'll release the ID tonight if they're able to do the death notification. Beverly Anne will have her cell on until eleven thirty."

"Will do. I'll be sure to give Sergeant Fazio a call." I can tell by the way she emphasizes *Fazio* that she's irritated I refer to the sergeant by first name only.

May returns to her grooming, this time pouting her thin lips and slicking on light pink lipstick while glancing into a compact mirror. But then she turns to me.

"Isn't your boyfriend on this one?"

"Yeah, like that helps."

I stare more at the picture on my computer screen and pick up my phone. "Hey, C-Lo, I think the killer was out there on the water about the same time as you."

"No way, man."

"Yeah. You see anything?"

"Nah, I didn't see nothing except the sheriff's boats chasing my ass back to shore."

Before I log off my computer, I shoot Liz, the news researcher at our paper, an e-mail asking her to search for information on Agnes Clark and also to dig up background on the Phantom Fleet.

I'm always looking for features stories to work on when the crime beat is slow.

With my bag slung over my shoulder, I hover at Kellogg's desk until he looks up.

"When's the last time someone wrote about the Phantom Fleet?" I ask.

Kellogg pushes his large frame back from his desk and scratches his chin, grunting. His eyes narrow as he thinks.

"I'm gonna say 1990. Some anniversary deal. Stanford wrote a small piece, but it was mostly a photo essay. C-Lo was the shooter. Got some cool shots. Why? You want to do a piece on it?"

"Yeah."

"What's your angle?"

"I was thinking maybe I could find some local guys who were on those ships and do a spread for the Memorial Day weekend."

Kellogg squints at his calendar. "That's about a month away. That'd work. Get up with C-Lo on it. Keep me posted."

In the car, I shoot Donovan a text. *On way home.*

My phone rings a few seconds later.

"There was something in her pocket." His voice is low, as if someone is nearby.

I wonder why Mr. Goody Two-shoes, Play-by-the-Rules Cop is telling me this. But then he continues, and my mouth grows dry.

"A Bible verse written on a piece of paper. A familiar verse."

"Jesus Mary and Joseph." I'm hyperventilating, and my face grows warm. With one fluid motion I crank the wheel and pull over to the side of the road right before the entrance to the Caldecott Tunnel that connects the East Bay to Oakland. Frank Anderson, the man I'm convinced killed my sister, sent me Bible verses a few years ago.

"Probably a coincidence," Donovan says. "A lot of killers are religious freaks."

"Right." I press my forehead to the cool glass of the driver's side window.

"But it might not be."

"Right." I stare at the taillights of cars passing me until they become blurry red streaks.

"I'll meet you and Grace at the after-party tomorrow," Donovan says. Every Sunday after mass, my huge Italian-American family gathers at my grandmother's house for a giant feast we've dubbed the "after-party."

I'm bringing those *pignoli* cookies I bought last week. Unless you ate them all," I say. I hid the cookies in a tightly sealed bag in the back of the freezer so Donovan wouldn't eat them all before Sunday.

"Nah. Haven't seen them. Where are they anyway? I love me a *pignoli* cookie with my coffee in the morning."

"I'm not telling you," I say, laughing. Hiding them behind the frozen plastic container of sauce worked. I'll have to remember that.

"By the way," he says, growing serious again. "I'm calling Agent West."

Because of the Bible verse found on the body. We haven't spoken to the FBI agent for a while. If there is any chance Frank Anderson has surfaced—and the Bible verse could mean that, or mean nothing at all—West needs to know. West is an old friend of Donovan's who took over Caterina's case a few years ago. He figures Anderson has either stopped kidnapping girls or has taken his predilections off the grid, somewhere very far away where his crimes wouldn't make it in the NCIC—the National Crime Information Center—database that tracks crime across the country.

"One more thing," Donovan says. "This isn't for print, either—the piece of paper was not soaked. It was damp, but not wet like it would've been if it was in her pocket when she was in the water."

I think about that for a second. Someone stuck it in the woman's pocket after she washed ashore. If only the fog hadn't concealed that man on the boat so quickly.

IN SAN FRANCISCO, I pull into our garage and don't get out of my car until the door closes. Once it does, I grab my bag and punch the security code for our private elevator to take me to our condo. When it opens, the lights in the kitchen and living room, which are on timers, are lit, and soft music plays through the intercom system. I hate coming home to a dark and quiet house.

I feel a little pang when I walk past Grace's empty room. She spends the night at my mom's frequently—usually when Donovan and I are working late unexpectedly—but even so, I still miss seeing her warm little body asleep in her pink sheets.

After changing into a pair of baggy shorts, tank top, and a hoodie, I head for the kitchen. Dusty comes out of his hiding spot and winds his gray body around my legs as I dip into the container of cat food and give him a healthy portion. I fill a small bowl with salted almonds and head toward the end of the galley kitchen to our makeshift bar on the counter—a big silver tray with bottles of alcohol. A large silver mirror reflects the colors on the sparkling bottles, but I reach underneath to the built-in freezer below and pull out a bottle of Absolut vodka.

After pouring three fingers worth, I retreat to a small cubby in the living room where my laptop rests on a tiny desk. I pop almonds into my mouth as I log into my e-mail account. It doesn't take long to find the e-mails I'm looking for.

Frank Anderson last wrote to me right before I got pregnant with Grace about six years ago. He sent four e-mails, each one containing at least one Bible verse.

I click on the first one he sent. My heart is pounding.

Subject line: *Sins of the Father.*

Inside, the e-mail reads, *Exodus 20:5 You shall not bow down to them or serve them, for I the Lord your God am a jealous God, visiting the iniquity of the fathers on the children to the third and the fourth generation of those who hate me.*

I dial Donovan.

"Was it the first one he sent? The ones about sins of the father?"

"Stand by." I hear some rustling of papers. "It said, 'I am a jealous God, visiting the iniquity of the fathers on the children.' That was it. Not the whole Bible verse, just a part of it. Listen, I gotta go."

He hangs up.

Taunting police was never Frank Anderson's style. And this killer's MO is different. This killer likes women, not little girls.

In any case, I'm glad Grace is with my mother, sleeping safely in a house with an alarm system in a gated community. It's late, so when I dial my mother's number, I'm not surprised that she doesn't pick up. I leave a message telling her I love her and Grace. I'll wait to tell her about the Bible verse when we know more. I don't want to alarm or upset her for no good reason. After all, it could be nothing.

Caterina, older than me by a year, was kidnapped from in front of our house when she was seven. Some off-road bicyclists found her little body six days later. It wasn't until I was older that I realized she'd been kept alive somewhere for days. The horror of imagining what she went through during that time has helped keep me in therapy as an adult.

Several years ago, before Grace was born, I got a lead on the person who I believe killed Caterina. Frank Anderson had recently been paroled from prison as a convicted sex offender. By the time I came across his name, he was on the lam, dodging his mandatory check-in with authorities.

With the help of Liz, the news researcher at our paper, I tracked down a house owned by his girlfriend. He escaped out the back of the house seconds before I found him. His girlfriend was later found dead of a drug overdose. After that, he began sending me the e-mails with the return e-mail FA2858. It didn't take me long to figure out that "FA" stood for Frank Anderson, whose birthday was 2-8-58. The e-mails stopped shortly before I got pregnant with Grace.

After a lazy Livermore detective dropped the ball, trying to trace the e-mails and working my sister's murder as a cold case, we turned to Special Agent Noah West. But now the case has grown even colder. Anderson has gone underground. I thought I was safe.

Now I'm not so sure.

Chapter 6

Sunday

IN THE MORNING, I'm unusually anxious to see Grace, so I skip mass at Joan of Arc's and head straight to my mother's house as soon as the sun rises.

I drove Donovan's car back from Roe Island last night. He was going to hitch a ride back to the police department and use his assigned detective vehicle for the rest of the weekend.

The guards at the entrance to my mom's neighborhood, tucked at the foot of Mt. Diablo, examine my pass and then open the gates, waving me in. The streets are deserted at this early hour except for one lady briskly walking a small white dog. I wave at her as I park.

Stepping out of the car, the air is cool, so I pull on the parka Donovan left in the backseat. When he got to the crime scene last night, he traded the light jacket he wore on the beach for a heavier leather one he keeps in the trunk. I pull the collar up against the chill morning air and dig my hands deep into the pockets. I'm at my mom's front door when I feel something in one of the pockets. Something velvety and square. I pause on the front steps fingering the small box, knowing what it is before I pull it out. The tiny black velvet box fits in my palm. It's from my favorite jeweler in North Beach. Their emblem is on the bottom. I turn the box over and over in my hand, closing my eyes. My heart is racing. No wonder Donovan was acting so nervous last night on the beach at sunset.

I'm tempted to open the box, but I stop myself. It wouldn't be right. It's like cheating on a test or opening your Christmas presents early. My sister was always the one who did that and then tried to wrap them back up. I'm pretty sure my mother could always tell that she'd snuck a peek. Me, I'd rather wait and be surprised.

No wonder Donovan pulled me aside last night and was so tongue-tied before he was interrupted by Finn's phone call. After that, the freaky guy approached Grace. That is so the story of our relationship and our life. Our jobs and our past always getting in the way, always a wedge between us.

The thought that Donovan was about to propose to me fills me with an odd anxiety. We have talked about getting married. We will get married one day. So why does finding this ring make me so nervous?

I push those thoughts aside and creep into the silence of my mother's house. My first stop is near the door, where I punch in the code disarming her alarm. The only sound is the ticking of the grandfather clock in the corner and the sound of a shower running somewhere.

I pause at the mantel, where my mother has all the pictures of her family.

There is only one picture that has all of us from when I was little. We are at a family picnic in Solvang, and my dad and brothers are in the background, roughhousing. Caterina and I have our arms looped around each other and are making goofy faces. My mother is looking behind us at my father and two brothers. Her mouth is open as if she is saying something. I don't know if it's a real memory or I've made it up from looking at the picture so many times while I was growing up, but in the picture she is scolding them in a mock serious voice for goofing around during the photo. But her harsh words are betrayed by a glint of merriment in her eyes.

That was before. When our lives were like a dream. When we seemed invincible—as if nothing could ever touch our charmed existence.

Only a few months later Caterina and my dad were dead and buried.

For a long time I worried that having a child would take away my love for my sister, but having Grace in my life has only proved what my grandmother always told me—we have an endless and infinite capacity to love.

Suddenly, staring at the picture, I feel a sense of urgency bordering on desperation to see Grace and scoop her up in my arms, to make sure she is safe, even though I know she is asleep in my mother's guest bedroom no more than fifteen feet away.

I crack Grace's bedroom door. She thinks this bedroom is hers and hers alone, even though I keep telling her that Nana decorated it for all her girl grandchildren. The boys sleep in a bedroom full of cars and trucks, and Grace sleeps in a room filled with fairies and mermaids and a giant tree painted on the wall with pictures of our family hung on the branches in pink-painted frames.

The door creaks a little as I push it open, and Grace mumbles in her sleep and turns over. Standing beside the bed, I lean over her so I can feel her sweet, warm breath on my cheek. Her hair is slightly damp at her temples and I smooth it back, inhaling the scent of the baby shampoo we still use on her hair.

"Gracie?"

She smiles in her sleep, and I can't help but smile back. I lean over and kiss her cheek. When I pull back, her eyes open and she throws her arms around me. "Mama!"

"Hi, darling."

She clutches me. "I missed you, Mama."

"Didn't you have fun with Nana?"

"Yes." Her face grows serious. "But you forgot bunny at home, so I couldn't fall asleep."

"Let's go make some pancakes," I say. "You can crack the eggs."

She's out of bed and out the door before I rise from the floor where I'm kneeling.

"She needs a little sister or brother," says my oldest brother, Marco, as we sit back under the grape arbor, watching his six-year-old daughter, Maria, and Grace weave flowers into wreaths in my grandmother's backyard later that day.

Marco's short, curly black hair has recently become dotted with silver. He and Caterina were the only one of us siblings born with curly hair and deep olive skin, which makes his dark blue eyes even more striking. He must have inherited his eye color from some distant relative, because he's the only adult Giovanni I know with blue eyes. His wife, Sally, is nearly platinum blond with blue eyes, so now there is a whole generation of little Giovannis with blue eyes.

Sundays, after mass and church services across the Bay Area, my big family convenes at my grandmother's house for an all-day eat fest for my favorite part of my week. Hanging out with my family grounds me and bolsters me for the ugliness I'll have to deal with in my reporting job.

As soon as Marco says Grace needs a playmate, I expect my mother to materialize beside me. She wouldn't miss this conversation for the world if she could help it. But she's deep in conversation with my aunt Lucia.

However, my brother Dante's bionic ear must have heard something, because he sidles up to us. Although Marco is very distinguished looking, Dante's the looker in our family. Unlike me, he's always been able to pull off the *la bella figura* attitude my mother taught us. Today, a gray silk shirt and black pressed slacks set off his dark good looks. His shirt is undone several buttons, revealing a tanned and hairless chest. He would deny it if I ever said anything, but I'm convinced he goes to a tanning salon to keep that bronze hue, and I'd bet my last cannoli that he gets waxed, as well.

Between the silky folds of his shirt, a braided gold chain rests on his chest. The Italian horn—a *cornetto*—and the *malocchio*, a hand with two fingers pointing out, hang on the thick chain. My brother Marco wears an identical necklace.

Wearing the horn and the hand is supposed to ward off the evil eye—*malocchio*—and grant you good luck.

But it didn't protect my father. He was wearing his *cornetto* when he died. My grandmother gave his to me a few years ago. I used to wear it nestled on the same chain as my miraculous medal every single day, but once I became a mother, the necklace was put aside in my jewelry box in exchange for a simple diamond necklace Donovan bought me when Grace was born. As if reading my mind, Dante absentmindedly caresses his *cornetto*. And then turns to me.

"I hate to harp on you about babies, but let's face it, Ella, you're not getting any younger." He wraps his arm around his wife, Nina, who has big brown doe eyes and hair shorn in a pixie cut, and who—despite having four kids—is as willowy as a high school girl. "You don't want to be an old mother."

"Leave her alone," Nina says, swatting Dante away with a laugh and rolling her eyes for my benefit.

"Don't be so sexist or I'm telling Mama," I say. "She didn't raise you to be a chauvinist pig."

"Gabriella's right," Nina says. "Mama Maria would chew you out if she heard you saying that."

"I doubt it," Dante says, flashing a grin that has made women melt since he was five. "Mama wants a new grandbaby more than anyone."

Dante dated his way through every pretty girl in our high school and then every woman at Diablo Valley College before he met Nina in his philosophy class and fell hard. She was a softspoken poet who hoped to get into the MFA program at Berkeley. But her dreams flew out the door when she got pregnant at nineteen. I always wonder if she regretted meeting my brother even though she appears to adore her life.

Standing, I squint against the sunset to watch my daughter, pretending I didn't hear Dante's prodding.

Dante starts comparing the shine on his shoes to Marco's even more expensive Italian loafers, teasing Marco about a small scuff. Even Marco does *la bella figura* better than me. I give up. I ignore my brothers' banter and focus on my daughter.

Donovan is over by Grace now, crouched down, showing her

and Maria how to tie the wreaths into a crown. As soon as the wreaths are on their heads, they take off around my grandmother's garden with arms stretched out like they are flying. They look like little fairies in the flowered wreaths and their Sunday dresses.

Like a specter, my mother is at my side.

"Ella, I don't mean to be a pest, but Dante has a point. You should have all your babies when you're young. Trust me, it's easier that way."

I was a fool to think she didn't hear what we were talking about.

I know better than to argue, even though the thought of having a baby right now makes me squirm. My mother misreads my expression.

"There's nothing wrong, is there?" she says, her forehead creasing with worry.

My brothers stop their good-natured bickering and look up.

All eyes are on me, and I squirm. After Grace was born, I immediately started taking the birth control pill. I'm way too superstitious to risk giving Grace a sister fourteen months younger. That's too much like Caterina and me. I refuse to tempt fate that way. But I can't explain why I'm still on the pill years later.

"Everything is fine, Mama." I force a smile and wrap my arm around her in a sideways hug. I lean over and pick a sugared strawberry off my dish of *panna cotta* on the table. The remains of our regular Sunday feast—platters of meatballs, pork chops, and Italian sausages, giant pots of pasta with marinara sauce, bowls of fresh vegetables, and loaves of fresh-baked bread—all have been cleared. All that remains on the large tables are pitchers of water, bottles of wine, and several types of desserts, including wine-soaked peaches, the *pignoli* cookies I brought, and cannolis.

"It's been a while since we've had a new baby in the family,"

Marco says, pressing on, shoulders back, reveling in his role as Patriarch of the Giovanni family. He beams, looking at Sally, two of their young daughters squirming on her lap, angling for the best position. She looks at me and blows her blond bangs up in the air in mock frustration. She wouldn't have it any other way.

A new baby. Going back to the newsroom from my three-month maternity leave meant holing up in a smelly upstairs bathroom using the obnoxious breast pump and feeling like a cow on an assembly line. More than once, something big would go down on the scanner while I was pumping and Kellogg would send someone else out to cover a story *on my beat.* And it wasn't uncommon for me to be stuck covering a crime scene way past the time when I should have been pumping and having to keep my arms tightly folded over my chest to keep from revealing tennis-ball-sized stains on my shirt.

And that was after Grace was born. While I was pregnant, it only took one time huffing and puffing up a steep driveway and being engulfed in black smoke from a house fire that made me admit I wasn't at my best.

I told Kellogg I was done covering fires and hoofing it around outside in 100-degree heat while I was pregnant. He was not happy, but he knew better than to argue. Underneath it all, he gets it. He's a dad. He's divorced and sacrifices everything for his kids. He sleeps on the couch in his one-bedroom apartment to make sure his boys feel like they have their own bedroom at his place.

"Sally can handle another one," I shoot back at Marco, using a spoon to scrape up the last bits of panna cotta. "She's like Mother Nature, for Christ's sake," I say, gesturing to his wife with my spoon, who is now holding their fifteen-month-old son, Anthony, while watching their other children play.

"Ella!" my mother says.

"Well, it's true." I lean over and scoot Marco's untouched panna cotta toward me. He slaps my hand away.

"I mean your language," my mother says. "We all know Sally wants eight kids. We're talking about you giving Grace a little playmate."

"What? I'm not taking the Lord's name in vain. I could've said 'for fuck's sake.'"

My mom shakes her head. Marco frowns. He believes only buffoons curse. I told him he should try working in a newsroom for a day and see how clean his mouth stays.

Three sets of eyes stare at me.

"Quit ganging up on me. Next thing you know you'll start harping about us getting married again." As soon as I say it, I cringe. No reason to give them any more ammo than they already have. Not only have I put my foot in my mouth but my timing is also impeccable. Donovan has appeared at my side. I grab him around the waist. Maybe he'll deflect this attack.

Instead, he gives me a kiss. It is chaste, but still it's in front of my family, so it makes me blush.

My mother is grinning when I pull back, which makes my face flush even warmer.

"Sean, we were just talking about you and Ella."

"Oh yeah?" he says, completely oblivious. He obviously needs to spend more time with my family if he doesn't realize my mother is about to release a Scud missile in his direction.

"It would be nice if Gabriella could still fit into my wedding dress when you guys get married."

His eyes widen. He looks at me, and his eyebrows draw together. I raise my own eyebrows and shrug as if to say, *You want in on this crazy family, be my guest.*

He jams his hands in his pockets and clears his throat as my mother gives him the eye. "Uh, I think she looks great. I mean, sure she's gained a little bit of weight, but it looks good on her. She's perfect to me."

I freeze, a spoonful of Marco's panna cotta halfway up to my mouth. Good Lord, he thinks my mom is telling him she thinks I'm fat.

"I don't mean that," my mother says and bursts into tinkling laughter. "I mean you guys should get married before your baby comes."

Now Donovan draws back from me, eyes wide with a question. He thinks I'm pregnant and have told my family before I told him. Mother Mary.

"Ma!" I need to stop this nonsense right now. "When we decide to get married and have another baby, I promise you that you will be the first one to know. Swear to Christ."

"Ella. Your language."

"I work in a newsroom, Ma. That's the censored version of what I really want to say." I'm done. I grab my wineglass, tip my head back, and gulp until not a drop remains. Then I grab the bottle off the table, pouring more wine in my glass, grab another cannoli, and head toward a stone bench in the garden, leaving everyone openmouthed, watching me.

Donovan remains behind, trying to make nice probably. He loves my family. He's crazy. He should run for the hills.

Chapter 7

Monday

"Got a follow on the dead girl from Saturday?" Kellogg leans on the wall of my cubicle Monday morning, making the entire thing shake with his weight.

"Waiting for the morgue to ID her," I say after I hurriedly swallow the last of the Italian sub I was scarfing down at my desk even though it's only eleven in the morning. "Cops say 'it's under investigation.'" I use air quotes and roll my eyes.

Kellogg strokes his beard. "Your boy isn't slipping you the skinny on this one?"

"Hardly."

"You'd think there'd be some advantage to having a boyfriend on the force."

"You'd think," I say, making a face.

"Why don't you see what you can dig up off the record, because the *San Francisco Tribune* is kicking your ass on this one." He throws the paper down on my desk and walks off.

Andy Fucking Black. I'm afraid to see what he's written. It's a rare day when I don't devour all the newspapers before leaving my house, but today was one of them. It was one of my less-than-ideal-Italian-Mama mothering moments. Grace spilled her chocolate milk down her dress and then her cereal all over the floor, so I spent my morning consoling her, getting her changed, and cleaning up a big mess. Then she decided to flop on the floor and refuse to put on the clean clothes, saying she didn't care if her Tinkerbell shirt was stained brown, that's all she wanted to wear. By the time I dropped her off at my mom's, I was already running late. Such a superfun way to start my morning. It was so crazy, I didn't even have time to eat breakfast so I had to eat the sub I brought for lunch early.

I stare at Kellogg's retreating form. Is he telling me to talk Donovan into giving me off-the-record info on the murder? I glance down at the *Trib* and scowl when I see Andy Black has IDd her—Agnes Clark, 22, went to college in Santa Cruz—before the morgue released it officially. Damn. I've had the ID since Saturday night, but I'm trying to play by the rules so her parents don't read about her in the paper before they are officially notified of her death.

I dial the morgue.

"Hey, Giovanni." It's Brian, my best source at the coroner's office.

"You releasing the ID on the Roe Island vic?"

"Can't find next of kin. See that asswipe Black splashed it all over the front page."

"Scum of the earth."

"Last address for family was in Livermore, but that was no good. Will let you know as soon as we do death notification."

For a second, my heart stops. Agnes Clark is originally from Livermore. Livermore was where we lived when my older sister, Caterina, was kidnapped.

I flash back to that day. Caterina and I were fighting over who could use the pink jump rope first. I had one foot out the door when my mom made me come back in to brush my teeth. While I brushed my teeth, I fumed at how unfair my life was. I was the youngest in our family of four kids, which meant last in line for everything. When I finished brushing my teeth, I ran into the front yard, but it was empty. Caterina was gone. I ran to the road and looked both ways. All I found was the pink jump rope in the gutter.

Shaking off the dark memory, I hang up and call Donovan.

"She was from Livermore."

"I know. West is on it. Made Anderson his top priority."

"Okay." After I hang up, I dig deep into my file cabinet where I have a folder in a plastic bag. Looking around to make sure nobody is looking, I take out the picture of Frank Anderson—a mug shot from his arrest. He looks like a drill instructor. Blond crew cut. Defined jaw. Square face. Dark, deep-set eyes with an angry, threatening look, as if he wants to leap through the camera and attack.

The more I think about it, the angrier I become. Why hasn't Frank Anderson been at the top of West's priority list this entire time? My heart is racing as I dial.

"West."

"Did Donovan tell you about the Bible verse?" I don't waste time on niceties.

"Yes. We're looking into it."

"It's part of the same Bible verse that Anderson e-mailed me."

"Yes, I'm aware of that. But I don't want you to get your hopes up." He fills the silence. "I know this looks like a lead on Anderson, but it is still a long shot." He clears his throat.

I stare at the giant TV screen. It is showing footage of the Roe Island murder scene. The volume is down, so I don't know what they are saying. Nothing new, I'm sure.

"The profiler I spoke to this morning says that serial killers spouting Bible verses is about as common as redheads named Murphy," West says. "I thought so but wanted to double-check with her before I got back to you."

I don't answer.

"Look at the Green River Killer," he says. "Killed forty-eight women. Was a bit of a church freak, read the Bible at work and talked about religion with his coworkers.

"Many serial killers will turn to religion right before they start their killing sprees. We think that because of strong religious upbringings, they might be sexually inhibited and turn to killing to compensate. As you probably know, it's never a sex thing, it's a power thing. Anderson is not the only serial killer obsessed with Bible verses; I can name three others off the top of my head who sent Bible verses to newspapers or whatnot before or during their killing sprees."

"Does Donovan know this?"

"Just told him a few minutes ago."

I hang up, not knowing whether to feel relieved or disappointed.

Later in the afternoon, I call my mother. She doesn't pick up at home and then doesn't answer her cell. I don't know why we even bothered getting my mother a mobile phone, because half the time she forgets it at home anyway.

Finally, I reach her at the flower shop and ask about Grace.

"She's watering the roses right now," my mom says.

My mom often takes Grace to her flower shop on the days she doesn't have school and after her morning kindergarten classes. My daughter loves it. She knows more about flowers than I do. Her favorite is a type of peony called Red Grace, which my mother began carrying in her flower shop after Grace was born.

"Do you and Donovan want to stay for dinner tonight when you pick up Grace?"

"Thanks, but I think I better head straight home. I promised Grace I'd let her help me make lasagna tonight."

I don't tell her that I'm looking forward to a quiet night at home, lounging around in my pajamas with my husband and daughter. After we put Grace to bed, we can open that bottle of wine I've been saving. It was what I had planned for Saturday night before Donovan got that call about a murder. He worked for a few hours last night after we left my mother's house but promised he'd be home for supper tonight.

"She's going to be as good a cook as your Nana at this rate," my mom says with a laugh.

"I hope so. I'll call you when I'm done here and on my way."

"Sounds good," she says. "Don't forget to pack her bathing suit tomorrow morning. I promised her I'd take her to the beach. Might as well take advantage of this heat wave."

Later, my cell rings at the same time I hear something about a dead body on the police scanner.

DOA—dead on arrival. Found on the shores of Martinez nearly underneath the Benicia-Martinez Bridge, a little more than two miles away from Roe Island, where the college student was found on Saturday.

I glance down at my cell. Lopez.

"I just heard," I say without preamble. Standing up, I can see Lopez across the newsroom in the photo department, leaning down and gathering up his photo gear, his phone pressed to his ear.

"Meet you at my car in five," he says. "Maybe we'll beat Pretty Boy to the scene."

Donovan is going to another murder scene outside his jurisdiction, this time in Martinez? Lopez knows something I don't.

I gather up my jacket and bag and a notebook and head for the door.

"Another body in Suisun Bay," I say as I pass Kellogg. "No official ID yet on Saturday's 187." I'm not a slime reporter. I'll wait for official confirmation even if it means losing a scoop.

"We got room on A1," he says.

Chapter 8

THE BODY WAS found in the shadow of the Benicia-Martinez Bridge.

The industrial road leading to the shore of Suisun Bay is lined with what looks like the exposed innards of a factory floor turned inside out. Big white holding tanks interconnected with hundreds of gray or rusted pipes of every size imaginable tangled together in a maze. The stark ugliness of the plant is made worse by the gray skies above. I can't see why anyone who didn't work at the plant would be out in this area voluntarily. Makes me wonder whether the dead body washed up out of the bay or was dumped.

"What is all this?" I ask Lopez, gesturing out the window at the factory we are passing.

"Chemical processing. They regenerate the leftover sulfuric acid from the refineries," Lopez says. He is the paper's institutional memory. He's been working there longer than anyone else in the newsroom. A lot of people underestimate Lopez because he's smaller, but he's all sinewy muscle and ex–Green Beret. He's always packing heat, and the rumor is he saw some crazy shit in Vietnam.

The night I went after Jack Dean Johnson, Lopez was who I wanted at my side. At the time, I thought Johnson had killed Caterina. But she wasn't one of his twenty-four victims. Johnson had kidnapped my niece, Sofia, I found Sofia and stabbed Johnson to death to stop him from shooting Donovan. I was too late. He fired his gun. Luckily, Donovan was wearing a bulletproof vest.

Andy Black is already there when we pull up. He's stalking that same buxom Channel 4 reporter. I'm surprised she hasn't wised up to him yet.

Lopez pulls his Honda in behind a line of cars that includes a few TV news vans parked on the curve at Mococo Road. On the drive, Lopez told me that Rosarito got another call from a tipster about this body, just like they did about the one on Roe Island.

"Why is a tipster calling Rosarito?"

"Don't know, man. It's some squirrely shit for sure."

I look around but don't see Donovan's car yet.

As soon as I crack the car door I expect the rotten-egg smell of sulfur but instead am engulfed in a breeze that brings with it the decaying stench of the swampy bog before us.

In the distance, the Phantom Fleet seems less threatening during the day than it did the other night. Across from that, on the far shore, lies the border of Rosarito and Benicia.

We can't see the body from where we park. But I can see a cluster of cops gathered around something down a brush-covered hill and closer to the swampy shore area. Lopez and I make our way down the slight incline. There isn't anything to hang the crime-scene tape on, so they have two community service officers holding it up, barring our way. Sort of ridiculous when you think about it. The CSOs holding the tape look embarrassed.

Lopez has taken off, skirting the crime scene, going closer to the water and snapping off shots. He's clearly hoping to get another interesting shot of the cops at the crime scene like he did Saturday.

I'm about to ask one of the CSOs if the Martinez Police Department's public information officer is around when he tells me to back up. He and his buddy on the other end of the crime-scene tape are walking forward toward the road up above. Pretty soon all the reporters are herded back onto the road, most grumbling. The TV reporters are stooping down, wiping muck from the bottom inch of their heels that stuck in the mud. I know better. I'm wearing my ballet flats.

A few seconds later, two Martinez PD SUVs come around the bend. Without even braking, they head down the hill to the swampy marsh, parking in a way that blocks any view of the cops hovering around the body. Two more squad cars follow and park on the shoulder of the road next to the hill. The CSOs secure the crime-scene tape on the cars and hop inside the vehicles. I'm looking around at the cars when I notice one is a Rosarito Police Department cop car. I whip my head around. Then I see him.

Donovan is heading my way. A few TV reporters are pushing microphones in his face. Behind him, Andy Black from the *Tribune* scowls. He knows better than to ask my boyfriend for information.

But the blond Channel 4 reporter in the low-cut top and shellacked hair doesn't.

She keeps pace with Donovan. She grabs his arm when her stiletto heel catches on something. She loses her balance and partially falls into him. Her grating giggle travels across the marshy bog. Donovan, who hasn't noticed me watching yet, steadies her. He basically picks her up and moves her aside, freeing himself from her clinging grasp. He says something that wipes the smile right off her face. He turns back and walks away, leaving her looking after him.

Right then, he looks up, meets my eyes, and gives me a wry grin. My heart swells with pride that he's mine.

As he grows closer, the merriment in his eyes fades and his eyebrows draw together as he looks at the crime scene. He runs his hand through his messy hair, which is always a sign he is upset or worried.

By crouching down a bit and glancing through the tinted windows of the SUVs parked to block my view, I look for anyone holding a piece of paper they got off the body. Is there another Bible verse? But all I can see is another cop taking Donovan aside. I'm on tiptoe, watching, as they both lean down out of my sight line.

Damn.

The Channel 5 cameraman is at my side.

"Fancy meeting you here," he says, not taking his eye off the camera viewfinder.

"You filming?" I try to stay out of the way and keep my mouth shut when TV cameras are rolling at crime scenes.

"Nah, just trying to see what the body looks like."

"What do you got?"

"Couldn't see shit." He puts the camera down and heads straight to the Channel 5 reporter. He gestures and points toward the shore.

We are both thinking the same thing — a serial killer is at work. Right now I think I'm the only reporter to know about the Bible verse. If it is a serial killer at work, there will most likely be another verse. The thought sends a ping of anxiety ricocheting through me. It still doesn't mean it is Anderson.

Lopez is at my side. "Kicked me off the beach, man."

"What did you get?"

"Long blond hair. Youngish. Wet, but more like she was doused with water than drowned," he says, chewing on a toothpick.

A commotion erupts behind us. It's the Martinez Police Department's public information officer, Lieutenant Ted Miller. Reporters gather around him. The PIO is a distinguished cop in his forties, with a thick head of black hair swept back from his forehead. He's wearing dark green pants and a matching polo shirt, as if he just stepped off the fairway. A glance at his shoes confirms this. He must've been pulled off the golf course to come to a murder scene. He faces the crime scene so the cameras are forced to turn their backs on the shore where the body lies. I unearth my reporter's notebook and a pen and gather with the other reporters.

"Thank you all for coming," he says.

He talks for a few minutes but is keeping most of the murder information close to the chest, because by the time he is done, I only have four sentences written in my notebook. His information basically confirms what I heard on the scanner. When and where a body was found. Appears to be a woman in her twenties. Police are investigating.

I'm hoping no other reporters make the connection, but that would be too much to ask.

Black, who is the first reporter called on, brings it up immediately.

"Is there anything linking this body to the one found Saturday?" Black says.

Before Lieutenant Miller can answer, it becomes a free-for-all with reporters blurting out questions.

"Do you think a serial killer is at work?" the Channel 11 reporter asks.

"Are the two women connected in any way?"

"Is this the work of one person?"

Finally, when everyone shuts up for a second, Lieutenant Miller answers.

"We are not prepared to release that information at this time." He scans the crowd for other questions.

"Can you confirm that this woman also has ties to Livermore?" Black asks.

My heart pounds in my throat. The cold from the ocean breeze shoots up my spine at the same time my heart pounds in my throat. Is this victim from Livermore? And how the fuck did Andy Black find this out before me? I can already hear Kellogg scolding me for letting Black get one up on me. But worse than that, why is a serial killer targeting women from Livermore? I feel like I'm going to vomit, and I lean over, my hands on my knees. Black shoots me a look, and I immediately straighten up, swallowing the bile that rose in my throat.

"We've only just learned about this death an hour ago," Miller says. "So we are in no position to confirm anything about this victim."

"When will you release the woman's identity?" Black pushes on.

Lieutenant Miller's face is deadpan for what he says next. "As God makes little green apples, I'm going to do everything I can to make sure no reporters receive the victim's name until her family is notified. So even if I had her name confirmed—which I do not—I'm in no hurry to release her name to a reporter who doesn't have enough respect to wait until a victim's family is notified before he prints it in the paper."

A few reporters nudge each other and whisper. Black doesn't even have the dignity to blush or look away.

"But isn't it true that in the past week and a half, two women have gone missing who are originally from Livermore?" Black asks, undaunted by the scolding.

"That's all for now," Lieutenant Miller says and turns his back on us.

I'm suddenly chilled and hustle back to the car. Inside the car, my phone buzzes with a text from Donovan who must have seen me leaving.

Have Grace stay at your mom's, it says. *I won't be home. Patrol car watching our place tonight.*

Is that necessary? I text back.

Won't hurt, he writes.

One reason we rented our condo is its secure underground parking, private elevator, and state-of-the-art security system, but I won't mind a cop car outside my door if I'm there alone tonight, because I can tell that Donovan is worried.

What's going on? I write back.

Later.

Bible verse?

My phone remains silent. I text the same question three times as Lopez and I drive back to the newsroom.

Donovan never responds.

Chapter 9

THE GRUMPY WATCH commander I reach by phone at the Livermore Police Department says no missing persons reports have been filed in the past two weeks in his city.

I text Donovan again: *Was she also college student? Where?*

But he doesn't respond to my text.

I've just filed my murder story when Lopez swings by my desk. He has his camera bag slung over his shoulder and is jingling his car keys.

"House fire. Maybe a kid injured." He presses one finger against the earbud in his ear. The cord trails down to where a scanner is clipped to his belt. "Three-alarm."

Usually most house fires are one or two alarms. Three alarms means they've called for additional firefighting vehicles and firefighters.

Lopez nods. "They've got two ambulances on standby. Sounds like they're searching for a kid inside one of the houses."

I close my eyes for a second. It used to be so easy to write about death. Opening my eyes, I stare at the framed photos on my desk.

Grace's little face, nearly identical to Caterina's picture beside her. The only difference is Grace has dark brown curls and light freckles, while Cat's skin was olive and her hair blue black. But their eyes are exactly the same, deep, knowing dark pools glinting with life and merriment.

A kid injured in a fire is nothing new for me. But it was easier before I became a mother. While it was always difficult to write about a child's death, now the very idea makes my heart pound and my stomach somersault.

Lopez waits. Not saying a word.

"Let's do this," I say, standing and grabbing my bag and a notebook.

As soon as we get within two blocks of the house fire, we look for a parking spot. The street is blocked off with ambulances, fire trucks, trucks from the gas company, and TV vans. And this is around the corner from the actual fire. Huge, billowing streams of smoke show us where the fire is.

Lopez and I park and make our way around huge fire hoses snaking across the wet streets. At least three fire trucks are pulled up right in front of two houses that still have flames shooting out of them. Another four trucks are across the street. We split up, Lopez hurrying ahead to get shots of the flames and me scanning the crowd for someone who might be able to tell me something.

People stand in clusters, talking and watching the fire consume the two houses. A firefighter walks a few feet in front of me. I hurry to his side and hold out my press pass, which is on a chain around my neck.

"Excuse me, I'm with the *Bay Herald*. Can you let your public information officer know I'm here?"

He casts a quick glance at me. "Sure. Wait here on the corner."

As he walks away, I make a face. I'm not staying a block away from the fire when the rest of the world is in for the close-up.

I'm heading closer to the fire when a burly man with a badge on his helmet appears before me.

"Looking for me?" I say with a smile. It's Rick Mason, the public information officer for the fire department. He is decked out in fire gear, but his ready grin is still there under his bushy moustache.

"Sorry I wasn't," he says, smiling even bigger. "Didn't know you were here."

Sort of what I figured. And why I didn't wait on that corner.

"What can you tell me?" I ask.

"Still sorting it all out," he says. "Why don't you wait across the street from the fire, there's another reporter there, someone from the weekly paper. I'll come over when I know more."

I'm about to ask him about the kid I heard about on the scanner when his radio crackles. He speaks into it and hurries off.

A reporter from the weekly? They don't usually cover much in this area. I remember my days on a weekly, busting my butt and wondering if I'd ever get a break at a big daily.

When I cross the street, I see a skinny guy with sideburns standing there, hands dug deep into his pockets.

"Hey, you with the weekly?"

He looks up in surprise.

"I'm Gabriella. With the *Bay Herald*. Been here long?"

He sticks out a hand. "Michael Dillman with the *Pleasant Valley Weekly*. I live right around the corner. I heard this on the scanner and walked over."

"What do you know?"

"Not much." The kid digs his hands even deeper into his pockets. He has a book bag slung over one shoulder. We stare at the fire for a few seconds.

"How long you been at the weekly?" I ask.

"Three years. My father keeps getting on my case. Tells me I'm not a real journalist until I work for your paper."

I scoff. "That's absurd. You are a real journalist. We all have to start somewhere. I worked at weeklies. They're great training grounds. Do you have a card?"

Red creeps up his jaw to his ears. "No, we don't have business cards."

"That's okay." I dig around in my bag. "Here's my card. Let's get you in to talk to the editor about working for us someday."

"Really?" The corners of his mouth turn up in a grin.

"Hell yes."

I know firsthand that plugging away at a weekly for a few years is harder than some of my colleagues have ever worked. Many of them graduated with a master's in journalism and landed at my paper with very little boots-on-the-ground training.

I glance around. Rick Mason is nowhere to be seen. The clock is ticking and deadline is looming.

"Screw waiting around," I say. The kid's eyes widen.

I walk over to a group standing nearby.

"You guys live here?"

"Right over there," one woman says, pointing to a house down the block.

"Do you know who lives in those houses?"

"Yeah. Dan and his family. His son is right there, across the street. A man with some kids lives in the blue one," she says.

The flames are extinguished on the blue house, and the firefighters are concentrating on their efforts to contain the fire at the green house, which still has spurts of flame shooting out of the attic roof and window. A ladder truck holds a firefighter with a hose, who's leaning close to the roof and aiming a high-pressure hose on it. Right when I think how dangerous it is, the ladder lowers. A few seconds later, there is a loud popping noise and flames shoot out a window right near where the firefighter was.

The people around me gasp.

I head back toward the weekly reporter.

"Dillman, take a walk with me." I don't wait to see if he follows, but when I get across the street and am in front of the man in pajama pants, he is by my side.

"Heard you were Dan's son," I say to the man, who is shading his eyes to watch the firefighters work.

"Yes." He bounces up and down, his eyes darting around him.

"Did everyone in your house make it out safe?"

"Yes, thank God," the man says, tugging on his pajama pants.

I sigh with relief. Nothing about a kid yet.

"I'm with the *Bay Herald*, and he's with the *Pleasant Valley Weekly*," I say. "Can you tell us what happened?"

The son in the flip-flops describes how he was watching TV when he heard a loud popping noise and a bang, and when he looked up, his window was engulfed in flames. The fire had leapt from the house next door and broken through his windows. The two houses are only about five feet apart.

"I ran screaming from my room for my mother and my grandmother," he says, pointing at a bottom window. "My grandmother's room is in the attic, so we ran up there. I had to pick her up and carry her on my back. When I got to the bottom of the stairs, I looked behind me and the stairway was filled with flames."

"Grandma okay?"

"Yeah, they're giving her oxygen over at the ambulance around the corner," he says, now pointing behind us.

I scribble as fast as I can, trying to get every word. I glance over at the weekly reporter to see if he is getting all these great quotes, but he stands there holding a pen and nodding. I shoot him a glance with a raised eyebrow. He has no notebook.

I rummage in my bag and hand him one. He looks at it like he doesn't know what to do. I mimic scribbling notes on mine. Maybe this is what his dad means about becoming a real reporter?

When I get done interviewing the son and get his phone number, I see Rick Mason heading back toward where we are supposed to be waiting. I nudge the weekly reporter. "Let's go."

He follows me back to the sidewalk where we are supposed to be waiting, but Mason turns and heads toward the house on fire instead of where we are standing.

Just then Lopez shows up, and I introduce him and Dillman to each other.

Dillman tries to give me my notebook back. It is open, and there isn't any writing on it. I give him another look. Come to think of it, I don't remember him scribbling notes during the interview.

I push it back at him. "Keep it," I say, watching his reaction.

But Dillman isn't looking at me. He's watching Lopez. He blushes and quickly stammers to Lopez, "Thanks. I forgot my notebook."

Lopez gives him a grin. "It's cool, man."

Dillman's face only returns to its natural color after Lopez lopes across the street and starts shooting more pictures.

A few seconds later, Rick Mason comes to give us the information. For once Rick isn't smiling.

It's bad. A five-year-old girl dead. The same age as Grace.

I try to swallow, my throat suddenly dry. And it gets worse.

"The father was able to get his wife and three other kids out of the house, but no matter how many times he ran inside, he couldn't find the five-year-old. He went in several times until finally the smoke was too powerful for him to handle," Mason says, his eyebrows knit together under the brim of his fire helmet. "When firefighters arrived, they found the girl. It took them a few times searching the house. She had been hiding from the fire under one of the beds."

That poor girl must have been so frightened. And her father, how can he ever get over losing her? He tried so hard to save her. My eyes begin to water, and it has nothing to do with the billowing smoke that engulfs us every time the wind changes direction.

I shoot a glance at Dillman. He's listening intently but still not taking notes. The notebook is open and he holds a pen a few inches above it, but the page remains blank.

"You okay?" Dillman asks after Mason walks away.

"I've got a five-year-old daughter," I say.

Dillman squats down to tie the shoe on his sneakers. "Oh man, that's rough. How can you cover the cops beat with a kid?"

I shake my head. "I don't know. Maybe I shouldn't. We were at Ocean Beach over the weekend, and when some guy came up to say hi, I totally freaked out. I'm so paranoid, I worry it's going to mess her up." I start flipping through my notes to make sure I got everything I need.

Dillman stands up again and frowns. "No, you got to be careful nowadays. You never know who is okay and who is a creep. Sometimes the nicest guys end up being sickos and nobody who knows them even knew it."

We sit there in silence for a second before he turns to leave. I touch his sleeve.

"I'm serious about calling me. I'll introduce you to the executive editor, Matt Kellogg. Get some clips ready to show him. Three to four of your best stories." Remembering how he didn't take notes, I add, "Even if he's not ready to hire you right now, he probably will have some good advice on building a career as a reporter."

"Thanks." He nods and gulps.

"What are your strengths? What can I tell Kellogg?" I dig around in my bag for my pack of gum.

"I'm good at talking to people." He nods as if he's trying to convince himself this is true.

"Okay. What else?" I offer him a piece of gum but he declines with a shake of his head.

"I got a photographic memory."

I pop a stick of bubble gum in my mouth. "Yeah. Like what?"

"If I'm out at a scene, like this, you know. I can go back and see it exactly in my mind. Like in your notes." He closes his eyes for a second. "Your third page said, 'bottom of the stairs, stairway filled with flames.'"

I flip through my notebook. It's there. "Fuckin' A."

Red spreads across his cheeks and up to his ears.

"Is that why you didn't bring a notebook and didn't take notes?" He nods sheepishly.

"You lucky son of a gun," I say.

"I also can read upside down," he says. "One time I was in the mayor's office sitting across from him asking him about some rumors he'd been paid off to approve a housing development. He kept trying to cover up a piece of paper on his desk, but I saw it. It was a check for thirty thousand dollars from H&B Housing."

I blow a bubble and turn to him. "Wait? You're the one who wrote that story that got the mayor investigated?"

He nods.

"Wow. You need to talk to Kellogg. I'll set it up."

"Thanks. Better run back and get this fire written up," he says. "Just so happens tonight is our weekly deadline."

After he rounds the corner, I give the scene one last look. A few houses away, a woman stands in her yard behind a fence. I introduce myself.

"I don't really know the family in the blue house," the woman says. "When I came out, the mother was running up and down the street wailing, while her husband was inside trying to find their daughter. She had on a bathrobe and no shoes. I gave her a jacket and some boots. She didn't say anything, just kept shivering and keening. When the firefighter brought her daughter out, the little girl was limp, and the mother buckled onto her knees in the middle of the street. Was the most heartbreaking thing I've ever seen."

As she tells the story, she covers her face, her shoulders heaving with sobs. I put my arm around her for a second and then hold out my pack of gum without saying a word. She takes it, wiping the tears off her face with the back of her hand. We sit and chew our gum silently, staring at the charred remains of the house across the street.

Although many of the stories I write unearth the seedy, dark side of the world, there are days like this that reveal the basic decency and humanity so many people have when it comes to other people. I know I could probably talk to a few more neighbors, but the fire is finally out and the streets are starting to clear. This story is too close to home. The cause of the fire is under investigation, but it could have been anything. And even with working smoke alarms, the little girl still died.

I've never wanted to be anything but a reporter and I've never wanted to cover any other beat except the crime beat, but covering stories like this one might do me in. Now that Donovan and I have moved into our spendy condo, I can't afford to quit my job if I wanted to. But I just don't know if I can hack it anymore.

Being a mother has changed everything.

With a heavy heart, I find Lopez, and we head back to the office in silence.

Chapter 10

GRACE IS HAPPY to stay the night at Grandma's house. I agree with Donovan that it's smart to have her stay there. I miss her but feel better knowing she is tucked away at my mother's house, just in case Anderson is back.

I will do anything to protect my daughter and my family. It's why I take shooting lessons. And why I train in military-style Budo martial arts. As I get to the Bay Bridge, I shoot a guilty look at the dojo in Oakland where I usually train. I've been going there for five years and am close to getting my black belt. But I haven't made it there very often these past few months. Life has become even busier lately as Grace gets older. Play dates and soccer and ballet. Thank God for my mother, who can often pick up the slack when our jobs get in the way, like tonight.

After I pay the toll and am merging into traffic on the Bay Bridge, I call Grace to say goodnight and "tuck" her in over the phone.

First I talk to my mom.

"I don't think it's really anything to worry about, but there have been two recent murders lately that have Donovan on edge," I say. "He thinks maybe we should be a little extra careful until they get this guy. But I don't want you to worry."

"What is going on?"

I spill it all—everything about the murders and the Bible verse—as I merge into traffic.

"I know it might seem a little paranoid," I say hesitantly.

My mother is silent for a second. "No. You're right. It is better to be cautious. I wish we didn't have to be like this, but I just accept it is part of life now."

"Thanks, Mama. I never worry about Grace when she's with you. . . . Thanks for understanding."

I feel guilty, because a small part of me is also relieved I get to skip the morning routine with Grace tomorrow. This morning was such a disaster. I yelled at her and then felt awful about it. I know she'll be a perfect angel for Nana. She always is. What I saw this morning was a sharp reminder that every time I think I've got it together as a mother, the universe is there to remind me that I'm not even close.

When Grace gets on the line, she is very chatty, telling me all about working in the flower shop. She loves having sleepovers at my mom's house. My mother lets her help cook and then gives her ice cream for dessert.

Halfway across the bridge, I tell her it's time to say her bedtime prayers.

"Are your eyes closed?" she asks before we start.

"Sort of." I am squinting. I obviously can't close my eyes while I'm driving. It's silly, but I don't ever want to lie to her. But, like other parents, I guess I already do lie. Case in point: The Easter bunny. The tooth fairy. Santa Claus. But those are white lies. What I really want to do is lie when she is old enough to ask me if I really killed two men.

Right now, though, my heart is full to bursting listening to her voice. That poor family whose house started on fire will never tuck in their little girl again. You can never take a minute of this life for granted. My job makes me hyperaware of the fragility of life. As a mother, I'm still learning to walk that tightrope between being overprotective and being grateful for each small magical moment I spend with my child. It's been a balancing act, reconciling the two worlds I live in.

At work, I'm pulled into the depths of darkness, talking to people who are grieving, or coaxing information out of convicts. When I return home at night, I'm confronted with innocence in the form of my small child, who knows nothing of the evil in this world, who is wrapped in a magical cocoon of her family's love.

Before I had Grace and even before I met Donovan, I was out drinking with some homicide detectives, and they were talking about why they stopped to have a drink every night before they went home. They needed that middle ground, that neutral space, that alcohol to serve as a barrier, a passage between dark and light—the life of a murder cop and that of a father and husband.

Now I get it. Some days it takes me a glass of wine out on the back deck before I can enter the world of innocence within my home. Donovan gets it more than most husbands would. And I never give him beef when he stops for a drink after work.

"Mama?" Grace's voice draws me back. I pull it together enough to sound cheery as we say goodnight, making kissing noises into the phone. Then she says something that tugs at my heart.

"Mama, when are you and Daddy going to get married?"

"Did Nana tell you to say this?" I say in a teasing voice, thinking of the black velvet box.

"No," she says and is quiet for a second.

"Does it bother you that we're not married? We told you that we love you and that we're a family no matter what, if we are married or not."

"I know," she says. "But Sofia and Maria and Lucia and Dominick . . . all my cousins . . . their moms and dads are married."

Hearing her little pleading voice makes me vow to examine, at the very least, the resistance I have to getting married.

My therapist, Marsha, claims it boils down to my fear of abandonment. That for some irrational reason, deep down I believe that getting married will result in me losing Donovan.

I'm mesmerized by the red taillights of the cars in front of me, remembering what Marsha thinks about my reluctance to tie the knot. It sounds crazy. It *is* crazy. But I worry that what she says is true. Traffic has grown thick on the Bay Bridge. I should hang up and pay more attention to the road.

"Grace, let's talk about this more with Daddy. Maybe tonight or this weekend, okay? I know. We can go out to breakfast at Max's Opera Plaza and have banana nut pancakes and hot chocolate and talk about it on Saturday morning, okay?"

"Okay." Her voice is quieter than usual.

After I hang up, I feel a mixture of sadness and guilt. I'm not sure why the idea of getting married freaks me out so much. But it does. It has ever since Donovan first brought it up years ago.

When I pull onto Grant Avenue in North Beach, I see the squad car waiting in front of our condo. I pull up opposite and roll down my window.

"I'm Gabriella Giovanni. Thanks for waiting for me," I say. I don't recognize the cop.

"No problem. Donovan did me a solid a few years back. Plus, it's dead in the city tonight. If something big goes down, I'll have to bail, though."

"You're staying out here all night?"

"I work until five. Got some coffee, and I'm listening to the classical music station."

"Can I bring you something? Something to eat?"

He holds up an empty fast-food bag and pats his belly. "I'm good to go. You go on in and get a good night's sleep."

"Thanks." I wonder what he'll do if he has to go to the bathroom, but I decide not to go there. Cops must have some plan for when they are on stakeout. I hit the garage door opener and pull into the private garage under our condo. Like always, I don't get out of the car until I see the garage door close behind me.

I feel a little sheepish having a cop on Code 5 stakeout outside our condo all night, but also a bit relieved after what Donovan told me about the Bible verse. I don't think I have anything to be worried about, but it's better to be safe.

Holding the kubaton that hangs from my key ring, I head toward the elevator, punching in our access code. The small, sharp, pen-sized metal weapon can disable someone much bigger than me if I jab him in the right spot.

Upstairs, the timers we use mean the condo is lit and the soft crooning of Bono singing U2's "Sometimes You Can't Make it On Your Own" is piping from the sound system. I scoop up a meowing Dusty and head straight to the master bathroom. I lock the door behind us, then unlock the gun safe. Grabbing one of Donovan's Kel-Tec P-11 semiautomatic pistols, I unlock the bedroom door and quietly go from room to room, heart pounding, as I check the rest of the condo. Once I'm convinced the place is empty, I change into a tank top and sweatpants, pour myself a double shot of Absolut, and crank up the stereo, which is now playing U2's "Vertigo."

I know I have nothing to worry about, but even the remote possibility that Anderson is back has me spooked.

Lounging on the couch with my feet up on the coffee table, I grab my chess book, read a page, then throw it down. I can't focus. I joke that my idea of peace is having the condo to myself for a few hours, cranking the music I love without anyone asking me for anything, but it's not true. Far from it. Tonight, for some reason, I'm uneasy, on edge. I turn off the stereo but regret it after every little noise seems louder than normal. I dial Donovan's cell. When he picks up, I hear voices in the background.

"Everything okay?" he asks.

"Wanted to let you know I'm home. Your cop buddy is out front, and once I got in, I cleared the condo. I'll sleep with a gun on the nightstand."

He is quiet for a second. "I'll try to stop by later and grab a few hours of sleep."

I don't answer.

"Anything else going on?" He's wondering why I called. I'm not the needy type of girlfriend who calls all the time for reassurance. I reach for the TV remote.

"I'm lonely and sort of creeped out and sad," I say, flipping through TV channels with the volume muted.

"I thought you said you checked the apartment?" He sounds distracted.

"I did. But I miss you. And Grace," I say and turn the TV off.

At the last minute, I add in more. "And I covered a fire where a little girl died."

Someone is talking to him, and he sounds distracted. I don't think he heard what I said about the fire. "Gotta go," he says. "Be home by midnight."

A few minutes later, I turn the TV back on again and flip to the news to see what the TV reporters dug up on the murder and the fire, drawing my legs up on the couch and pulling a soft blanket over me. They don't have anything I didn't already have. I flip the station to *Austin City Limits*. I don't recognize the musical act.

The next thing I know Donovan is nuzzling his unshaven jaw into my neck.

"Mmmm," I say sleepily, reaching up to wrap my arms around him.

"Your hair smells like smoke," he says, his low voice right next to my ear, sending a shiver through me.

"House fire."

"Some good that would've done you," he says, gesturing to the gun on the coffee table. "You didn't hear me come in. I even called your name."

"Oops," I say and tilt his head, guiding his mouth to mine.

We never make it to bed.

"My neck is jacked up," Donovan says in the morning, sitting up from where our bodies are tangled on the couch. He rubs the back of his neck and grimaces.

"I know," I say. "I've got a crink, too. I think we're too old for that."

"Which part?" he says, his eyes full of laughter. I sit up and start kissing his neck where he's rubbing it.

"Or else we need a bigger couch," I say.

Donovan stands and stretches.

I lean back and watch his naked body in admiration as he heads to the bathroom for his shower. I strip off my clothes and join him in the shower, and it's a long time before we come out. My fingers are like prunes by the time we are sipping espresso and munching on sourdough toast. We are still in our bathrobes, and every once in a while my wet hair drips droplets of water on the tile floor.

"This is nice—a morning to ourselves. But is it okay if I miss Grace, too?" I say, washing down my second slice of sourdough toast with a sip of my milky cappuccino. "That fire story was heartbreaking."

"Yeah. A damn shame." He stands up behind me, leaning down, lifting my hair off my neck so he can kiss it. "Hey, I have an idea to take your mind off of it."

Instead of answering, I stand and untie my robe, letting it drop to the floor.

Chapter 11

Tuesday

It's close to 10:00 a.m. by the time we are both dressed and ready to go. I'll stay late at work to make up for my tardy start. With my bag slung over my shoulder, I lean in to kiss Donovan good-bye but draw back when I see the look on his face. He's at the kitchen table with the *Tribune* spread before him, and he's reading Andy Black's story about the fire. I've already read it.

Luckily, Black had the same information I had on it.

"Ella." He pauses and takes a deep breath, and my heart stops for a second. He points to the picture of the crime scene under the bridge. "We found something in her pocket."

I close my eyes for a second.

"Bible verse?"

He nods his head so slightly that I nearly miss it. The muscle in his jaw is working overtime, clenching and unclenching, and his eyebrows are knit together.

"Son of a bitch." Another Bible verse. "Is she still a Jane Doe?"

He shakes his head again. "Kelly Dance, twenty-three. College kid. DeAnza College in Cupertino."

Despite what my gut is telling me, my mind says that there is still a chance the Bible verses might have nothing to do with me. Like West said, a lot of religious freaks kill and justify it in the name of God. I try to convince myself that it's all a coincidence, until his next words:

"She's also originally from Livermore."

Black was right. An icy wave of cold fear travels down my spine.

Donovan stands and takes my face in his hands, searching my eyes.

"We have to consider the possibility that these murders are a message."

Heat flushes my cheeks, and I'm suddenly dizzy.

"Anderson?" I ask, my mouth so dry the name comes out with difficulty. Now it is suddenly real, not just a fear I've kept bottled up inside.

Donovan breathes out loudly and nods. "Same Bible verse as the second e-mail he sent you. The one about thou shalt not kill. It's like the first one— he shortened the verse again. 'You have condemned and murdered the innocent one.'"

"What are we going to do?" My voice is shaky.

Donovan shakes his head and exhales. "I'm going to figure it out. Let me make a few calls. You can go to work, but watch your back. Take Lopez out to any crime scenes with you. Grace should stay at your mom's until we know more."

"Okay." The word comes out as a whisper.

My phone is on the nightstand, so I head back into the bedroom. I've missed a call from my mom. When I call back, her house phone rings and rings. I glance at the clock. I feel guilty. I usually call her and Grace first thing in the morning on the nights Grace sleeps over, but instead I forgot because I was getting busy with Donovan.

When her voice mail picks up, I leave a message.

"Mama? That second body had another Bible verse. I hate this so much, but we should probably be careful. Maybe stay home from work today. And you should probably tell Marco and Dante."

I hang up and cringe. My family hates my job for good reason. I've put their lives in danger more than once. The worst was when Jack Dean Johnson kidnapped my niece Sofia. Even though she was rescued before anything bad happened, I'm still filled with guilt over that.

"I left a message for my mom, but maybe I should just skip work today and spend the day with them?" I say to Donovan.

"Sure, you could do that," he says, absentmindedly reading the paper.

I bite my lip, thinking. I'm unsure. Am I overreacting? After all, my mom's house is secure.

Glancing down at the *Tribune* spread out on the table, I see Black's story on the slaying. He interviewed the parents of the woman who was found on Roe Island Saturday. Scooped the hell out of my story. Damn it. I need something more. I have to ask even though it's going to irritate Donovan. But he knows I have a job to do. He's filling his to-go mug with the rest of the coffee in the moka pot.

"I need to use the Bible verses. Is it going to hurt the case?" I ask Donovan.

"I doubt it, but I'll check with Beverly Anne," he says. "Did you decide to go in to work?"

I nod, but inside I'm still uncertain.

"Grace will be fine with your mom," he says. "You already suggested they stay home today, lay low. Her community is like Fort Freaking Knox. I'll call the rent-a-cops who work there and tell them to do a few extra patrols around her house if that makes you feel better."

"Okay," I say, telling myself it *is* okay as I head for the door. Grace is with my mother. She'll be fine. My mom's number is unlisted, and just like us, her property records for her home are under a fake name. We've lived this way my entire life. Once Caterina was taken and we learned evil does exist, we've taken precautions. Grace is safe with my mom.

My mother is very protective of Grace and very concerned with keeping her safe. It's one reason I don't send Grace to day care and have my mother watch her. Since she was born, it has been hard to trust anyone else with Grace, to get over the feeling that I'm the only one that can protect her. I've fought against this fear for years in therapy. When she was a baby, I nearly quit my job because I was worried that I needed to stay home to keep Grace safe. Marsha convinced me that this was irrational thinking and quitting my beloved job would be an extreme overreaction I would regret.

Besides, I know that other than me and Donovan, there is nobody I trust Grace with more than my mother. She won't let anything happen to her. I can't raise my daughter to live a life filled with fear, spending more time worrying than living.

IN THE NEWSROOM, the press release Beverly Anne sends out about the second body is not much help. Even so, I dutifully write a short story about how investigators are looking into the two deaths as the work of a serial killer.

Those two words—"serial killer"—will ignite their own shit storm when they appear in 24-point type on the front page. I dial Donovan.

"My story is lame. I have to include the Bible verses. Nobody will know it is directed at me. Except us and the killer."

He's quiet for a minute, and I can feel the tension through the phone line. "I haven't heard back from Beverly Anne to get the okay."

"All I need to know is if this will hurt your case?"

He sighs. "Stand by."

I hum a Replacement's song for a few minutes until he comes back on the line.

"I told them I couldn't control you, which God knows is the truth, and that you were going with the Bible verses. My lieutenant said if this blows our case, it's my ass."

"Oh come on, do you really think that would blow your case? It's not like this is something only the killer would know. The whole crowd of cops saw the piece of paper, right?"

He's silent.

I realize this is much more than just whether it will blow his case.

"Will you be angry with me if I print it?"

I hold my breath, waiting. Even after eight years together, I'm still learning how to be part of a couple. I probably always will be a work in progress.

"No." He says it so quietly I barely hear him.

"Thanks. I love you." I hang up and rush over to Kellogg's desk to tell him about the scoop.

"How come every fucking whack job in California thinks that invoking the Bible gives him license to kill?" Kellogg says.

I shrug.

Back at my desk, I try my mom's house phone and then cell phone again, but there is no answer. I disconnect and dial the number to her flower shop.

"Hey, Jane, it's Gabriella. Is my mom there today?"

"No, she told me she was watching Grace and wouldn't be in."

"Great, thanks." Good, they are staying home like I suggested.

I try her house phone again. Nobody picks up, so I leave a voice mail. "Mama, will you give me a call when you get this?"

A flicker of worry runs through me, but I brush it off. Once, when my mother was watching a three-year-old Grace, she didn't pick up the house phone and I panicked. When her gated community's security team arrived at her house, she and Grace were in her garden in the backyard sitting on a blanket and having a tea party.

I text Donovan: *Did you make sure security is checking on my mom's place?*

After I hit send, I'm ready to write my front-page scoop.

It takes me an hour. When I'm done, I head over to the news research department. I only have a few weeks if I want to write a story about the ship graveyard for Memorial Day.

Liz, my favorite news researcher, smiles when she sees me, her soft brown eyes lighting up behind her rhinestone eyeglass frames. Over the years, Liz and I have become close friends. She is the best librarian this side of the Mississippi. She should have left the paper and retired to Florida, where her family lives, long ago, but she would never leave her tiny Berkeley bungalow and yard overflowing with flowers. Besides, she'd be bored without the thrill of the daily hunt for information.

"Hey, sugar." She tosses her long hair, which is neatly weaved into a thick braid. When I started at the paper, her hair was brown, but now it is streaked with gray. A native Berkeley resident, she dresses in long, flowing skirts and Birkenstocks, and I suspect she might grow her own marijuana, but I've never asked.

"Anything new on Anderson?" I feel duplicitous asking after the recent killings, but Liz would be suspicious if I *didn't* ask about him.

"No, sorry." Her eyes grow soft with pity.

Liz checks her online sources at least once a week to see if Frank Anderson has applied for a driver's license or any other type of legal documentation that might indicate his whereabouts.

Liz knows everything about my past and Anderson.

After a few minutes, I'm loaded with a stack of documents Liz printed out about the Phantom Fleet. In addition, she hands me an aerial-view map of the fleet and the surrounding bay.

"I've always been fascinated by that ship graveyard," she says. "I can't wait to read your story."

When I get back to my desk, there are two messages on my cell phone—one from my mom and one from Donovan.

My mom says she was driving and couldn't pick up. Maybe she is going to work after all. I bet Grace talked her into it. Grace loves the flower shop. *She will be fine.* The flower shop is on a crowded and fancy Main Street shopping district not far from the police substation.

Donovan's message says I should go ahead and pick up Grace after work and head home. He has arranged for an off-duty cop to be outside our condo 24-7 until further notice. The cop will come inside and "clear" our apartment before we go in. Every day. I hope it was the nice cop I met the other night. He didn't make me feel paranoid or silly about him being there.

I hate being babysat like this, but I'll do it if it means my daughter is kept safe.

I'm staring off into space, facing the newsroom wall with the big-screen TV. A commercial for Baja California in Mexico is playing. The screen shows clips of a giant cactus, people frolicking on the beach sipping giant margaritas, and whales dipping in and out of the dark waters.

When I see the whale's hump gracefully rise and curve out of the water, it hits me.

I'm back to that day with the whale six years ago. The day I almost died and have otherwise tried to forget. I was tied to a dead man in a small boat by a crazed former cop out to seek revenge against Donovan. Before he left me alone in the middle of the ocean, he fired a gun into the bottom of my boat. As I fought against the idea of my death, a whale came to the side of the boat. When I looked into that big black eye brimming with intelligence and emotion, I made peace with the idea of my death.

Then I was rescued.

Later that night, I remembered an old wives' tale I had heard about coming face-to-face with a whale. Lore suggests that if you see a whale, you must go immediately to sleep and remember your dreams. When I'd heard the story, the storyteller had been cut off before she'd revealed the significance of the dream, whether it was prophetic or what. When I did fall asleep that night after I saw the whale, I had a nightmare that I've pushed back deep into a black hole in my mind.

But now, sitting at my desk in the newsroom, snippets of the dream come back.

I dreamed of a little girl laughing and playing on the beach. But then a long shadow fell on her. In my dream I couldn't see who cast the shadow, only the face of the little girl. It was filled with an unspeakable terror.

Now, remembering the dream as I sit in the newsroom, it seemed that the little girl *was* Grace. How could I have dreamed about my daughter before she was ever born? Isn't that impossible? My mind must be replacing the girl's face with my own daughter's features. Like how we think we have a memory of something from our childhood that we've seen in pictures.

Now, remembering this, I sink into my desk chair, dizzy, heart booming in my ear.

The other day I watched Grace on the beach as a long shadow appeared over her and that man leaned down to grab her arm. But she is fine. She didn't look up at him with fear or terror. She was smiling and chatting animatedly with him.

For a few seconds, I'm lost in this memory, staring at the big-screen TV in the newsroom that is now showing CNN footage of the White House. Then, with a jolt, I remember that yesterday my mother mentioned taking Grace to the beach today. Because Grace stayed at her house last night, I didn't have a chance to send over Grace's swimsuit, so I assumed they weren't going to go. My mother often keeps clothes from her other grandchildren in a tiny bureau to use as spare clothes for visiting grandkids who get messy. Fear slithers up my spine, and I'm groping through my bag, searching for my cell phone at the same time it rings.

And I know.

Grace.

Chapter 12

"Is this Gabriella Giovanni?"

"Yes." I bite the word out. I'd recognize the official voice of a cop anywhere. A wave of panic rises into my throat.

"This is Officer Kirkpatrick from the San Francisco Police Department. Is your mother Maria Giovanni?"

"Yes." At his words, my vision starts to close in on me, an oscillating circle of black. A few years back, I was shopping with my mother when she bought a new wallet. I filled out the little card that came with the wallet, naming myself as my mother's emergency medical contact, never imagining a day would come when it would be used.

I must answer yes, because he keeps talking. "She's being taken to the hospital. It looks like she was attacked, hit in the head, at Ocean Beach."

"Where's my daughter?"

Silence.

"Answer me, goddamn it. My daughter was with my mother. Where is she now?"

He clears his throat. "The witness who found your mother says she saw a man carrying a little girl up to the street. We're still trying to figure out what's going on, ma'am."

"Who? Who has her? Where is she now? Where is my daughter?" I'm screaming, and the edges of my vision are red and black and closing in.

"You're going to have to speak to the watch commander here at the scene," the officer says.

I've slung my bag over my shoulder and am running through the newsroom toward the door to the back parking lot. "Then get me the goddamn officer in charge and quit wasting my time."

My voice is frantic. So much so that people in the newsroom—who don't blink an eye at someone standing up and screaming "fuck"—actually look up from their computers and stare. A few people have halfway risen from their desks.

As I run, I catch a glimpse of myself reflected in the window. I don't recognize myself at all. I'm wild-eyed and deranged looking. My heart is thrashing about in my chest and I can barely breathe. I hear some grumbling and other conversation on the other end of the phone that I can't understand, and then a man's voice is on the line.

"Sergeant Don Jackson here."

"My name is Gabriella Giovanni. My mother is Maria Giovanni and my daughter Grace was with her." A sob catches in my throat. For once, words fail me.

"Mrs. Giovanni, we are doing everything we can to find your daughter."

I'm in the parking lot now, racing toward my car. He has to be wrong. My daughter can't be missing. She had to have run and hid when someone attacked my mother. Now it's just a matter of letting her know it's safe to come back out. As I reach my car, I ignore the image that pops into my mind of wide-open Ocean Beach with nowhere to hide.

"She is hiding. She wouldn't just leave my mother's side like that." I choke the words out, nearly out of breath from running and hyperventilating.

Not willingly she wouldn't. I push that thought aside, but then I remember what the officer said. A witness saw a man carrying a little girl away from the beach. *No!*

I'm starting to see black again on the edge of my vision as I put the key in my ignition.

"Please remain calm," the sergeant says. "A team of officers is searching Ocean Beach and surrounding streets. We'll find her."

"What about my mother?"

"Your mother is in an ambulance on the way to San Francisco General."

"Okay, okay," I say, trying to calm down. And then what he says next sends me recoiling in fear. He tries to be matter-of-fact about it, but I know why he is asking. I throw my car into reverse in the newspaper parking lot. I hop a curb and leave a strip of rubber as I pull onto the main road.

"If you have a picture of your daughter, it might help to bring it to the police station so we have it in case we need to file a missing person's report."

Oh my God.

"I'm not going to the police station. I'm on my way to the beach. My daughter is probably just hiding. I'm sure you'll find her before I even get there." My voice is panicky, frantic. Next he's going to ask for her medical and dental records, isn't he? And her little hairbrush so they can get her DNA off it? *Oh my God. Oh my God.*

I've covered a lot of missing kid cases, so I know too much about what happens when a child disappears. She can't be missing. She has to be somewhere nearby on the beach. Maybe some nice strangers took her somewhere for help.

I screech to a stop at a red light, the nose of my car sticking into the intersection.

"Mrs. Giovanni, you still there?"

So many things run through my mind. *My daughter can't be missing. You have to find my daughter. Where is Grace?*

I grit my words into the phone. "When you find her, call this number immediately. I need to call her father."

As soon as I hang up, I dial Donovan with shaking hands.

"I'm almost there," he says, his voice jagged in a way I've never heard before. The fear is entangled in his steely words. I don't ask how he's heard.

"Oh God, Donovan..."

"Don't go there, Ella. Don't even think about it." His words are fierce, desperate, and angry.

"It was that guy. From the beach."

"We don't know that. We don't even know if the witness account of seeing someone with a little girl is right."

"I know. I know." But even to my own ears, I don't sound convincing.

"Calm down, Ella." His voice is so matter-of-fact that I'm incredulous. "We've also got to consider that she was taken. That someone hit your mother over the head in order to kidnap Grace."

"Who would do such a thing?"

"I've been thinking," he says. I want to tell him to shut up right then. I want to tell him not to finish what he's about to say. If he doesn't say it, it can't be real or true. But I know, deep inside, what he is going to say before the name comes out of his mouth.

"Frank Anderson."

He's said it out loud. I thought that if I didn't say it, it couldn't be true. If I pushed it down deep inside, I could make it go away, make it impossible. But he's said it out loud now.

There is not enough air in the car. I roll down my window and gulp in the air streaming through my window, blowing my hair in a tangle around my face. Frank Anderson took my sister, and now he's got my daughter.

Donovan and I stay on the phone but don't talk. I cut off a few cars leading up to the bore of the Caldecott Tunnel and cause a cacophony of honking.

"Are you okay to drive?" Donovan finally asks. "Don't kill yourself getting to Ocean Beach. Your mom needs you. Grace needs you, Ella."

I don't answer. Suddenly, I'm angry at everyone. Donovan. My mom. And especially myself. I'm furious I didn't take off work today to keep Grace safe. And what kind of person doesn't even go to the hospital to check on her mother who was hit on the head? What kind of daughter am I?

With cold calculation I prioritize my love, organize it into little boxes. I know it's monstrous to do so, but I can't help it. There is nothing that will stop me from going to that beach and finding Grace.

"Stay strong, Ella." Donovan's voice startles me back to the road in front of me. I was driving on autopilot.

"Okay." But I don't ease up on the gas pedal, snaking in and out of cars in the darkness of the tunnel.

"Hang up and drive."

"No."

"Put me on speakerphone," he says. "Can you at least do that for me?"

"Okay." I punch the speakerphone button and set the phone on the passenger seat.

"Keep talking to me. It's going to be okay. We'll find her. It's going to be okay."

I can't tell if he's trying to convince himself or me.

Emerging from the Caldecott Tunnel into Oakland, the sight of the San Francisco skyline across the bay makes a wave of panic rise into my throat and lodge there like a wet dishrag. Ocean Beach is so far away. It will take me forever to get there. I'm punching my steering wheel when I realize they didn't even tell me how serious my mother's injury was, and God forgive me, I didn't ask.

My mother has been my guardian angel for the past five years since I've become a mother myself. She has helped me through the most challenging and difficult days of motherhood.

When Grace was a newborn, my mother saved my life.

The first few weeks after Grace was born were full of sleepless nights punctuated by nursing every two hours. I was so grateful to have a baby in my arms after suffering a miscarriage previously that I was determined to do it all on my own and soak in every minute of it. My mother kept offering to help or to take Grace for a night so I could get at least four hours of sleep in a row, but I didn't want to leave my baby's side. When I wasn't nursing Grace or rocking her to sleep, I was walking around in a haze where nothing seemed real. I felt like I'd been transported to an isolated planet for new, sleep-deprived mothers and that there was no escape.

When Grace finally did sleep in fitful chunks of time, I would curl up on our bed near her crib and stare at her chest moving up and down until I drifted off into a light slumber, only to awake at each little grunting animal noise she made. One night, I prayed to God to keep me sane. I knew I was losing it and falling into that special crazy caused by sleep deprivation. After all, a few governments use sleep deprivation as a form of torture and method of interrogation. I remember reading an article about rats who had been kept awake for several weeks and ended up dying.

But at the time, I felt it wasn't my choice not to sleep. I truly *wanted* to sleep, craved sleep, lusted for sleep. But I wasn't willing to forego my motherly duties to do so.

Donovan was at a loss. He wanted to help, but I refused to pump my breast milk at first and said that she "needed" me to be with her at all times. Every attempt to lure me out of the house or away from Grace failed. I refused to be away from her, even for a trip to the market. Going out to dinner with Donovan was not an option. I was convinced I had to be around her to keep her safe. Without me around, something bad would happen.

It was only when I started laughing and crying hysterically one night and talking deliriously that Donovan and my mother plotted my kidnapping. My mother came over with a breast pump and threatened to call my therapist if I didn't use it. So I pumped milk for a few days and agreed to go out to lunch with Donovan on Friday to keep her from calling my shrink.

But I was still walking around on autopilot when Donovan took my arm and led me to his car that Friday afternoon. My mother held Grace and waved from a window as we pulled away. It was only then I noticed my small overnight bag in the backseat.

"What the hell? I thought we were just going to lunch."

"We're going on a little field trip. Don't argue with me." He reached over and grasped my hand in his.

I pulled away from him. "I can't leave her. What kind of mother leaves her newborn baby? A shitty mother, that's who."

He burst into laughter, and I glared at him.

"Ella, you are a wonderful mother. You have to believe me when I say this is not only for your own good, it's good for Grace. She'll be fine."

We pulled into the big, swooping driveway of the Fairmont Hotel, perched on one of the tallest hills in the city. I hadn't been here since the night I met Mayor Adam Grant. A pang of sadness trickled through me as I remembered his untimely death.

Donovan handed the keys to the valet and grabbed my overnight case out of the backseat as I stood there, numbly, wishing I'd worn something nicer than a black cotton dress that probably had a trail of baby spit-up splashed down the back.

When we got inside, I found out Donovan had paid for a weekend at the Fairmont Hotel. For me alone.

After he checked me in, we found my room on the tenth floor. Inside the opulent charcoal-gray-and-beige room, Donovan helped me undress as I stood there like a zombie. I stared at him as he helped me change into some new pajamas, men's-style in pink silk. Then he tucked me into bed, handed me the phone, the remote, and the room service menu, and told me he'd pick me up at 11:00 a.m. on Sunday.

When I came home, I was a new woman. Grace had survived the weekend without me. And I had survived the weekend without her.

BUT I CAN'T survive without Grace now. Never. I'm still so lost in memories of that weekend when she was a baby that when traffic slows in front of me, I have to slam on my brakes.

I want to scream as I come to a stop, waiting for cars to merge into the toll lanes to enter the Bay Bridge.

At one point, I scream, "Fuck. Fuck. Fuck. Please let Grace be there when I get to the beach."

"Ella?" I had forgotten Donovan was on the other end of the phone.

"Okay."

"Where are you now?"

"At the tollbooth."

"I just got off the bridge. I'm a few minutes ahead of you," he says, sounding like he is panting.

I swerve to avoid the line of cars waiting to pay the toll, then ride on the shoulder until I'm at the express FasTrak lane, cutting off an angry driver who honks in a long, drawn-out, obnoxious blare.

The tollbooth is a blur as I zip through and then punch the gas, accelerating past all the other cars on the bridge until the path is clear. All the while, I'm screaming inside my head. Every now and then a sob escapes like a loud gasp. But my eyes are dry. I cannot cry. I have to stay strong.

"I'm pulling into the parking lot at the beach now. I'm going to hang up and find our little girl. I'm going to find her. I will call you as soon as I do."

I exhale in a long, jagged breath. "Okay."

What I really want to say is *Don't hang up. Don't leave me here alone.*

Chapter 13

ONCE I GET off the freeway, the drive to the beach through San Francisco is a blur. I don't remember a second of it. All I know is that when I pull up into the parking lot at Ocean Beach, it is full of ambulances, fire trucks, and more police cars than I've seen in one place in a long time. The beach, the scene of so many happy memories with Grace, appears nightmarish, even though I know it's my own dread playing tricks on me. Everything casts long shadows. Voices sound eerie, whipped around by the wind. People trudging through the deep sand seem to be in slow motion.

As soon as my tires hit the parking lot pavement, everything speeds up. I don't even bother to close my car door, just leave it open and race like I've never run before for the beach, where I see Donovan huddled with a group of cops.

I race past a reserve officer, who puts out a hand to stop me. I push his arm away like he's a rag doll. Before I get to the group, they notice me. Donovan looks down at the sand, and I stop in my tracks. They found her. She's dead.

For a second, I don't notice that Donovan is in front of me, speaking to me. "Pull it together. Grace needs you to be strong. If we're going to find her, you need to be the strongest you've ever been in your life. Do you understand?"

I nod, slowly, staring over his shoulder at the group on the beach.

"They need you to go to our place."

"No. I'm not leaving here without my daughter," I say, jerking away from him, my hair flying in my face.

He grabs my face and waits until I meet his eyes. "She's *our* daughter, Ella. And you're going to do this. You're going to do this for Grace. Do you understand?"

I don't answer.

"You have to trust me to make sure everything is done right here, and you need to make sure everything we need to do at home is done. There are certain things that need to be done when a child is missing. You know this . . ."

The days following Caterina's kidnapping are a blur of nightmarish proportions. It only comes back to me in snapshots. Now, on Ocean Beach, more than twenty-five years later, everything rushes back to me in sharp slices.

MY MOTHER AND father holding each other and weeping.

The first and last time I ever saw my father cry.

My dad's body at the bottom of the basement stairs.

My mother being taken away in a squad car to identify Caterina's body. Her ramrod posture. Her vacant eyes. Her pale face. All the members of our big Italian-American family calling and bringing food by our house.

My brothers, both angry at the world, punching each other until they are out of breath, then punching holes in the wall, overturning furniture, blasting rock music. And my mother, ignoring my brothers' bad behavior as if they are ghosts only I can see. And throughout all of it, our home invaded by police officers. Some in uniform, some in regular clothes. All with grim expressions on their faces.

I watched all of it as if I'd been a ghost myself, spying on this family that was wailing and screaming after the last guest left for the night. Wondering why I didn't feel anything. I didn't feel sad. I didn't feel angry. I wasn't like them.

I was six years old and wondered if maybe I was *dead*. Every once in a while I would bite the inside of my mouth to prove I was alive and could still feel pain. I crept around the outside of my family as a specter. The week she was missing, I didn't sleep in the room I shared with Caterina. I grabbed my blanket and stuffed rabbit and slept on the couch in the den and nobody said anything to me about it. Nobody even noticed. Once, the entire family went to the police station and left me behind. They were halfway there before someone noticed I wasn't in the car. Instead of turning around to come get me, my mother called a neighbor, who came to sit with me until night fell and my family came home with defeated expressions and posture.

"BE STRONG, ELLA." I snap out of it and realize Donovan is standing in front of me at Ocean Beach. He has a cigarette hanging out of his mouth. I stare at it, mesmerized. I haven't seen him smoke for six years. When he said I know what happens when a child is kidnapped, I realize he didn't mean Caterina. He meant from my work as a reporter. "Grace needs you to be strong. Do you understand?"

"My mom?"

"Unconscious. Your mother is a strong woman. She's a fighter," he says as he takes a long drag of his cigarette and his eyebrows draw together. He exhales over my right shoulder. "We'll find Grace. She's a survivor like you and your mother."

"Are you sure?" I'm begging him to tell me everything is going to be okay, even though I know he can't.

A man starts slogging through the sand, headed our way. Gray tips his tightly trimmed Afro. He wears a black suit with a Garfield tie resting on his belly. "I'm Sergeant Jackson." He is all business. "Mrs. Giovanni? I'm going to need to go back with you to your place and explain what we need to do there. I promise you, ma'am, we will do everything in our power to find your daughter and bring her home safe. I give you my word that I will not stop looking until she is found."

Donovan has let go of my arm and is talking to some detectives a few feet away on the beach. Someone hands him a cigarette, and he lights it from the small nub that his cigarette has become.

"I need to go see my mother."

"I understand your need to go to the hospital, but right now, it's really important we take care of some matters at your home. Right now your mother is unconscious."

"She's in a coma?"

"Why don't we head back to your place and do what we need to do. I have a call in to the hospital to alert me the minute your mother's condition changes."

"But she can't be alone. I have to go to her." I start to rush away but stop. Instead of rushing to my mother's bedside at the hospital, I need to help the police find Grace.

Donovan is back with us, eyes darting this way and that, as if he can't decide what to do or where to go. I know how he feels.

Sergeant Jackson stands right in front of me so that he is all I can see.

"You need to come with me back to your place. We need to get some pictures and set up a phone line. I promise you as soon as your mother's condition changes you will be the first one to know."

I feel a hand on my arm at the same time I hear the bone-vibrating thud of helicopters. When I open my eyes, I see it's the sergeant's hand. Donovan has his fingers over his eyes, rubbing them as if trying to wake up from this nightmare we're in. He wraps me in his arms and whispers in my ear. "I'm going to find her, Ella."

When he pulls back, the pain in his eyes nearly shatters me. He can say whatever he wants. I've heard and seen it before: a cop promising to find a missing child and then going to his deathbed regretting the promise he couldn't keep.

Donovan takes his cigarette out of his mouth and kisses me on the forehead like I'm a child. Then he turns away and heads back to the group on the beach.

Sergeant Jackson takes my arm, and I let him guide me back to the parking lot.

Chapter 14

THE SKY IS darkening as night falls upon the city. As we make our way to the parking lot, time becomes distorted. It feels like I'm in purgatory on this walk that seems like it is taking forever. Every fiber of my being wants to stay on this beach. The last place Grace was seen.

She must be so cold in just a swimsuit. She must be so scared. *Stop. Don't go there. You can't go there.*

Over the years in therapy, I've learned how to compartmentalize my fears and anxieties, to redirect my thoughts, but this—this is the off-the-charts terror. So I chant, *Grace will come home safe. Grace will come home safe. Grace will come home safe.*

Don't think anything else. Don't go there. Stay strong for Grace.

I'm not sure if it works, but it keeps me from toppling to my knees.

I give the sergeant my keys so a reserve officer can follow in my vehicle, then I get into the passenger seat of the sergeant's squad car. I'm a mass of mush, as if my bones had disintegrated. Another officer carrying a small notepad wordlessly hops in the backseat behind the Plexiglas.

"I'll ask you all this at your place, but just off the top of your head, has anyone threatened your mother or daughter?" the sergeant asks, staring straight ahead as he pulls out of the parking lot.

"No," I say.

"What about you?"

"Where do I start?" I give a strangled laugh at the irony, and the sergeant shoots me a concerned look. I tell him about my sister's kidnapping and murder. I tell him how the FBI suspects Frank Anderson took my sister, and now I'm worried he's back and killing women. My teeth chatter as I say this. I'm shaking.

Even though it is seventy degrees outside and he has small beads of sweat on his brow, Jackson cranks the heat full blast, reaching into his backseat with one hand and pulling a blanket around me as his car screeches through the city streets. When I finish telling him about Anderson, he exhales loudly.

"Detective Donovan mentioned this Anderson guy," he says and quickly darts a glance my way. "He said the feds are working on it, but we need to put out the word, as well."

The sergeant grabs his phone and makes some other calls. I tune out, saying the chanting prayer in my head to keep it together. *Please bring Grace home safe. Please protect Grace. Please help us find Grace.*

I want to get the words right, but I don't know what to say. Protect her? Bring her home? Keep her safe? All of it.

The sergeant hangs up. "Anything else odd lately?" he asks me while he looks straight ahead out the front windshield, hands gripping the wheel at ten and two o'clock like they taught us in driver's training.

I flash back to the man on the beach last weekend. I describe him to the sergeant as best as I can.

"At first he seemed young, twenties, although I think he was my age, thirties. His hair was dirty blond and cut like a little boy's in a sort of bowl haircut. I think that's what made him seem boyish. And his sort of effeminate facial features, like pink lips. And his eyes. They were weird. Icy blue. They weren't evenly spaced. It's hard to describe, but there was something odd about them." My voice is shaky.

"Yes, your husband mentioned that man."

I don't tell him I'm not married.

I squeeze my eyes together, trying to remember what the man was wearing.

"He had on Converse sneakers. I remember that. I think white or maybe black."

What else? I think. *What else?*

"And baggy jeans. He said he was from Marin and was having drinks in the city or something."

"Did you see him get in a vehicle at all?"

"No, he just walked off down the beach," I say. "We packed up and left."

Sergeant Jackson is quiet for a minute.

"Do you think he took my daughter?" I ask. "Someone took her. Why else would they attack my mother?"

"I'm calling in a sketch artist," Jackson said.

"If Frank Anderson took my daughter, I don't want to waste time looking for this guy just because he was weird. Who do *you* think took my daughter?" I'm verging on hysterics.

"Ma'am, we will follow every lead we can until we find her. First let's go over what she was wearing. The witness said the little girl had on a swimsuit. Maybe yellow and white. Do you know which one? We'll want to look through her clothes at your house to make sure that is what she was wearing."

"No. She doesn't own one like that," I say. Then I remember she was probably wearing a hand-me-down swimsuit that had been one of her cousins. "Maybe it was borrowed. Oh, God, I don't know. My mother would know. I don't know."

"Does she have any physical characteristics that might stand out," he asks. "Such as a scar or missing front tooth? Or has she ever had surgery or broken bones?"

"Yes. Her pinky. She broke her left pinky last year running down a hill. It is still a little bit crooked. It healed oddly, and the doctors didn't want to do surgery just to straighten it."

It was so silly. It was the first day of spring. She was running in the park and got carried away running down a steep hill, falling and bending her finger back. We had to keep her pinky duct-taped to her ring finger for a month. I bought pink, purple, and polka dot duct tape to keep it interesting. The sergeant is going to ask for X-rays. As soon as I think it, he does.

"I need the name of her medical doctor so we can get copies of those X-rays. How about missing teeth? Any teeth come out yet?"

"No. Not yet. Just a loose front tooth. None missing yet."

A memory of her asking about the tooth fairy streaks into my mind. "Mama, how does the tooth fairy get in our house? Does she fly through the window or use the front door?"

"Nobody knows," I told her. "But I think she must use magic, don't you think?"

Grace nodded her head vigorously so her curls bopped around. "Yes. Magic. Like the leprechauns, right?"

"Exactly."

AT OUR CONDO, I sit on the couch as a team of cops goes through Grace's room. I can't bear to see what they take. I know another team is at my mother's house.

I've called my brothers. I didn't stay on the line to talk, just blurted out what was going on and hung up.

A spasm of guilt streaks through me that I haven't called to check on my mom at the hospital, but I know my brothers and sisters-in-law are going to be with her. Plus Sergeant Jackson promised me I'd be the first to hear if her condition changed. I can't bear to call my grandmother. I'm worried she might have a heart attack or stroke from the news.

I found two pictures of Grace—her school picture and one of her profile as she tries to catch a butterfly hovering by her face. A police reserve office takes them out of my hands as if they are delicate and precious and breakable and puts them in an envelope before he takes off at a run out the door. Our condo is filled with people I don't know. Some in uniform, others in plainclothes. They all blur into one big mass to me.

The clock on the wall, a big retro school clock, ticks away like a doomsday bomb. It is 4:00 p.m. The police say it was 3:00 p.m. when the woman who found my mother on the beach saw a man carrying a little girl near the parking lot.

Grace has been missing for one hour. None of this is real. It can't be. This isn't happening. It's all a bad dream. I've written so much about missing children that the statistics are engraved on my brain. Every second that passes is vital. The first three hours are the most critical when it comes to finding a child alive.

Statistics show that about 75 percent of abducted children who are killed are dead within three hours of being abducted. According to the U.S. Department of Justice, the first forty-eight hours a child is missing are the most critical in terms of whether the child will be found safe.

The DOJ stats show that out of the more than seven hundred thousand children reported missing each year, most end up being communication misunderstandings, runaways, or custody disputes. Only about 115 kids are stranger abductions.

These facts run like ticker tape through my brain, and at the end, there is only one conclusion: We are running out of time.

Chapter 15

I'M SITTING ON my couch in a daze. Sergeant Jackson kneels at my side.

"We got info entered into the NCIC and NCMEC," he says. "We've issued an AMBER Alert. Bloodhounds are out searching the beach. We've got a team from Hamilton Air Force Base working with U.S. Coast Guardsmen doing a grid search for the square mile around the beach. We're doing door-to-door searches within that mile. We've got a sheriff's helicopter up with their infrared camera scouring the city and beaches, and another one searching the Marin headlands. We've got roadblocks and are distributing pictures of Frank Anderson." He ticks things off on his fingers as he speaks. "The FBI is gathering a response team. Coast Guard is out on all nearby bodies of water."

He trails off.

Coast Guard. Searching the waters. Looking for her body.

I sneak a glance at the clock. It is 4:30 p.m. She's been missing for ninety minutes.

"I'm going to need you to make a list of everyone you know," he says, tapping his pen on his thigh and walking away, pacing near the window.

On a yellow legal pad off the coffee table and with my hand shaking, I list every person I know, along with their address and phone number. Some techie-looking guys come in. They fiddle with the phone jack. After a few minutes, a thick, boxy phone console is on the table, connected to a tape recorder with wires.

Sergeant Jackson reappears. "Any calls you get, you hit record. John here will trace them. Also, I want you to keep a pen and pad near the phone. If the call comes in on your cell phone, write it down. If it's on your house phone, hit record, and write down the name and number on the pad. Record everyone, even your husband."

Boyfriend.

"Got it?"

I nod, acting like I have it together. The sergeant stares at me. I wonder if my eyes are bulging. I rush to the bathroom, clutching my cell phone and throwing the door open in time to collapse on my knees and dry heave into the toilet. When I'm done, I wash my face, avoiding my own eyes in the mirror.

Slumping back to the floor, I grab my phone off the bathroom sink and dial the hospital, which connects me to my mom's room.

"Ella. I'm so sorry." It's my aunt Lucia, my mother's sister. "Your mother is still unconscious. If it makes you feel any better, she looks good. Like she's sleeping. I'm sure she's going to wake up soon. You just concentrate on finding your little angel." I hear her voice catch for a second. This is the second time my family has been through this. My aunt was there with my mother when Caterina was taken.

When Grace was four, I took her to Caterina's grave. She'd been asking about the picture I keep on my nightstand of Caterina and me. She didn't really understand that Caterina was a child when she died.

"Where is Aunt Caterina?" She would ask me this, and I never knew how to answer.

"In heaven with God," I would say.

"Oh." But her little face would scrunch up. I would sometimes catch her holding the picture and talking to Caterina. She called her "Sis" in her play chatter.

"Sis, let's go play dolls. No, I don't want to eat my peas. I don't like peas. Well, then you eat them."

I loved how vivid her little imaginary world was, but it also filled me with grief that my daughter and sister would never meet.

"I'm going to Caterina's grave today," I told Grace one morning. "I'm going to drop you off at Nana's first."

"I want to go. I want to see Aunt Caterina," she said, leaping up from her pile of stuffed animals and yanking open her dresser drawer to get dressed.

I hesitated. "You know she's not there, right? It is just a place Mama likes to go to remember her." It was so hard to explain.

"Do you talk to her there?"

I waited a second and then said yes. "But she can't answer you, right?"

"Right."

"Okay. Let's go." She grabbed her little pink sweater and headed for the door.

At the grave, she stood there, solemnly looking at the little black-and-white picture of Caterina embedded into the grave marker.

"She's pretty."

I smiled. "You look exactly like her except for your hair is dark brown instead of black and you have freckles."

"Angel's kisses?" Grace tugged on one of her curls absentmindedly. And then she smiled. "I'm glad." She reached up and grabbed my hand. "Can we go now?"

I nodded.

"Bye Caterina," Grace said and skipped to the car, singing something under her breath.

"ELLA?" MY AUNT's voice jolts me back to my San Francisco bathroom.

"Aunt Lucia, what do I do? Please help me. Tell me what to do."

The line is silent for a few seconds, then she clears her throat.

"This is not your sister, Ella. They will find her. Do you understand?"

I can't even choke out an answer. Instead, I click the disconnect button.

A WOMAN WITH blond hair held back by sunglasses on top of her head walks in my front door. I'm standing in the doorway of my bathroom, leaning against the doorjamb and trying to get the motivation to walk into the living room full of cops, when I spot her. She wears a chic black tunic and leggings with cute red ballet flats that I automatically admire, which sends a zing of sickening guilt through me. I shouldn't have another thought in my head except Grace. Not another motherfucking thought.

She stops to speak to one of the uniformed police officers milling near my door, and he points my way. The woman heads toward me, lugging a large sketch pad and fold-up easel. A giant black tote bag is slung over one shoulder. She carries it all effortlessly. When she gets close, she sticks out her free hand.

"I'm Anissa Kennedy," she says, giving my hand a firm shake. Her gaze is somehow professional and sympathetic at the same time. "I'm a forensic sketch artist with the San Francisco Police Department. I've worked with them for the past fifteen years. Before that I was a professional artist, but after my best friend was murdered, I wanted to put my talents toward something that would really matter in this world."

I was right. What I saw in her eyes was the empathy that only a person who has lost a loved one to violence can truly have. We are members of a melancholy tribe that recognizes one another on a subliminal level deep down inside.

I nod, and she continues.

"I'm going to ask you some questions so we can come up with a composite sketch of the man you saw on the beach the other day," she says, shifting the sketch pad to her other hip. "It might be a little bit tougher, since a few days have passed, but I bet together we can come up with something that looks like him. You ready?"

"But it's not him." My voice comes out warbly. *It's Frank Anderson.*

"Let's just get your description down as best as we can." She pats my shoulder. "Just in case he saw something when he was on the beach. You don't need to worry about anything else." She glances around at my crowded living room. "Can we go someplace quiet?"

I lead her to our bedroom.

When I close the door she says, "I always like to point out that a composite sketch is not a hard piece of evidence but, rather, an investigative tool."

"I'm ready."

Anissa sits on a pink velvet chair near my dresser, and I sit on the bed while she asks her questions. She hands me a thick catalogue. I flip through it as she sets up her easel. The catalogue has hundreds of face shapes. Eyes. Eyebrows. Noses. Lips. Cheeks.

"I know this is hard for you, but I need you to try to relax as much as possible. What I'm asking you is information you know, even if you don't think you know it," she says, testing out some pencils on a scrap piece of paper. "You have all this information in your memory. I'm just going to help you access it."

"Okay," I say, staring off into space.

"The first, rough sketch is going to be done quickly. Then I'm going to show it to you, and we'll fine-tune some of the details, okay?" She sharpens one pencil and sets it on the easel.

I nod and meet her eyes. It feels like even turning my head takes enormous effort.

"The first thing we're going to talk about is the general face shape of this man. So turn to that page, please, and we'll go over them."

I flip to the beginning of the catalogue and look at the face shapes. I find one that is square-ish, with a Superman-type chin, and show her. She nods. Glancing occasionally at the picture I pointed out, she concentrates on the sketch.

We work on developing a sketch for what feels like forever and no time all at once. When I look up, an hour has passed. It is five thirty. Grace has been missing for two and a half hours.

The picture Anissa holds up at the end is a good likeness of the man I saw on the beach. I wish I could run it by Donovan to see if he agrees.

"It's him."

She purses her pink lips and nods. "I'm going to sign and date the front, and then I want you to sign the back."

After I sign the back, she opens my bedroom door and says a name I don't recognize. Standing there waiting, Annisa asks, "How accurate is it on a scale of one to ten?"

"Maybe an eight?"

But even though it is close to what I remember, I don't trust my memory. Pulitzer Prize-winning *Miami Herald* crime reporter Edna Buchanan cited studies showing eyewitnesses are bunk. "What about all those studies of eyewitnesses and how people can't really remember?" I ask.

"Don't you worry about any of that," Anissa says, gathering her things. "If it makes you feel better, I have a good track record with my drawings. Eighty percent of the time when there is an arrest, the suspect looks like my sketch."

She walks to the doorway of my bedroom, where a detective in a blazer and khakis waits. She hands him the sketch and he leaves.

Anissa gives me an apologetic look. "We're getting it to the media and making copies as soon as possible. We want to still make the six o'clock news."

"But that guy is not the one who took Grace," I say.

"They still want to question him. He might have seen something that day when you saw him on the beach," she reminds me.

She's right—if Frank Anderson knew the spot where my mother took Grace to the beach. He knew to find her there. That means he might have been stalking us for a while. He might have even been there the other night. What if that guy who touched Grace's arm is working with Frank or saw Frank on the beach that night?

When I finally take a step out of my quiet bedroom, the scene in the rest of my condo seems like sensory overload. The TV is blaring, showing footage of Ocean Beach and one of the snapshots of Grace I gave the sergeant. They've blown up one of my favorite pictures of Grace. They've cropped the butterfly out of the picture so the entire frame is taken up by her little face and mop of dark brown curls. I want to kneel in front of the TV and run my finger along the glass, tracing her tiny pink lips, small smattering of freckles on her nose, and giant dark eyes.

But it was just a teaser for the lead story we will see in a minute, so the picture disappears and instead the screen shows two television anchors looking grim.

I want to go hide in my room. Our small condo is filled with cops, and it makes it hard to breathe. In all the chaos, I barely notice my sisters-in-law, Sally and Nina, rush in, eyes puffy and red from crying. They scoop me up in their arms and hold me close, breathing into my hair. I fall into their arms, suddenly weak. They are all weeping, but my eyes are dry. My daughter has been kidnapped and I haven't shed a tear.

"They'll find her. Don't worry, they'll find her," Sally says, clutching my hand, her blue eyes shot with red. Nina's heart-shaped face is filled with fear. She doesn't say a word, only tucks my hair behind my ears and looks into my eyes. She can't disguise the sorrow in her eyes, and she doesn't try. She squeezes my hand. Words are not needed. We huddle on the couch, holding hands, my knuckles white. We all grow quiet watching the TV, waiting for the newscast to start.

Sergeant Jackson is on his phone by the window. I can hear him talking about a vehicle. A ripple of hope fills me. How did they get a vehicle description? He is describing a big white van without windows, jotting notes and repeating it back to whoever is on the other end of the line. A kidnapper van. In the newsroom, we've always jokingly called big vans without windows "kidnapper vans." Now it seems like the worst joke ever.

As soon as he hangs up, the news starts, my cell phone and the house phone ring at the same time, and the clock on the wall strikes 6:00 p.m. My heart sinks.

Those first three critical hours have come and gone.

Chapter 16

WITH BOTH PHONES ringing, I reach for my cell and Sally answers the house phone, reaching for the pen and paper where we are supposed to record the calls. Donovan is on my cell. The thump of helicopter blades nearly drowns him out. He is shouting.

"I'm going up in the air," he says. "They've got someone pulled over in San Mateo. White van."

"Where?" I realize how loud I've said it when everyone in the room stops and stares.

"Stay put." Donovan is shouting over the noise of the helicopter starting up. "I'll be at the van in seven minutes. Will call you then."

He hangs up. I stand, holding the phone to my ear even though the line is dead.

Sergeant Jackson hangs up his phone and hurries over. "Just sit tight there for a few until we know more. If it's her, I'll personally escort you there in my vehicle, lights and sirens. Got it?" He puts his hand on my arm. I stare at it. He doesn't think it's her.

He clears his throat. A shiver of apprehension goes through me before he even speaks.

"I need the names and numbers of Grace's medical doctor and dentist." He must see the look of horror on my face, because he quickly adds, "Standard procedure in cases like this."

Cases like this. I scream it in my head but manage to keep my lips pressed tightly together. I know this is standard procedure, but how can this apply to my life? To my daughter? *Motherfuck. Motherfuck. Motherfuck. He's talking about dental records and the tiny X-ray they took when she broke her finger running down that grassy hill last summer. No, no, no, no. Things used to identify a body.*

Sally is busy talking to someone on the phone. She twirls a strand of her blond hair around one finger as she does. It sounds like some family member. Every once in a while she glances over at me. Clutching my cell in my hand, I pace, waiting for Donovan to call back. I stop by the door, slip on my shoes, hang my bag over my shoulder, and grab a sweater. I'm ready to run out that door as soon as Donovan calls.

Please dear God let the van have Grace in it and let her be okay. I will do anything you want if you bring her home safe to me. I will let her become a nun if that is what you have planned for her. I realize I'm in the bargaining stage of the grief process, which makes no sense because I'm not really grieving. There is no reason to grieve. Grace is missing. We will find her. Besides, as far as I know, God doesn't make bargains.

I wander into the hall and stop at Grace's bedroom. Things are out of place, but the cops didn't ransack it like I've seen elsewhere.

A few of the drawers on her little white dresser remain pulled out. Her bed is mussed up. I grab a fistful of the covers in my hands, wishing they hadn't taken her pillow, wondering why they took her little pillow. Her brush is missing from the top of her dresser. A stack of papers is on her little art desk. They've been flipped through. I sit on the floor next to the desk, not letting go of the cell phone. A few times I check to make sure the battery hasn't died.

Picking up a few of Grace's drawings, what must be a cross between a smile and a grimace spreads my lips apart as I choke back a sob. I flip through her crayon scribbles. One makes me pause. It is three stick figures in a row. Me, Donovan, and a tiny figure with brown crayon hair that is Grace. It is what we are wearing that stops me in my tracks. Donovan has on something mostly black. Black pants. Black shirt with a white stripe down the middle. He also has on a top hat. Or at least what looks like one. Grace has drawn me in a long, white gown that trails off behind me. The white blob on my head trailing off behind me must be a veil. Both Grace and I are holding little clusters of red circles that must be Red Grace flowers. Her favorite.

It's our wedding.

The last time I spoke to Grace on the phone, I realized how badly she wants her parents to be married. I've ignored her pleas and dismissed them as childish.

I'm so sorry, Grace. I didn't know how important it was to you.

I should have realized. Because most little kids want their parents to be the same as everyone else's. When you are little, anything different is difficult to understand. The differences you grow to embrace with age are hard to accept when you are a child figuring out how things work in the world.

My cell rings. I shoot to my feet, shoving the picture into my bag as I answer.

"Wrong van." It's Donovan. There is so much sorrow and disappointment in those two words that my knees collapse. I stretch my entire body out on the little rag carpet in Grace's room, pressing my face into the knotted folds of pink and green and squeezing my eyes together as tightly as I can.

No.

The phone is still in my outstretched arm. I hear Donovan's voice, but I can't make out what he is saying. I don't care what he is saying. Unless he tells me he has found Grace, I don't care about anything else.

My sister-in-law Sally finds me on the floor later.

Donovan must have hung up, because he's no longer on the line.

I glance at the time on my phone. It is now seven. Four hours have passed since Grace disappeared. I don't think I have it in me to get up off the floor. I've been lying here for what feels like forever, although it's really only been an hour.

"Marco called," Sally says.

I stare at her feet beside my head. She has on black Chanel flats. "How's Mom?" I ask.

"I don't know."

I arch my head to look up at her, and her forehead crinkles in confusion. "Wasn't Marco at the hospital?" I ask.

"No. He and Dante have been out at the beach helping the search."

I'd thought my brothers would rush to the hospital to be with my mother, but they are out trying to find Grace.

"I should go see Mom." I scramble to my feet.

Sally rubs my arm. "There's nothing you can do there. Last time I talked to Aunt Lucia, she could barely hear me because of all the noise in the room. Mom's hospital room is packed with aunts and uncles and cousins. The nurses are losing their minds. She's probably pretending not to wake up so she doesn't have to deal with all of them."

The image of all my Italian aunts and uncles, crying and praying the rosary and arguing in my mother's hospital room, makes me smile.

But I quickly grow somber. How can I sit here smiling when my mom is unconscious and Grace is . . . God knows what she is going through? I don't even realize I'm yanking at my hair until Sally gently moves my hands away.

"Ella, I came in here to tell you that Sergeant Jackson wants to speak to you."

I take a deep breath, stand up, and head down the hall. When I walk into the main room, I see my cousin Tricia making coffee in my kitchen. With her big eyes, skinny body, and massive mop of black curls, she looks just like Cher in *Moonstruck*. She drops everything on the counter and rushes over, scooping me up in her arms, weeping so hard that the front of my shirt is instantly wet.

She pulls back, wiping her nose. "God, I'm sorry." She looks away, then thrusts a stack of papers at me. "I had my coworker print out these fliers off the police website. They are all over Ocean Beach and the neighborhood surrounding it."

Tricia works for the San Francisco Child Protective Services office. I'm afraid to look at the flier, but I pick one up with a trembling hand.

Grace looks out at me with her innocent smile, and I feel like a giant hand just wrapped itself around my heart and squeezed it, trying to make it pop.

The flier describes her like this:

"Grace Giovanni is a white female with brown curly hair and

brown eyes. She is 2'5" weighing 32 lbs. Her left pinky finger is slightly crooked. She has pierced ears with pink and white flower earrings. Last seen wearing a yellow flowered swimsuit and no shoes."

Sergeant Jackson hovers at my shoulder.

"Now, all of this is just a precaution in case we don't find her in the next few hours," he says. "I'm going to tell you what happens if they don't find her by about two a.m., just so you are prepared. At that time, most of the searchers will go home to catch a few hours of sleep and they'll be back out first thing at dawn. Some of my guys are still out there, but I have to say that most of the square mile surrounding the beach has been thoroughly searched. We will keep them out there until two just in case. But honestly, there's a good chance, a really high likelihood, that she's not in the area anymore and was taken somewhere else. That's why we really need to shift our focus to getting the word out as far and wide as we can. I've scheduled a press conference for ten in the morning tomorrow, and I think you and the father should be there."

I nod but think, *We won't need it. She'll be home by then. She has to be home by then.*

"I've been talking to your sister-in-law Nina, and she's going to set up a volunteer center tomorrow—"

He's interrupted by a commotion at the door.

Donovan.

He stops in the doorway, and our eyes meet across the room for a second. Behind him, I see the diminutive form of his mother.

Mrs. Donovan. I don't call her this to her face. Her first name is Fiona, but I try not to use that. I try to avoid calling her anything to her face because it is so awkward.

I've been with her only son for eight years now but have only seen her less than a dozen times, usually on a holiday or some big family event. She lives in Sacramento, where Donovan's six sisters live. Once a month Donovan takes Grace up there to see them. It's usually the one Saturday a month I'm scheduled to work in the newsroom. It's not that I don't want to go, it's just become a tradition for him to take Grace there when I work a weekend shift.

I *think* Donovan's mother likes me, but I don't know for sure. What I do know is that she doesn't approve of us "living in sin," as she told Donovan once. I don't think I'm going to be fully welcomed into her family until I'm legally married to her son. And a stubborn part of me is angry about that. I'm the mother of her beloved grandchild. Doesn't that count for something?

It does. I know it. She adores Grace. And the ravaged look on her face right now tells me she's hurting.

Sergeant Jackson is at Donovan's side, and he pulls away to speak to him.

"Can you take a look at this sketch and confirm that it's the guy you and your girlfriend saw."

"Fiancée," he says stiffly. I remember feeling the small velvet box in his jacket pocket. The picture Grace drew flits back into my mind.

We're going to get her back and then we're going to get married.

The words fly into my head before I realize it, and then I decide they are true.

We will get her back and get married to celebrate.

Then I notice Mrs. Donovan is in front of me.

"Gabriella, we came as soon as I heard," she says. One hand with long mauve nails pats her bright red hair while she looks around in a daze. Her eyes are red.

"We?"

"Jamie is parking the car. She drove."

Donovan's sister came, too. "Thank you for coming."

Her hands, wrinkled and filled with age spots, fiddle with her old-fashioned handbag, undoing and resnapping the clasp. "We won't be any bother. We're staying over at the Marriott at Fisherman's Wharf."

"You can stay here," I protest, but she shakes her head.

"We don't want to be a bother. We just want to help. What can I do?" Her manner is matter-of-fact despite her red-rimmed eyes, and I realize she needs to feel useful, like she is helping.

"I've been meaning to get into the kitchen and help my cousin Tricia make coffee and set out some food, but I just haven't had a chance to do it."

Fiona sets down her purse, straightens her shoulders, and says briskly, "Don't worry about it for another second. It's taken care of. Send Jamie into the kitchen when she arrives." She marches into the kitchen, and Donovan looks my way. His eyes are filled with gratefulness. I give him a slight smile and instantly feel guilty. How can I even consider smiling right now?

I make my way over to him and grasp his fingers like a lifeline. He continues talking to Sergeant Jackson but squeezes my hand so tight it hurts. I relish the pain.

"I just got done meeting with Agent West," he says to Jackson. "He's got a BOLO out for Frank Anderson. If there is a volunteer center set up, I want criminal background checks run on all the volunteers," Donovan says, rhythmically squeezing my hand. "I want a camera filming everyone who signs in. I want a list given to me of everyone who volunteers, and I want a cop stationed at the volunteer center."

Sergeant Jackson hesitates for a second, mouth wide open,

looking like he's about to protest, but then he closes his lips and nods. "Whatever you say, boss."

He's with a different department and outranks Donovan, yet he is deferring to him in this case. I'm filled with gratitude. He is preventing this nightmare from being even worse. If we wanted or needed things done and the police pooh-poohed us or dismissed our concerns, this would get ugly fast. Donovan has good reason for his demands. Donovan knows what I do. And what Sergeant Jackson probably knows. There is a chance her kidnapper will show up at the volunteer center and sign up to help search as a sick thrill.

Looking around, I see that our tiny condo is packed with people. Everyone is busy doing something to help find my daughter. My phone rings. It's Aunt Lucia again. She spoke to the doctor and wants to fill me in on what happened to my mother. With my phone pressed to my ear, I rush to my bedroom and lock myself inside so I can listen where it is quiet.

I take notes as she talks. What she says is very confusing to me—I think she had a hard time understanding what the doctor was saying—so after I hang up, I grab my medical handbook and look up what she told me.

Chapter 17

ACUTE SUBDURAL HEMATOMAS, severe bleeding on the brain after a head injury, are the deadliest of all head injuries. The injury can cause a person to lose consciousness and slip into an immediate coma. Sometimes, as in my mother's case, the doctor will maintain a medically induced coma to give the brain an opportunity to heal itself.

Treatment involves waiting for improvement and/or brain surgery to relieve the pressure on the brain. If the blood doesn't drain on its own, surgery is necessary. This surgery could involve drilling a hole into the skull and suctioning the blood off the brain. Or a large section of the skull could be removed, briefly or for an extended period, to relieve pressure on the brain.

Despite not-great-odds of survival, those who do survive have a chance of finding all symptoms disappear as soon as the blood disappears.

Only 50 percent of the people who suffer acute subdural hematomas survive.

After reading this, I tell Donovan that someone else has to answer the phone. We have to go see my mother.

Every minute with her has suddenly become increasingly precious.

THE CITY IS muted and muffled in low-lying fog. Our drive to the hospital is a slow crawl, with Donovan gripping the steering wheel and hunching forward, concentrating on trying to see the taillights of the car in front of us. I'm numb. I feel like a zombie. I feel disconnected from my body.

My mind wanders to memories of Grace and her first reaction to the fog. She still can't quite understand that she can't hold the mist in her hands. I glance at Donovan, and he seems lost in thought, as well.

Then I'm thrown violently forward, and my seat belt locks up as Donovan slams on the brakes. We come to a screeching halt, the sound mingling with shrieking horns. When I look up, the hood of another car is a few inches from my passenger side window. My heart is racing, but I sit back in a daze.

I barely register Donovan flinging open his door and rushing to the other car's driver's side window. Donovan's face is red, and I wonder idly if he's going to reach in and yank the man out of his car. Even though I keep my window up, I can hear him screaming at the driver, a man in a tie who is now out of his car, pointing this way and that. Donovan's face is nearly purple as he gets right in the guy's face and yells something about nearly killing us and running a stop sign or something. The man backs down. He is biting his lip, and then he must be apologizing, because he holds out his hand for Donovan to take. I look away. None of it matters to me. Not really. Finally, a line of cars honking behind us spurs Donovan back inside. He doesn't even look at me. Only starts the engine and we drive on.

Even the scare and Donovan's anger don't lift my brain from its own foggy state. I almost feel as if I'm still at home, dreaming. Everything is unclear, unfocused. Nothing seems to matter. Nothing except my mom getting better and finding Grace.

It is only when we pull into the hospital parking garage that I feel the pain I've been pushing down. My daughter is missing and my mother is in a coma. I make a choking sound, but Donovan doesn't notice the noise, only comes around to my side of the car to take my hand.

When we step off the elevator in the hospital, Donovan tells me he's going to grab a coffee and will meet me in a minute in my mom's room. He's doing this so I have some time alone with her. He knows I need it.

When I arrive, my aunt Lucia is in a chair pulled up to my mother's bed. She puts down the paperback she is reading and stands to hug me.

"Anything?" I ask when I pull back, glancing down at my mother, who could be sleeping instead of in a coma.

Aunt Lucia shakes her head. "I'm sorry."

Fury spreads out from my core, making me clench my fists. I want to pick up that metal chair and hurl it through the window. My fingers open and close as I imagine clawing at Frank Anderson's face, gouging deep enough to draw blood.

"Gabriella?"

"What? Sorry," I say, my aunt coming back into focus before me.

"I'm going to go get some coffee downstairs and I will be back," my aunt says, leaving me alone in the room, which is silent except for the sounds of the machines and my mother's breathing. Tubes come out of her mouth and her nose. More lead from under her blankets to plastic bags on the side of her hospital bed. Seeing them fills me with a rising panic that I have to beat down. *Stay strong. Giovannis don't melt under pressure.*

I TRY TO swallow down the mass of flesh that is closing up my throat as I sit down in the seat still warm from my aunt's body. I lift my mother's limp hand and hold it to my cheek. Tears prick at my closed eyelids, but I swallow back my tears. I need to be strong. For my mother and for Grace.

"Oh, Mama. I'm so sorry this happened to you," I whisper.

I gently lay her hand back down on the sheet and reach over to smooth back her silky black hair from her forehead. Besides the angry stitches, she could be peacefully asleep. The nurse told my aunt that it is good to massage her feet because it helps her circulation. My mother's also wearing compression socks, which inflate and deflate to keep circulation going and protect against blood clots. They are acting like she's going to be here awhile.

I lift the covers and massage her feet and calves for a few minutes. It feels weird to care for my mother in this way. When I was a child, my mother used to come into my room at night when I woke crying from growing pains. She would sit patiently on the edge of my bed and massage my calves until I fell asleep. Such selflessness. She must have been exhausted after working long hours at her flower shop and taking care of us three kids, but she never once complained and would sit there for an hour if it took that long.

When I'm done with her feet, I sit back near her head. I press my cheek to hers, resting there until I hear Donovan clearing his throat at the end of the bed.

Chapter 18

Wednesday

It's 5:00 a.m. Grace has been missing for fourteen hours.

I stare into the mirror at the deep black hollows nestled under my eyes. Donovan is in the shower. He's been in there for more than thirty minutes. I have to go to the bathroom, but I don't want to go in there because I'm afraid of what I might see. Is he crying? Is he punching the porcelain tiles? Is he on his knees praying and wailing and keening with the water pouring down on his face?

I can't go in there. If I see him like that, I will shatter into a million pieces.

As I stand in front of my open closet, my clothes blur in a smear of colors. What do you wear to have a polygraph done so the police can rule you out as a suspect in your child's disappearance? What do you wear to a press conference announcing your child's kidnapping?

There is a lump in my throat, a furry foreign something lodged there that makes it hard to breathe. When I walked by Grace's room earlier, it was all I could do to not throw myself on her bed.

I didn't sleep last night. Everyone left our place around two in the morning. I spent the night huddled on the couch, staring at the phone, willing it to ring with information on Grace. Every once in a while I dozed off for a few seconds. Once I woke, frantic, when I didn't feel my cell phone in my hands. It had slipped off my lap onto the couch.

Donovan paced the apartment all night long, back and forth, occasionally going onto our deck for what seemed like hours but was probably only minutes, coming back smelling like cigarettes. When he was outside, the noises of the house, the hum of the refrigerator and lights, seemed amplified and taunted me. Life without Grace summed up in an eerie silence.

All night I tried to stop my thoughts from going to the deepest, darkest territories in my mind—the places where Caterina's murder lives. Memories of my mother being stoic when Caterina was missing remind me that I need to pull it together. *You're a Giovanni. You need to be strong for Grace. Get it together.* My mind shouts this, but my body disobeys, staying immobile.

The sound of the shower turning off nudges me out of my reverie—one long nightmare that has seamlessly blurred into today. I don't know how long I've been standing in front of the closet.

Staring at the silky colors on hangers before me, I focus on a beige blouse.

LAST YEAR A woman wore a similar blouse at a news conference not long after a drunk driver killed both her children. She and her husband invited reporters to interview them at their million-dollar house in one of the exclusive East Bay neighborhoods.

We gathered in her living room only weeks after she and her children—her eight-year-old son and seven-year-old daughter—had walked to the ice cream shop. Although they'd been on a wide path set back from a parkway, a drunken driver had gone off road and struck the children, killing them both in one fell swoop.

Along with the other reporters, I sat on the couch in this beautifully appointed home full of the best things money could buy and felt how empty this couple's life was without their children. When they finally came into the room, I couldn't stop staring. Both were impeccably groomed. The mother looked like she'd had her hair and makeup done for the red carpet. Her expensive outfit—wool slacks, silk blouse, and gold jewelry—gave her a chicness I couldn't achieve on my best day. I remember thinking that if I'd been her, I'd have been unwashed and in my pajamas, not graciously welcoming a bunch of nosy reporters who had invaded my home.

I'M STARING AT my clothes hanging so neatly, when Donovan's hands on my shoulder startle me. I jump slightly but go back to my immobile state. I want to turn to him, but I'm frozen, facing the open closet, staring into the void.

Donovan's hands travel over to the base of my neck. I'm still wearing my clothes from yesterday. He unzips the back of my dress from behind. Slowly, gently, gingerly. He pulls one arm out of one sleeve, then the other arm. The dress falls in a heap at my feet. He lifts my feet one at a time, helping me step out of the dress. Then he tugs my tights down. He lifts one foot to remove one leg of my tights. Then the other.

I stare at the closet. Goose bumps rise on my bare skin—my arms and legs and back. The blacks and reds and pinks and greens merge, all swirling together. In front of me, Donovan reaches into the closet and unbuttons the back of a turquoise shift dress I wore to a wedding last year. I blink as his figure comes into focus before me. Distantly, I note he is dressed in slacks and a dress shirt and tie. His damp hair is sticking up in that sexy way I like so much.

He turns and nudges my arms into the air, slipping the dress over my head. He guides my head through the opening. He pulls my arm through one armhole. Then the other. He nudges the dress down around my chest to my waist. He shrugs it down around my hips and then stands behind me. He zips up the back, slowly, carefully, so it doesn't grab my bare skin. Then he kneels at my feet again, lifting each foot one at a time as he slips them into sandals. His fingers graze my ankles as he tightens the straps.

I stand, staring straight ahead. Not able to focus on anything in front of me except the blurry colors of the clothes in my closet.

He takes my hand and pulls me over to the pink velvet chair in front of my vanity. He gently bends my legs at the knees until I'm sitting, staring at a woman in the mirror I don't recognize. A pale-faced woman with deep, dark hollows under her vacant eyes. The woman in the mirror's face crunches up, grimacing in a mixture of pain and sorrow and anguish. I close my eyes, not wanting to see any more. I keep my eyes closed as, slowly and tenderly, Donovan brushes my hair. When he stops, he kneels in front of me until I open my eyes and the only thing I see is his face. I want to meet his gaze but I'm too afraid to look into his eyes, so I close my eyes again. The kiss on my forehead is like a whisper, and then he is gone.

Chapter 19

It's 7:00 a.m. Grace has been gone for sixteen hours.

I've been sitting on my bed for an hour. Staring at the red numbers on my digital clock as the minutes pass. The doorbell rings, and like an alarm, it launches me off the bed and into the living room. I'm on autopilot, yanked out of my catatonic state, as I buzz in the officer who is going to monitor the phone while we are gone. A headache forming at the base of my skull is a welcome relief from the clawing panic that I'm barely keeping at bay. I hold my head for a few seconds, then open the door, looking right through the man before me. All I see is a uniform.

"I'm Officer Craig."

I don't ask him if that is his first name or last.

He hands me a coffee. I take it with a jerky motion, like a robot.

Donovan opens the glass door to our back deck, stubbing a cigarette out in a soda can as he stands in the doorway. Our eyes meet and hold. It doesn't take more than a quick glance to see his eyes are bloodshot.

"Aw, geez, I'm sorry. I should've brought two coffees," Craig says, seeing Donovan.

Donovan grabs his keys off the end table by the door and pats the officer on the shoulder. "No worries, man, it's all good. Make yourself at home. Watch some TV. We'll be back soon." Without looking back at me, he heads out.

I linger behind for a few seconds. Even though the officer is here to catch any calls that come in, I'm reluctant to leave the house. If news comes in about Grace, I want to be here.

Casting a glance behind me at the cop hunched on the couch with the phone in front of him and the TV remote in his hand, I take a deep breath and follow Donovan.

DONOVAN AND I stand awkwardly in the lobby of the San Francisco Police Department's Central Station, waiting for Sergeant Jackson to come get us. I've got my hand under Donovan's blazer, resting on his back. I feel like I have to be touching him or I will freak out. The woman behind the desk is trying not to stare, but she keeps eyeing Donovan. He is bouncing lightly up and down on his toes, jaw clenching, eyebrows knit together, anger and fear and frustration coming off him in waves.

The door to the inner office opens.

"Who wants to go first?" Sergeant Jackson says, holding the door wide. He's not smiling, and a shiver of apprehension trickles through me.

Donovan clears his throat. "You're doing your job. I get that. But this is bullshit. And it's a waste of time when all your resources should be concentrated out there looking for my daughter." His words taper off into a low growl. The way he's working his jaw, I know he's about to explode.

Jackson doesn't crack a smile. "Standard procedure, Detective. You know that."

Any deferential treatment from last night is gone.

"I'll go first," I say, squeezing Donovan's hand and stepping forward. "Let's get this over with." I turn to face him. "Come get me if . . ." . . . *you hear anything.* He knows what I mean and nods without meeting my eyes. His fingers are clenching and unclenching in fists. He yanks a worn orange plastic seat away from the wall and straddles it backward.

Before the door to the lobby closes, I look back to see if Donovan is watching, but he has put his head in his hands, running his fingers through his messy hair, staring at the worn tile floor under his shoes.

IN THE INTERVIEW room, Sergeant Jackson introduces me to a slim man wearing a cardigan and Buddy Holly glasses. "I'm Corey Carter. I'm the examiner who will conduct your polygraph today."

A laptop on the table has wires stretching out from it in a neat row. A video camera in the corner is on, recording everything that happens in the room.

"I'll leave you two to it," Jackson says and leaves the room.

I glance at the big clock on the wall. Eight o'clock. Grace has been missing for seventeen hours.

As soon as the door shuts, Carter turns to me. "Don't be nervous. I'll walk you through this and get you out of here as soon as I can. Go ahead and have a seat."

I let out a breath I didn't realize I'd been holding. "Thank you," I say quietly and sit down across from him.

"Why don't we take a few minutes and get to know one another," he says, giving me a smile. "I'm a dad. Have a fourteen-year-old son and twelve-year-old daughter. I grew up in San Mateo and went to San Francisco State. As a parent, I can imagine this is about the worst thing that's ever happened to you in your life, and I'm sorry about that. So let's try to make this go smooth and get it over with so we can get you out of here."

He looks up at me over the screen of his computer but keeps tapping away at the keyboard.

I nod. But I'm not supposed to be here. This is not right. It's all a mistake. Every cell in my body wants to run far away from here. For a second, I imagine myself sprinting for the door and running down the halls of the police station until I'm outside, where I can breathe again. But then I focus back on the examiner's words and fold my hands under me on the chair to keep them from fidgeting.

"This is going to take a while," he says, now glancing at a stack of papers. "If you need to use the bathroom, please let me know. Let's go over your medical history, your prescriptions, if you see a therapist and some other factors that might affect the results. We're going to talk about why you're here, and I'm going to go over all the questions I'm going to ask you before I hook the polygraph up. There aren't going to be any surprises. Feel free to ask any questions. I know this feels like you are being treated as a suspect, but I can tell you that sometimes this process jogs people's memories and helps them remember information that they didn't realize they had retained. It's a little tedious. We go over the questions several times. In addition, the blood pressure cuff inflates and deflates, and that causes discomfort for some people. So let me know how you are doing. Any questions?" He looks up at me.

I shake my head. He pushes a stack of papers toward me.

"Now, after you sign these release forms, we'll get started."

I glance at the door, wishing with all my heart that Donovan would come rushing in and tell me they found Grace safe. This is all a mistake. Every tick of the clock takes Grace further away from me. I need to stop time. I need to slow it down.

I reach for the forms. My hands are shaking, and when I take the documents, they rattle loudly. Without reading anything, I sign them quickly, in a messy scrawl that will serve as my signature.

"Why don't you tell me a little bit about why you're here. Remember, this is just pre-interview stuff," he says when I hand him the signed documents.

I'm trying to form the words, but my throat feels clogged with mucus and I can't talk. I can barely breathe.

"You're hyperventilating," he says. "Just take ten deep breaths in and out. I'll do it with you. First breath. Breathe in, one, two, three. Now breathe out, one, two, three."

I do as he asks.

"Better?" He is untangling wires and peering under the table.

My voice wavers as I begin to speak. "My daughter. Grace. She's five years old. She was on the beach with my mother yesterday and someone came up and hit my mom on the head and took my daughter."

My heart is pounding in my ears like I'm having a heart attack. He hands me an open bottle of water that has materialized out of nowhere and I gulp it down, splashing some on my lap.

"Do you know how a polygraph machine works?"

I nod. "It measures your sympathetic nervous system." I researched polygraph exams once for a story about a woman who confessed to killing her infant son, when her boyfriend was the one who actually did it. The polygraph showed she was lying about the confession. It was inadmissible in court, but she retracted her confession before the trial when she found out her boyfriend was sleeping around.

His smile spreads across his face before he can stop it. Then he becomes serious again.

"Good, good," he mumbles, looking down. "Then you know it is okay—in fact, expected—to be nervous during the exam, correct?"

I nod.

"Let's go over the questions. Remember, these are sort of like the practice exam. Do you know who took your daughter?"

I swallow. "No."

"Did you take your daughter?"

Angry heat rushes to my cheeks and I grit out the word. "No."

What a waste of time. The clock is ticking and I'm stuck here in an outer ring of hell. My muscles twitch, and I'm eager to leap up out of my seat. I have to go find my daughter.

Closing my eyes for a second, I remind myself that Donovan is waiting in the lobby for me. I have to pull it together. I take a few deep breaths and answer the next question. The more I delay, the longer I have to sit in this room instead of being out there trying to find Grace.

Be strong for Grace.

Once I decide this, several more questions go by quickly. He asks if I've ever committed a crime. Then he asks this: Did I ever kill someone?

I wait until his eyes rise from his laptop and meet mine.

"Yes." I know my eyes hold a challenge. *Judge me if you will.*

I almost feel his slight intake of breath. I surprised him. I have killed twice in self-defense.

"Do the police know you've killed someone?" he asks in a

monotone voice, but I can feel the tension in the air as he waits for my response.

"Yes." I lift an eyebrow as I say this, and he quickly looks down. When he is done asking questions, he seems more flustered than when we began.

I explain the circumstances in which I stabbed Jack Dean Johnson and killed a former cop who shot at Donovan.

I have killed. I am a killer.

And there is no doubt in my mind that, if given the chance, I would kill the man who has Grace. If Corey Carter asks me if I would ever kill someone again, the answer would be an instant yes, and his machines would show I'm not lying.

He is chewing on his bottom lip a bit, looking at the screen. Then he looks up at me.

"I think we're nearly ready to begin. I'm going to place some rubber tubes around you at your chest and stomach to monitor your breathing, and I'll also put the blood pressure cuff on your arm to look at your pulse and fluctuations in your blood pressure. These monitors will be attached to your fingers to record changes in your skin glands, and pads under your thighs and feet will monitor and record any movement."

After he hooks up all the recording and monitoring apparatus, he tells me to look straight ahead at a blank wall and not move during the exam.

An hour and a half later, I stand to leave and become so dizzy that a circle of black starts to close in on my vision. I clutch at the table so I don't pass out.

Carter helps me back to my chair. I sit with my head between my knees. After a few seconds, I look up and drink more from the bottle of water he hands me.

"You want me to call a doctor?" he asks with a frown as I stand on wobbly legs.

I haven't slept. I haven't had anything to eat. My daughter is somewhere out there—just thinking this sends a wave of panic through me—and my mother is unconscious in a hospital bed. I should be anywhere but here. I have to get out of this little room. Now.

I don't answer, only shake my head and walk out.

Chapter 20

Donovan is in the lobby.

"Just got done," he says, gripping my arm. "They brought in two examiners, one for me, one for you. Some type of professional courtesy, I guess."

"More like they want us done in time for the press conference," I say, nodding to the steps outside, where there's a podium with a police seal on it. The clock says ten to ten. Grace has been gone for nearly nineteen hours.

"Jesus H. Christ," Donovan says, seeing the crowd gathering outside.

"It'll be quick." I know that seeing our worry-ravaged faces might make Grace's disappearance real enough for people to start looking for her and the kidnapper. I have to believe that Grace is being held somewhere alive for some reason. I have to believe that she's out there somewhere unharmed. I can't let my mind go anywhere else. Every once in a while, in a deep, dark place in my mind, murky forms huddle in shadows and whisper to me what might be happening to Grace. I have to stomp the voices down, push them back, or I will be sucked into a black hole from which I'll never escape.

Reporters are beginning to cluster on the sidewalk outside the station. Glancing through the glass door, I see a commotion when several TV reporters jump out of their vans and, holding microphones, rush toward a group of people coming up the steps.

It's my family. All at once, my brothers and sisters-in-law are on the steps, reporters trailing after them until they burst through the door. Sally and Nina rush over to me and we stand, hugging. We all hold hands so tightly my fingers hurt.

"How's Mom?" I ask Sally.

"No change," she whispers, squeezing my fingers.

Once my family is inside, Marco, who is wearing a suit over a tight black T-shirt, stands in the doorway, facing the reporters outside and blocking their way.

"My name is Marco Giovanni. I'll be the official spokesman for our family. If you want to talk to anyone, go through me."

He rattles off his cell-phone number, and reporters scribble it in their little white notebooks.

"If you bother anyone else in my family, such as my sister, Gabriella, or Detective Donovan, you're cut off. I won't talk to you and I'll make sure you are left out of any information we give about my niece. So mind your manners and we won't have any problems. *Capisce*?" He glowers at them.

The reporters eye each other but don't say a word.

Marco closes the door. He walks over to Donovan and grabs him in a hug. I'm close enough to hear what he says in his ear. "Hope that's okay with you. I don't want you guys to have to worry about any of this."

"Thanks," Donovan says, clapping Marco on the back. Donovan was raised with six sisters. He says Marco and Dante are the brothers he never had. He knows they would do anything for him.

Sergeant Jackson comes out of the inner offices, holding a sheet of paper, and clears his throat. This time, instead of a Garfield tie, he has one with the Looney Tunes' Tasmanian Devil, Daffy Duck, and an Oakland Raiders logo. A uniformed officer follows with a stack of fliers.

"Detective? Gabriella? Can I speak to you for a second," Jackson says, and we follow him over to a corner. He hands me an eight-by-ten picture of Grace, the same one that is on the flier—all big brown eyes and dark curls.

"You guys churchgoing folk?" he asks, which takes me aback, but Donovan quickly responds.

"Yes, sir."

"Good," Jackson says. "There are certain things I'm going to ask you to say and certain things I'm going to ask you to avoid saying, okay?"

We both nod. Donovan gives my hand a squeeze. I loosen my grip. I was clutching his hand so tightly I'm worried my nails were close to drawing blood.

"I want you, Gabriella, to hold up Grace's picture when Sean speaks. Then, when you speak, he'll hold it," Jackson says in a low voice. "I want both of you to say Grace's name as often as you can. I want this sick bastard to look at her as a person, your daughter, and not an object to destroy."

I feel slightly faint at his words, but I swallow and nod. He continues.

"No matter what, do not show your anger or disdain toward whoever took your daughter. Instead, I want you to do the best acting of your life. I want you to look right in the cameras and tell the kidnapper—which by the way is a word you shouldn't use right now—that you forgive him and God forgives him and God wants him to let Grace be reunited with her mom and dad. If he's got a soft spot for God, which often people do, we want to work that. Can you remember all that?"

I nod, thinking of the Bible verses. I sneak a glance at Donovan. His jaw muscle is working as he chews the inside of his lip. A nervous habit.

We head back to the others, and I introduce Jackson to my brother Marco and explain that he volunteered to be the family spokesman.

"Good idea," Jackson says, shaking Marco's hand and handing him his card. "We'll keep in close touch."

Jackson clears his throat. "Everyone ready?"

We all nod.

"Let's do this."

OUTSIDE, AT THE top of the steps, my family stands in a semicircle behind the podium. I feel hands from everyone touching my waist and back and shoulder, sending me their support.

There are more than a dozen microphones taped to the podium. The police closed off the street below to traffic because the reporters and bystanders are spilling off the steps and sidewalk.

My friend Nicole, our court's reporter, is in the crowd. Her eyes are red-rimmed from crying. She called my cell phone three times yesterday, but I never picked up. She nods at me, biting back tears, and her thick blond bob bounces slightly. She holds her hand to her heart, and I have to look away.

To my relief, the police chief comes out the front door right then, and as all the reporters jostle for position, Nicole's sorrowful face blends into the crowd. I'm surprised that the chief is going to do the news conference himself.

"Thank you for coming this morning. When a child in our city disappears, we make it our number one priority to bring her home safely as quickly as we can. Part of that involves getting the word out, and that's where we are asking for your help. My staff is passing out fliers with information that I hope you share immediately with your public."

He goes on to read the contents of the flier.

I stare at the one in my hand, feeling numb, out of body, almost as if I'm watching myself from high above. Someone nudges me, and I realize the chief has introduced me.

I shuffle in front of the microphone. The crowd before me is blurry. I blink and focus on one face up front. It's the weekly reporter, Michael Dillman. He is nodding and encouraging me to speak. The world narrows so it is just the two of us. His eyes are telling me it is okay. I stare at him as I speak.

"Please, I beg you, help us find our daughter, Grace. Help us find Grace. Please share her picture with everyone you know, and please call the tip line. Even if you think it's nothing, it might be something important. You never know."

The weekly reporter gives me a solemn nod. Time to address her kidnapper.

"Whoever has Grace, I want you to listen." I take a deep breath and briefly close my eyes. When I open them, I look right into the lens of Channel 5, the best-watched news station in the Bay Area. "If you took Grace, I want you to know that I forgive you. I want you to know that God forgives you. Please just return Grace to her family. It's not too late to do the right thing. We understand.

We know that you want to do the right thing and let Grace come home to us. Thank you."

I back away. Donovan passes me the eight-by-ten photo of Grace he's been holding. I hold it in front of my face as he steps in front of the podium. The blood is rushing in my ears so loudly I don't hear anything else. I don't realize Donovan's done until he steps back beside me.

The chief returns to the podium, and the reporters jockey for position, all asking questions at the same time.

"That's all we are releasing at this time," the chief says and turns away.

As the reporters on the steps below begin to leave, I cast one last glance at Dillman. As soon as I meet his eyes, he looks down.

Back in the lobby, Marco walks into the center of the room and waits until we are all watching him.

"Tomorrow afternoon we meet at Nana's," he says. "The whole family will be there, along with some special security people we are bringing in to conduct our own search."

A look of surprise flashes across Donovan's face. He shoots a glance at Jackson, who is in the corner, busy on his phone.

"The police are fine, but we need more than them," Marco says. "If she is not back by tomorrow, we take matters into our own hands. We need to find Grace now. There is no time to waste. If she is not found, we will meet tomorrow at three."

My mind goes where I don't want it to go: today at three o'clock Grace will have been missing for twenty-four hours. I block this thought out and watch as Dante and Nina leave. They make such a striking couple. Nina makes her way down the sidewalk in a black pencil skirt, black silk blouse, and Louboutin heels, one hand holding onto Dante, in his dark suit with a black shirt and black silk tie. *They are dressed for a funeral.* The thought pops into my head before I can stop it. A few reporters start to approach them but see Marco standing in the doorway, watching, so they back off, talking among themselves.

Marco's wife, Sally, hangs up the phone, tucking her blond hair behind her ears.

"A tiny bit of good news, honey," she says, her pale cheeks now flushed. "The governor is willing to offer a ten-thousand-dollar reward to find Grace."

"Thank you," I say, pressing my lips tightly together. I know that wasn't the right response, but I can't figure out what else to say.

Jackson is shuffling papers. He hands me a pen and forms to sign. For Grace's dental and medical records to be released. I scribble my name, my hand shaking.

A few reporters linger on the steps, casting glances our way. Dillman is gone, but then one familiar face I'd rather never see again materializes out of the crowd. He's swinging the front door open.

Andy Black. My competition at the *San Francisco Tribune*. My one-night stand. The reporter who taunted Donovan about me, got a punch in the jaw from Donovan that ran on national TV, and then got Donovan suspended.

He starts to brush his way past us in the lobby, but then pauses and turns back to Donovan.

"How did your lie detector test go?" he asks. Donovan is already lunging for him. Marco grabs Donovan's arms.

Before I can react, Sergeant Jackson swoops in, grabs Black by his jacket collar, and nearly throws him out the front door.

"I was just going to use the bathroom," Black yells as the door closes. Outside, he makes a big show of smoothing out his jacket and pants before leaving.

The door to the inner offices swings open, and I'm relieved to see a familiar face.

Lieutenant Scott Strohmayer. He immediately hugs me.

"Let me know what I can do," he says, grabbing Donovan in a hug after me. "I've been out all night on the grid search."

"Thanks, man," Donovan says, giving him a hearty pat on the back.

We've been friends with Strohmayer and his wife, Mary, for the past five years. Grace loves hanging out with their twelve-year-old twin boys.

"Mary's recruiting people to spread the word and search as we speak."

There is so much I want to say, but all my dry throat can manage is the one word that counts. "Thanks."

Strohmayer glances outside at the few stray reporters milling around on the steps.

"You ready to get out of here?"

Donovan and I nod.

"Give me your keys," he says as he holds out his hand. "I'll pull your car around back to the employee lot. Meet me there."

Donovan hands him the keys and we head toward the back.

Out in the parking lot, Strohmayer leaves the car running and hops out. Donovan's phone rings, and I wait inside the car, watching, as he paces outside, smoking a cigarette and talking on the phone.

Strohmayer leans in my window.

"We'll find her, Gabriella." His mouth is set in a grim line.

I don't answer; I just try to form my lips into a smile of thanks. I'm not sure if it works.

Donovan hangs up the phone, steps on his cigarette, and hops in the car. He's not smiling. He meets my eyes and shakes his head slowly.

Dread fills me.

"It's not Grace," he says before I manage to speak. A mixture of disappointment and relief fills me. See, the thing about not knowing is that it also gives me another few seconds to believe Grace is alive. I sweep away that thought. Of course she is. *She's alive, goddamn it. She's alive.*

"They found another body. In Benicia this time. Another Bible verse." Something about the way he says it sends a series of alarms pinging throughout my body. My mouth is as dry as cardboard. The muscle in his jaw is working overtime, and his gaze is piercing.

"What was the verse?" I swallow back my dread.

"He shortened it again."

"Tell me what it said."

Donovan rakes a hand through his hair before he speaks, his voice wavering.

"'Vengeance is mine, I will repay, says the Lord.'"

It is the third verse Anderson sent me. Acid fills my mouth. There is not a shred of doubt now. There is no way for me to deny it any longer.

Frank Anderson has Grace.

Chapter 21

THE WIND IS whipping my hair across my eyes, lashing my cheeks as I stare at the gray-blue ocean that stretches for what seems like forever until it meets the same color sky.

I want to run down the length of the beach, screaming for Grace. I demanded that Donovan drive to the beach before we went home. Donovan and I walk to the spot where the waves dampen the sand without saying a word.

For the first time since Grace was taken, I allow myself to cry. I weep silently but violently, falling to my knees, digging my fingers into the sand. When I'm done, my face is covered in snot and tears. I wipe my face, now scratchy with sand, with my sleeve. When I stand and turn around, Donovan is gone.

I see him back in the parking lot, leaning against the car, smoking and watching me.

I've cried until the tears have dried up. Now what? I look around me, taking in my surroundings. The beach looks so harmless. A place where families pack picnic lunches and build sand castles. A spot where lovers lay on blankets or college girls come to work on their tans. A place that is now ominous in my thoughts. A nightmarish landscape that has sucked my child away from me.

How could she have been here one minute, laughing and playing in the sand, then snatched away from us the next? I whip my head around, looking down the beach in both directions as far as I can see. The sand is deserted on such a cool day. Roiling clouds overhead cast grayness upon everything in my sight. I'm standing on the shore of the Pacific Ocean, yet it feels like a desert, a vast, barren desert leached of color and life.

Get it together. Be strong for Grace. You owe her that. You're a Giovanni. You can do this.

Gooseflesh rises on my arms and I hug myself tightly. I realize with horror that at this exact moment I wish I'd never had a child. At the same time, I'm mortified that this even crossed my mind.

A rush of determination surges through me. I can't sit still on this beach, wallowing in self-pity. She's not on this beach. But she is somewhere. She's alive. I would know if she were dead. I have to believe I would know.

Some say there is an invisible cord that connects a mother with her children. I once read a *Scientific American* article about the incredible bond, both psychologically and physically, between a mother and her children. The article talked about microchimeric cells, which are cells from another person found within you.

In most cases of microchimerism, a mother and her child have exchanged cells, either across the placenta during pregnancy or transferred from mother to child during nursing.

Grace and I share cells. If she were dead, I would know. But I also know that is one question I never ask the parents of a missing child: Do you think she's still alive?

In the past, I've believed that most people have to cling to the hope, the slightest tendril of a chance, that their precious child is still alive to keep them from collapsing in a heap of flesh and bones. Now I know this is true.

Chapter 22

WE ARE BACK at the police station. While we were at the beach, Sergeant Jackson called. A task force comprised of police officers and FBI agents has been set up to find Grace, and he wants us to attend the first meeting.

When we are escorted back, the small conference room at the police station is full. People are poring over maps taped to the wall showing where searches have been done and what searches need to be done. They are also sharing information on the three women's bodies.

"We've got a rush on DNA analysis for the three vics," someone is saying as I walk up. "We can compare to Anderson's DNA."

Anderson's DNA is in the system. After killing Caterina, who knows what Anderson was up to throughout the years, but we do know one thing—details of the crime that put him away for a few years after that. He broke into a home and masturbated on a little girl's underwear. He got caught when the father returned home to retrieve a briefcase he had forgotten.

The man, an ex–pro wrestler, found Anderson in his daughter's bedroom with his pants around his ankles. He beat Anderson to a pulp before calling the police. There was some discussion that Anderson had to have reconstructive surgery in prison. I'm sure they didn't bring in the best surgeons for that.

Investigators were able to link him to several other break-ins, but Anderson had a documented history of mental illness from a military stint and pled not guilty by reason of insanity. He got out on parole after only eight years at the Napa State Mental Hospital.

I know it is good that they are trying to match the DNA, but that's not helping them find Grace. They can work on linking him to the three murders all they want as long as my baby is home safe with me.

A small table in one corner is filled with donuts and coffee and sodas. My stomach growls seeing the donuts, but I'm worried that if I eat, I will puke. That doesn't stop Donovan, who doesn't even like donuts, from grabbing three and scarfing them down in less than a minute.

I glance at the clock. It is one o'clock. Grace has been gone for twenty-two hours.

We stand in a corner with Sergeant Jackson and his boss, Lieutenant Bruce Campbell. The rest of the room is filled with plainclothes detectives from San Francisco, Martinez, and Rosarito trying to put their joint pieces together.

FBI Special Agent Noah West is also in the room. His gut hangs over his belt, and his swept-back hair has grayed. His forehead now has permanent creases. He is no longer the young buck agent I met five years ago. I suppose that seeing what he does would age anyone prematurely.

After everyone settles down into chairs, Donovan, West, and Sergeant Jackson stand at the front of the room. I stand against the wall off to the side.

As Donovan and West fill the other cops in on Grace's disappearance and our family's history, the connections between my sister's kidnapping and death and the recent murders become stronger:

All three women were taken and held for six days.

My sister was taken on a Tuesday, and her body was found on a Monday. Six days later. Grace was also taken on a Tuesday. If the pattern is repeating itself, and Grace's kidnapper intends to kill her in six days, we are running out of time. West passes out mug shots of Anderson. A few seconds later, someone hands me a stack. I take one and pass the stack on.

Fury crawls up my neck like a warm rash when I see his picture again. I clench my hands. And I know for certain. I would kill this man. If he were in front of me, I would rip his throat open with my bare hands.

"Find him." I say it in a low voice. Only one person nearby hears me and gives me a quick look before glancing away. My hand holding the photo betrays me with tremors, making the face on the photo jump around. I turn around and examine one of the maps on the wall behind me. They've searched every nook and cranny within a mile radius of Ocean Beach.

"I'm shooting photocopies up and down the state and as far north as Washington and as far east as Utah," West is saying in the front of the room, dragging his hand through his hair. "Every cop shop in the West is going to have this dude's mug on their wall.

"We're also having a sketch artist do an age progression photo. This was about a decade ago. We'll put both the sketch and the mug on one page. The composite sketch will show more wrinkles, less hair, etc."

West is very matter-of-fact about what needs to be done, and for some reason this calms me, makes my heart rate slow back down. I turn back around and face the front of the room. Donovan meets my eyes and gives me a barely perceptible nod. *Stay strong.*

"We've amped up the pressure to find Anderson's last whereabouts," West says, now chewing on a toothpick I didn't notice he had. "If he's been anywhere in this part of the state, we're going to find him."

I nod, meeting Donovan's eyes, but the truth is my faith in West has slightly evaporated. He's had more than five years to find Anderson, and he is trying to convince us he can find him in the next five days.

Then Sergeant Jackson gets up and talks about how his officers need to work with the FBI agents and set past differences aside in order to find a missing little girl. Cops usually resent the feds moving in, but this is standard procedure when a child is missing. I stare at the heads of the cops seated in the white plastic chairs. Nobody rolls his eyes or scowls. They are going to work together to find Grace. I'm so grateful I want to cry, but instead I pull my shoulders back and head for the door as soon as the meeting ends.

Chapter 23

Standing in the doorway of my mother's hospital room, I hold my breath watching my grandmother. It is two in the afternoon. My mother has now been unconscious for more than twenty-three hours, nearly an entire day.

Besides my grandmother's fervent whispering above my mother, the only sound is the beeping of the monitors. The breathing tubes obscure my mother's face. Wires trail from her throat, her arms, her mouth, and her face. Dread fills me seeing her like this. Donovan stayed downstairs to smoke, and I suddenly wish he were by my side.

My grandmother doesn't notice. Although her back is turned to me, her face is reflected, ghostlike, in the window. She holds a bowl above my mother's head. She speaks in a low murmur and drips drops of oil from a small crystal cruet into the bowl.

In an instant, I'm transported back to my childhood.

My grandmother and mother stood over my bed. My grandmother held a small bowl. My mother had my feet out of the covers and was doing something near my feet.

I sat up and my grandmother pulled back, mumbling something in Italian.

"Shhhh, *mia cara*. We'll be done in a minute. Lie back and close your eyes."

My mother came to stand beside me then. "Nana came over here tonight because she wants to make sure you are protected against the *malocchio*," my mother said and gave me a wink I nearly missed. It was a game. She was humoring my grandmother and wanted me to do so, as well.

But I didn't understand. Why did she need to protect me against the evil eye? What about Caterina? I glanced over to the place where Caterina's bed once was. It was gone. Then I remembered. Caterina was dead. She'd been gone for a while, but I still sometimes woke up in the mornings and forgot until I looked around for her. I hadn't spoken a word since they found her body in some bushes by the side of the road.

Then it hit me—they were casting out the evil spell they thought was on me that prevented me from speaking. I could talk if I wanted. I just didn't want to. To prove it, I opened my mouth to tell them this, but nothing came out except a little grunt. I clamped my mouth closed.

In defeat, I slumped back down and closed my eyes, wanting everyone and everything to go away. I didn't want to talk anyway. What was the use of anything? Caterina was gone. A monster took her and then my father died. They were both dead in the ground and buried. I was only six years old, but I knew then—monsters are real.

I reached up and angrily swatted at my grandmother's hands holding the bowl over my head. Water and something slimy splashed on my face, and my grandmother scolded me in Italian. I didn't recognize the words she used, and I didn't care. I just wanted her to leave me alone.

I rolled over until I was facing away from them, keeping my eyes scrunched tight until I heard their footsteps leave my room. Only then did I reach down to my feet to feel what my mother had been fiddling with. She had tied a silky ribbon around my ankle. I flipped on my bedside light and crouched, examining it. It was red like blood. I tore at it to rip it off, but it only stretched out and hurt my fingers.

I got out of bed and stood by my bedroom door, listening. I heard my mother and grandmother talking and then the front door open and close. I waited until I heard my grandmother's car drive away and my mother's bedroom door close. Then I crept into the kitchen like I did every night. My mother's kitchen shears were in the drawer. They felt giant in my fingers. In one smooth motion, the ribbon was off. I left it where it fell on the floor and put the shears on the counter, not bothering to hide my handiwork. I turned toward the kitchen table, where my uncle had left the chess game.

Each day he came over and moved a piece. Each night I got up after everyone else was asleep and moved my own piece. Chewing on a strand of my hair, I studied the board.

On that day, my uncle had moved his knight and now was about to take my queen. I knew I had two choices: move my queen or kill his knight. Quietly, I scooted a kitchen chair out and leaned over the board. The pieces cast long shadows from the tiny stove light.

I could take his knight, but if I did, he would not only take my pawn with his bishop but he would also put me in check. And then when I moved to get out of check, he'd take my queen anyway. So I'd lose my pawn and my queen.

Biting my lip, I looked at all the possible things that could happen if I moved my queen. If I did, he could put me in check in two moves. Then, for me to get out of it, he'd walk away with my rook and bishop. I couldn't let that happen. Without my rook and bishop, I'd lose.

As reluctant as I'd been to play chess with my uncle, I was then desperate for the game to continue. I sat and stared at the board, going over various combinations until I fell asleep, slumped on the table. In the morning, my mom found me there and woke me with a kiss to my forehead. I sat up, and she set the table for breakfast like she had done for the past five months, ignoring the chessboard in the middle.

I glanced at the board and finally admitted what I hadn't wanted to the night before: I was going to lose this game. No matter what I did, my uncle would have me in checkmate in three moves or less. Then I did what I had never done before—I tipped over my king. I resigned.

For the next few hours, I restlessly paced my room, glancing out my curtains every few minutes until I saw my uncle's car pull up. I waited until I heard him and my mother settle in at the kitchen table with their coffee cups before I came out.

My uncle, my mother's brother, owned an Italian shoe store less than a mile from our house. After my father died, he came over for coffee every single day.

On this day, I hovered in the doorway, spying on my mom and uncle. I glanced at the board. He had accepted my resignation and moved all the pieces back to starting position. But he hadn't moved a pawn to start a new game. I swallowed back disappointment that it was over. When my foot made a scuffing sound on the wooden floor, he looked over.

"Gabriella," he said, his eyes lighting up. "You were smart to resign. That little formation is exactly the same as the move that allowed Bobby Fischer to win the World Chess Championship against Spassky from the Soviet Union. It was Fischer's dream to win this match. And in the nineteenth game, it all came down to one move. Just like Boris Spassky, you saw by moving bishop to d7, my next move would have been king to g4, and one more move to win. It is a tricky one, and you were intelligent enough to see the outcome. That's why I think you are ready for this."

He leaned down and rummaged in a plastic bag at his feet. When he sat up, he had a beige rectangular piece of plastic with silver buttons on the top. On the front on each side were clocks, timers.

"I'm going to show you a new way to play," he said.

My mother cleared the dishes.

"Sit down here." He pointed to the seat across from his. We played three fast games. I liked punching the button after I made my move. The fast pace was exhilarating. In the third game, I saw it. The perfect move. Maybe even checkmate. I picked up my black piece and carefully moved it.

"Check!" The word flew out of my mouth before I realized it.

My uncle stopped, frozen, his hand hovering in the air above the chessboard.

At the sink, my mother dropped a glass, shattering it. She stood at the sink, her back to us, shoulders hunched over, quaking.

It was the first word I'd spoken in six months.

To this day, my mother will tell you that my grandmother broke the evil spell of the *malocchio* that night and that is why I started speaking again.

Me? I really don't know.

WATCHING MY GRANDMOTHER now in my mother's hospital room, I know that at the very least, what she's doing won't hurt my mother.

"Nana?"

She jumps, and a little drop of water from the bowl spills on my mom's cheek. I stare as it slowly dribbles down my mother's neck.

"I tell you about this at Christmas," my grandmother says, shaking her head. "It is time you know."

"What?"

"This. I get rid of the *malocchio* on your mother."

"I remember when you did it before. For me." I hover in the doorway, afraid to disrupt what she is doing by coming closer.

"It is a sacred ritual that was passed down to me by my nana. It can only be shared at midnight on Christmas Eve. It is time you know."

She sets the bowl down and holds her hand out to me. I walk over and put her hand in mine.

"Okay. It's a date. Why don't you go home, Nana?" I say, squeezing her hand.

She is about to protest, but then nods. "Yes, I'm very tired. Your uncle Dominic is supposed to be here soon. Any minute. I want to get home and get the house ready for everybody coming over tomorrow. I need to make coffee and some biscotti and maybe some ravioli."

"Nana, don't worry about that. Nina and Sally said they are bringing treats. You don't need to do anything except be there and relax. Go. Go on home and take a nap. I'll sit with Mama until Uncle Dom comes." I grab her and hug her, folding myself into her softness.

"I say the rosary for Grace today," she says, pouring whatever is in the small bowl into a bag, then tucking them both in her handbag.

"Thank you," I whisper in her ear.

I watch as she leaves the room, giving one last glance at my mother.

Chapter 24

If I squint as I drive along the shores of San Pablo Bay, I pretend I can see San Quentin in the distance, nestled across the bay in Marin County. But the smog is blocking my view. The day is gray and dull. It's how I imagine my heart must look right now. In thirty minutes, Grace will have been gone for twenty-four hours. An entire day.

Right after we left the hospital, West called. They have an address for Frank Anderson's mother, and we are nearly there. In the back of my mind, I can't help but wonder if West would have been able to find Anderson's mother years ago if it had been a "priority." I know the FBI's focus has been on terrorism since 9/11, but it is still disheartening to hear that my case was "shelved."

Donovan's Saab plummets into a huge pothole and back out again, and I grab for the dash. Road repair is the least of the city's problems.

Richmond can be one of the roughest areas in Contra Costa County. Last year the city was dubbed the ninth most dangerous city in the country. But it also has more waterfront—thirty-two miles—than any other Bay Area city. Last year, after a man was shot in the face at a teenager's funeral, a group was formed with the police chief and city officials' blessings to put fifty of the city's most lethal characters in a program to turn their lives around. Our paper's Richmond city reporter is writing an ongoing series about the program, which is still in its infancy.

Passing the Richmond-San Rafael Bridge, nicknamed "The Rollercoaster Bridge" for its curves and bumps, we pull off the freeway into an older part of the city, with apartments and strip malls and trash clogging the gutters.

Right when we pull up to the address, I look at the clock on Donovan's dash. Three o'clock. Grace has officially been missing for twenty-four hours. The longest twenty-four hours of my life.

I debate mentioning the time. Donovan takes his gun out of the glove compartment and tucks it into his shoulder holster before he leaps out of the car and furiously smokes a cigarette before we have to go inside. West pulls up in his dark blue Crown Vic a second later, and Donovan glances at his watch. I don't have to tell him how long Grace has been gone. He already knows.

Although the streets are empty, Donovan sets the car alarm before all three of us head up the cracked sidewalk to the squat apartment building before us. Apartment 3 is on the first floor, behind a barred screen door.

An emaciated woman answers our knock. She has long, stringy gray hair that is nearly yellow and wears a pilled sweater over sweatpants. I can't see beyond her into the apartment.

"Mrs. Anderson?"

Her eyes narrow and her arm flinches, ready to slam the door.

"I'm FBI Special Agent Noah West." West flashes his badge and wedges his shoe in the space between the door and the jamb. I stare at his shoe, some type of loafer. It looks like something an old man would wear.

"Detective Sean Donovan, Rosarito Police Department." Like West, Donovan flashes his badge. "We're here to ask you about your son, Frank Anderson."

She startles us by rolling her eyes. "Frank? You're here about Frank? I haven't seen Frank since he was five. That's why you're here? I thought you were the social services."

Her efforts to push the door closed come up firm against Donovan's foot.

"Who raised him then?"

"His father's mother. Lenora Anderson. She's probably dead and gone now, though. Last I heard she was in that home for old folks down the way on Crockett Boulevard."

Donovan withdraws his foot, and we leave to the sounds of her mumbling. "Thought they were the social services coming with my check."

INSIDE THE CROCKETT Boulevard care center, Lenora Anderson sits in her wheelchair in the sunroom, staring at nothing. When I see her vacant gaze, disappointment fills me. She is so old. As we watch, the nurse who escorted us says Mrs. Anderson is 102 and has good days and bad days. She doesn't know which one today will be.

The nurse nods toward Mrs. Anderson. "I'll leave you be. I'll be around if you need me." She busies herself with cleaning up some Scrabble pieces some other residents of the facility must have left. The care center smells damp and slightly sour and I try to breathe through my mouth. The sunroom is deserted for some reason, which doesn't make sense until I hear laughter and hooting from a room down the hall. It's time for *Wheel of Fortune* in the TV room, apparently.

West turns to me. "Why don't you try talking to her first?"

I'm surprised, but grateful.

Mrs. Anderson is facing a big picture window. She is tiny and shriveled, with wispy white hair in curls. A red-and-gold-colored crocheted blanket covers her lap. Beside it is a small teddy bear. I crouch in front of her, looking for any comprehension in her eyes. She smells like talcum powder.

"Mrs. Anderson?" I say gently, putting my hand on hers.

Her head wobbles on her neck as she takes me in.

"I don't know you," she says in a voice barely above a whisper. "Am I supposed to know you?"

"No. We've never met. I'm Gabriella Giovanni. I'm here to ask you about your grandson, Frank Anderson."

She looks blank and kneads at the blanket on her lap. "My grandson?"

"Yes, Frank," I push on. "Your son's child. You raised him, remember?"

"Frank." She lets the word roll across her tongue slowly, without revealing whether she remembers him or not.

I give Donovan and West, behind her, a look of despair. She doesn't remember her own grandson, whom she raised?

"I know Danny. My son. He was such a good boy. He was the light of my life." Her head wobbles as she speaks, and a big grin spreads across her face, then fades. "But he never comes to visit me. I think he's dead. They won't tell me that, but I know. A mother always knows."

Her words send a brief chill down my spine. *A mother always knows.*

"Maybe you could tell me about Danny?"

She doesn't answer. She smacks her lips together and leans her white curls back on the chair's cushion. Soon, the soft sounds of snores are coming out of her open mouth.

The nurse is at our side with a sympathetic look.

"I saw you on the news," she says, looking away as soon as she says it. "Why don't you come back in about an hour and try again?"

IN THE PARKING lot of the care facility, Donovan and West talk and smoke outside, while I lean back against the car seat, closing my eyes. I say a silent prayer. *Please bring Grace home safe.* I'm worried if I elaborate on that one desire, it will take power away from my prayer. So I say it over and over and over. *Please bring Grace home safe. And alive,* I add, suddenly worried that God's idea of "safe" might be different from mine.

I know I'm being ridiculous. When I was little, my grandmother used to tell me that the words you used to pray didn't matter. God always saw your heart and what you really wanted and needed.

As I sit there, Donovan's conversation with West only reveals itself in a word here and there drifting through the cracked car window. "Body. Benicia. Bible verse."

West walks to his car, and Donovan climbs in the driver's seat and puts his hand on my thigh.

"You hungry?"

No, I think, but I nod.

"West has a meeting," Donovan says. "We'll come back here alone in an hour or so. Right now, I need to eat. Those donuts at the police station didn't cut it. Let's go eat and come back in an hour."

As we leave the driveway, I wonder about something. "Where did they find that third body again?"

"On the shores of Benicia."

I sit up straighter. "All three bodies were found within a few square miles. Do you think he's dumping them close to where he's living or staying?"

Donovan gnaws on his inner cheek, nodding. "That's what we're going on," he says. "We've got detectives canvassing all the businesses around each murder scene to see if they saw anything suspicious, but also showing people in shops and houses Grace's flier, the composite sketch of the man on the beach, and Frank Anderson's picture."

I PICK AT some calamari at the restaurant and sip on a soda. Nothing seems real. The world around me appears flat and dull.

As I'm eating, my sister-in-law Sally calls and tells me that the family talked and they want to hold a candlelight vigil at Ocean Beach tomorrow night a few hours after the family meeting at my grandmother's. They'll only hold the vigil *if* Grace is still gone, she adds quietly.

I close my eyes as she says the word "vigil."

"Vigil" means that Grace is a missing person. It means she's been gone for much too long. My mind dips into a whirlpool of memories flying around, and as much as I don't want to, one huge question leaps to mind: Have they ever found someone alive after a vigil is held? I push the thought back down into the darkness before I even try to answer it.

"Gabriella?" Her voice startles me back.

"I'm here."

"People want to come together and pray, you know."

"Yes."

"I've already called Father Liam. He says he'll come and lead the prayer."

"Yes." Over the past five years, Father Liam has become something of a father figure to me in addition to being a spiritual counselor.

"Gabriella," her voice breaks. "We'll plan for it and then maybe won't even have to hold it, right?"

"Yes."

When I get off the phone, Donovan raises an eyebrow.

The words stick in my throat, and I have to take a few sips of water before I can speak.

"A vigil. Tomorrow night."

He closes his eyes for a few seconds, then opens them and nods, staring straight ahead.

BACK AT THE care facility, Mrs. Anderson is back in the sunroom but now has something orange smeared around her mouth. Her early dinner? Pureed carrots? I want to wipe it off but am worried she will recoil from my touch, no matter how gentle I am.

"Do you remember me?" I ask. Donovan sits nearby. We decided it would be less intimidating if it was only me talking to her.

"Yes. You wanted to know more about Danny."

A smile reveals a missing tooth off to the side, and her eyes grow glassy. "He was such a good boy." Her mouth closes, and she frowns, as if remembering something distasteful.

"Can you tell me about Danny as an adult?" I'm hoping to gently get to the part where Danny has a son.

Mrs. Anderson spends the next twenty minutes talking about Danny. The nap has done her good. She tells us what a great soccer player he was. How he opened up his own garage at twenty-two and then died when a car fell on him.

The sunlight is now streaming through the window, making her glow a golden color. She closes her eyes for a second and grows quiet. I put my hand on hers again. It's now or never.

"What about Frank? Was he close to Frank?"

"Danny died when Frank was just a grade-school kid."

I shoot a glance at Donovan.

"Do you remember Frank now?"

"Why, yes." She shakes her wobbly head, and her eyes grow wider. "I remember Frank." She narrows her eyes. "Why do you ask if I remember him 'now'?"

"This morning you didn't remember him." I pat her hand with mine. It feels like velvet.

"This morning? That doesn't make any sense. Why wouldn't I have remembered Frank? I had that boy since he was a child. I raised him. Why wouldn't I have remembered him?"

She looks at me beseechingly for answers.

"Well, Mrs. Anderson," I say. "Give yourself a break. I'm sure you have a lot to remember after a hundred and two years on this earth."

I smile and squeeze her hand.

"One hundred and two years old, huh?" She looks as if she is marveling at this number. "Well, that explains a lot."

She is such a sweet lady. I feel slightly guilty about what I'm about to say, but I know Grace's life might depend on it.

"Mrs. Anderson, I have something to tell you."

She tilts her head and listens.

"I think your grandson might have done some bad things. Frank might have hurt my sister, and he might have my daughter right now. I need to find him to see if he has my little girl."

"Oh good Lord, help us," she says, letting out a puff of air. "He saw his daddy get killed, so that might be it. He cut out of my house when he was fourteen. I never saw him after that. I'm sorry. I'm not going to be much help. I'm so sorry." Her eyes turn down with sadness. And disappointment fills me.

I'm about to stand up from my crouch in front of her when her eyes grow wide and she leans forward in her chair.

"But his son might know where he is," she says with a gasp of excitement, clutching the arms of her chair as she attempts to sit up straight.

"His son?" I lean forward, taking her hand between both of mine.

"Frank's son. He came to me one day. I hadn't even known I was a great-grandmother."

Frank Anderson has a son.

This stops me in my tracks. I shoot a glance at Donovan, who is reaching for his phone.

"He was a good boy. He brought me flowers and chocolates and spent the afternoon with me."

"When was this?"

She scrunches her face and closes her eyes, then opens them in defeat. "I don't know. I don't remember."

"What was his name? How old was he?" I find myself pressing her fingers in mine and let up the pressure, worried I'm hurting her. Donovan is behind her, tapping the buttons on his phone. Texting someone what we are hearing.

"His name is Frank, too, but for some reason he used that as his last name. His name is Anders Frank," she says in a matter-of-fact voice. "He seemed like a young man, but I can't tell how old people are nowadays."

"Can you tell me more about him? Do you have a picture?"

She licks her lips. "No, but I can tell you he was a nice young man. He told me he never even knew about me until he got in touch with his father. I guess his mother kicked Frank out when Anders was just a boy. It wasn't until she died a few years ago that he went looking for his dad."

"Did he say where his dad was living?" I hold my breath, waiting for her to answer.

"No. He said something about his dad hiding out. That's why Frank couldn't come see me, too."

Hiding out. From the law.

"Do you have any idea where I could find him now?"

She shakes her head.

"Did Anders ever mention any city names?"

"No. I'm sorry. No."

"Is there anything else you can tell me?" I lean forward. When she pulls her hand away from me, I realize I'm clutching it too tightly. "Anything about Anders? Anything at all? Did he drive very far to come see you? Does he live close?"

I don't realize how intense I'm acting until I see a tear roll down her face.

"I'm sorry. I don't know. I don't know. I'm sorry."

"Mrs. Anderson, you have been very, very helpful," I say, taking her hand gently again. She pats my hand with her other one. "If you remember anything, maybe you can tell the nurse and she can tell me. I'm so glad I came to visit you. I think you really helped us."

"I did?" she sort of sniffs.

"Yes. Thank you. Maybe I will come back to see you one day. Would that be okay?"

She nods and smiles, showing that gap. "Yes, I'd like that."

I turn to leave and meet Donovan's eyes. He's whispering on his phone as we leave the care center, but he gives me a big smile.

Frank Anderson has a son.

As Donovan and I head to the parking lot, he raises his voice, and I catch some of his conversation. "Birth records and all other database searches for the past twenty-five years. Anders Frank."

We have a lead.

Chapter 25

IT IS FIVE o'clock. Grace has been gone for twenty-six hours.

Donovan has texted West about Frank Anderson's son. While we wait for more information, Donovan says he wants to visit the murder scene of the third victim. Finn is busy with paperwork on the first body, so another detective, David Chilimidos, is going to meet us there. Chilimidos has been with the department for fifteen years, Donovan said. Apparently, he could've been promoted ages ago, but, like Donovan, he wants to remain a murder cop.

I glance out the window as we cross the Benicia-Martinez Bridge. To the right lies the Phantom Fleet ship graveyard. It seems like so long ago that I wanted to write about it for the newspaper. It feels like another lifetime. Why did I even care about something so unimportant? When it comes to life and death, why do we bother with so many things that don't matter one bit? For some reason my reporter job seems like a distant memory, a life I once lived or read about. At this moment, I can't fathom going back to work ever again. It's as if my life was paused, frozen, when Grace was taken.

A BLACK CROWN Vic is the only car parked down the dirt road in Benicia in a small, now muddy, parking lot of a small refinery. A few white tanks are connected with pipes that lead back to a bigger area with tall smokestacks.

"I thought you said she was another floater," I say, instantly cringing at my callous cop reporter term for a drowning victim.

"She was found in one of those holding tanks."

As we park, I eye the small white tanks, which are about ten feet tall. Donovan's Saab has kicked up the dust, and we wait a minute for it to settle before we open our car doors.

The other detective gets out of his car at the same time.

Chilimidos is about forty and lithe, with a frame like someone who studies martial arts. And the way he moves, with little effort yet coiled with tension, shows his relaxed posture could change in a heartbeat. He has on standard detective fare—black slacks, black blazer and tie, and shiny shoes that are going to be splashed with muddy dirt soon. "Hey, Chili," Donovan says.

The other detective just shakes his head and presses his lips together, suddenly serious. "We're going to get this guy," he says, turning to me. "We won't stop until we find her."

"Thanks, man," Donovan says and introduces me.

Then Chilimidos leads us over to one of the tanks. "This is why I wanted you to see." He points, and as I round the corner, I see it—a Bible verse written in blood on the side of the tank. When Donovan said they found another verse, I assumed it was on a damp piece of paper in the victim's pocket, like the other two. "We probably would've never found her inside the tank if it wasn't for this. He made sure someone found her."

"Whose blood is it?" It takes all I have to ask the question. I back away from the Bible verse, staring at the rust-colored letters that seem to drip off the tank.

"We think it is hers. Haven't confirmed it yet, but that's what we're assuming right now." Chilimidos glances at Donovan to make sure it's okay to share all this with me. Donovan gives him a slight nod and lights a cigarette.

"Did you ever get cause of death on the other two?" I ask.

"Both strangulations."

"And this one?" I walk around the tank, looking for anything that might prove it was Anderson. Of course, there is nothing except the Bible verse.

"Appears to be a straight stabbing."

A shiver races across my scalp even though the sun is beating down on my head.

"Got an ID on her yet?" I say.

"Medical examiner hasn't confirmed yet, but we've got her as Dawn Powers." I'm grateful he is answering my questions even though I'm not a police officer.

"What color was her hair?"

"Dark brown," Chilimidos says.

The other two victims were blondes. Why was this one different? Donovan is wondering the same thing. He moves closer to the tank, examining the writing.

"Is she a college student?" he says, taking a long puff of his cigarette and exhaling with squinted eyes.

"No." Chilimidos flips through his notebook. "An accountant."

"From Livermore?"

"San Francisco native."

I turn to Donovan. "What if this one is a copycat?"

He shakes his head. "I thought that for a second, too, but the fact remains that the killer has left his signature at all three murder scenes. A signature that only has meaning to me and you. A copycat killer wouldn't know about the third verse."

He's right. It's Anderson, alright. But why is this victim so different from the others? Maybe he couldn't find a college student from Livermore and got desperate?

From the Benicia hillside, we can see the puffing smokestacks from the Martinez refineries across the bridge, the Phantom Fleet, Roe Island—where the first body was found—and the swampy marshland under the bridge where the second body was found.

We follow the detective around the refinery as he points out places where possible evidence was found. He shows us some tire marks he photographed, the place where a small piece of plastic with blood on it was found, and the spot where they found a cigarette butt.

"Have they determined whether the DNA on the first vic matches Anderson?" I ask.

Chilimidos clamps his lips together and shakes his head. "Nope. It's a rush job, though. We are probably at the front of the line at the lab, now that the governor has spoken out about it."

"What?" I knew the governor had offered a reward.

"News conference this morning," the detective says. "Asked the people of California to keep their eyes out for Frank Anderson. They are distributing Anderson's picture and asked people to call the tip line if they know him or his whereabouts."

We tread through overgrown weeds that line the parking lot. Chilimidos pokes and prods them with a long walking stick he took out of his trunk.

Before we leave, I once more circle the tank where the woman's body was found. Donovan and Chilimidos stand and lean against the car, smoking and talking in low voices. I feel like I'm missing something. I don't know what I'm searching for, but I have the strongest feeling that this nightmare is all part of a game to him. A game I'm terrified to lose.

Chapter 26

THE DRIVE BACK to San Francisco seems to take an eternity. I stare out the window at the San Francisco Bay until we get on the Bay Bridge. The sun is setting behind the skyline and the Golden Gate Bridge.

It is seven o'clock. Grace has been gone for twenty-eight hours.

The closer we get to the city, the more anxious I feel. This feeling of claustrophobia makes me want to claw at the windows and escape from this car. Grace is not here.

I don't know where she is, but she's not here. Every fiber of my being tells me that she's not in San Francisco.

When Grace first disappeared, I was terrified to leave San Francisco, convinced she was somewhere nearby. I thought for sure I'd feel closest to her at Ocean Beach, where she was last seen. But that isn't the case. As we cross the Bay Bridge and drive over Terminal Island below us, my desperation grows stronger.

"She's not here," I mumble staring out the passenger window. Donovan is in his own world and looks over. "Huh?"

"Grace isn't in the city anymore."

He bites his inner cheek. He doesn't answer me.

BACK AT OUR condo, we settle onto the couch. I doubt I'll ever sleep again. Instead, I will sit on this couch staring at the phone. When we arrived and Officer Craig handed me the phone log, I ignored it. I figured he would've told us about anything important.

Now I pick up the yellow legal pad and scan it. The list of people who called when we were gone is a mixture of our friends and coworkers—Lopez, Nicole, Kellogg, Liz the librarian—but nobody who had any information on Grace's whereabouts.

Last night flew by because our apartment was filled with people. Tonight, sitting alone, the time seems to stretch and warp. Every time I check the clock, only minutes have passed. I can't decide if this is bad or good. In a way, it seems like the faster time passes, the quicker Grace will return home to us, but that's completely illogical.

At least every half hour Donovan goes out on the back deck to smoke. I'm tempted to join him, but getting off the couch seems like it will take more energy than I have.

At ten o'clock, when Grace has been gone for thirty-one hours, I finally break the silence.

"Donovan," I say. He looks up from a stack of paper. He's been going over all the details of the three slayings, looking for clues that might help us find Grace. "There's only been three murders tied to the three Bible verses Anderson sent me, right?"

"Yes, we've checked the NCIC. There aren't any other recent murders with Bible verses anywhere in the U.S."

He stops and looks at me. My mouth is parched, sucked of any moisture, but I need to say it.

"Frank Anderson sent me four Bible verses."

Donovan closes his eyes for a second, then opens them and nods without saying a word. He's thinking the same thing I am—will there be a victim for each Bible verse?

I'm floored by guilt. I sit here in my warm, cozy apartment, when my daughter is somewhere out there, maybe cold and hurt and crying for me. I can't believe that I felt relief that Grace was staying the night at my mom's so I didn't have to deal with another potential temper tantrum getting ready the next morning.

Maybe I don't deserve to be a mother.

Chapter 27

Thursday

It is only when my phone rings that I realize it's morning and that I drifted off into a torturous sleep filled with nightmare after nightmare tangled together. Instead of a few seconds of bliss forgetting that Grace is gone, I sit up instantly, fumbling for my phone on the coffee table. My heart skips into my throat. The number is unfamiliar.

"Giovanni." My voice cracks.

"I don't know if you remember me, but this is Michael Dillman. We met at the fire. I work for the *Pleasant Valley Weekly*."

"Of course I remember you." I sit up on the couch and try to sound friendly, but I can't hide the disappointment in my voice. I was hoping it was news about Grace. I practically begged him to call me about talking to my editor, but he was at the news conference, so he must know this is the worst possible time to call me. I squint, trying to focus on the clock in my dining room. It is 6:00 a.m. Grace has been gone for thirty-nine hours.

"I'm sorry to call you so early, but I just discovered something I thought you'd want to know right away."

I sit up and wait, too weary to even grunt.

"That guy. Frank Anderson. I know where he is."

THERE ARE MORE dead people than live ones in the City of the Dead.

Today, Donovan and I drive south to the City of Colma, aka the "City of the Dead," as the sun rises above the hills to the west. We check with the caretaker at the visitor center, then drive to one of the smallest of the seventeen cemeteries in Colma strung together across two square miles.

After we park, Donovan walks ahead, stomping, really, holding the guide. I drag my feet, hoping that the weekly reporter is wrong.

My mother took me here once when I was in elementary school.

I HELD MY mother's hand as we went to put flowers on her father's grave. Walking from the BART platform to the cemetery, we passed a small plaque that read, IT'S GREAT TO BE ALIVE IN COLMA.

I asked my mother what that meant, and she explained.

"More than two million bodies are buried here," she said, pointing to a population sign. "And only twelve hundred people live here."

"Yuck," I said and scowled.

As we walked, headed for a giant cemetery on the hill, my mother explained that at one time, people were not allowed to bury the dead within the San Francisco city limits. Colma, which lies on the outskirts of the city, was founded as a necropolis in 1924.

I didn't know what that meant, but she told me that it meant the entire town was created just to be a big cemetery. We wandered the rolling green hills through Jewish, Chinese, and Catholic cemeteries. We passed modest gravestones with only small markers and elaborate headstones with soaring angels or Virgin Mary statues. There was even a pet cemetery.

She pointed out the gravestones for Levi Strauss and William Randolph Hearst, but never could find Wyatt Earp or Joe DiMaggio's graves. I tried not to listen to anything she said or be interested in any of the famous gravestones. The only thing a cemetery meant to me was a place where my sister and father lay underground, never to be seen again.

TODAY IN THE Holy Cross Cemetery in Colma the last name I expected to see on a marker practically bites my ankles.

Donovan stands beside me and we dip our heads, silently reading the words that seem unreal. Seeing the small and unassuming grave marker, a simple rectangular slab of concrete, sends a wave of fury through me.

Anders Frank
"*Vengeance is mine, I will repay, says the Lord.*"
Dec. 5, 1955 to May 12, 2006

The man who killed my sister has been dead for two years. He changed his name. Frank Anderson—Anders Frank. What he named his son.

When Michael Dillman called, he said that he'd recognized Anderson's picture. Apparently, Anderson had come into the weekly shortly before he died, wanting coverage about some Veteran's Day event at the Colma Cemetery. He'd said a group of veterans was putting American flags on all the graves of fallen soldiers.

Dillman had written a small story about it to be nice, even though the San Francisco cemetery wasn't in his coverage area.

After the story had run, the man, Anders Frank, had called him, complaining about the coverage, saying the story really needed a photo. He'd been such an ass to Dillman that when Anders Frank's obituary had come across his desk not long after that, the young reporter had wadded it up and tossed it in the trash.

But after seeing Anderson's picture on the news, Dillman had called the funeral home and asked for burial information for Anders Frank. I stare at the grave marker. It looks recently weeded. A small United States flag is pushed into the dirt in front of the grave.

Using an assumed name, Anderson had been living underground in the Bay Area since 2002. He lived for three years within miles of me. Holy fuck.

I WAS WRONG.

Anderson doesn't have Grace.

Donovan is no longer at my side. He has wandered off near a huge mausoleum and is on his phone. I know without his saying it that he's calling the FBI, Rosarito and San Francisco detectives, basically everyone—and telling them to call off the search for Anderson.

Thanks to Michael Dillman, we've found Frank Anderson.

I feel numb. If Anderson doesn't have Grace, *who does*?

I stare at the grave marker. The last rays of the rising sun move over the slab, which has been in shadows until now. For the past half hour, as we walked through the cemetery, my phone has been ringing with calls from my brothers and sisters-in-law. I've ignored them all, knowing that if they found Grace, the police would call. My vision loses focus as I stare down at the grave marker. The words blur into one another. When I blink to clear the fuzziness, the rays of the sun that had spread across the gray stone slab disappear, leaving the marker once more in shadow.

Instead of being grateful to Dillman, Donovan is suspicious.

"Tell me more about this guy from the weekly," Donovan says after he gets off the phone.

"He's just a kid."

I don't know why I'm defensive. Maybe because I know how shitty it is to work at a weekly for years, dreaming of being hired by the daily newspaper. Dillman seems like a nice kid. Not a killer.

But Donovan is right, we need to find out more. I grab my phone and scan calls received, but when I dial the number Dillman called me from, an automated message says, "This subscriber is unavailable."

This sends a tiny alarm through me. I'm sure it's nothing. Goose bumps rise on my arms. They could be from the breeze that just picked up. Huge roiling clouds from the west have swept in, blotting the sun, just as this visit to the cemetery has obliterated much of the hope I had of finding Grace alive.

I was convinced down in the bottom of my heart that Anderson had taken my daughter. I was wrong. Which means everything I was clinging to is wrong. My entire theory on her still being alive was that Anderson had taken her and was holding her for the same six days he held Caterina and these murdered women before killing them. If it's not him, then who is it? I have wasted precious time and valuable resources on a bunk theory that has just been blown to smithereens.

The truth is I don't know who took my daughter. I have no leads, no clues, nothing.

A heavy pall falls over me. The winged shadows that have hovered in the periphery of my vision since I was a child are now closing in, and I don't have it in me to stop them this time.

Chapter 28

My brother Marco is alone with my mom when we walk into the hospital room.

It is eleven o'clock in the morning. My mother has been unconscious for forty-four hours. Grace has been gone nearly two full days, which means the odds of her coming home safe are drastically decreasing from here on out.

Marco jumps to his feet. I can tell by the dazed look in his eyes that he was sleeping. He shoots me a guilty glance.

"How is Mama?" I ask as he folds me in his arms. I press my face against his soft T-shirt, which smells like some expensive cologne.

He shrugs an answer to my question. She's the same.

"What did the doctor say today?"

"They did another MRI this morning to see if the blood was draining on its own or if they're going to do the surgery on Monday. They might try to bring her out of the induced coma tomorrow to see how she is." He looks away as he says it, then grabs Donovan in a bear hug.

Despair threatens to flatten me, lay me out prone on the floor. I push it down.

"There's more. This is so fucked," my brother, who believes swearing is for buffoons, says.

I look up, surprised.

"I wasn't sure if I should say anything, you guys have enough to worry about, but apparently the two radiologists are not in agreement with the diagnosis. The first one who claimed it was a grade 3 brain bleed is now off duty and won't be back until next week. The second radiologist said that she doesn't agree with his diagnosis. She thinks it's closer to a grade 1 or 2. She's the one who wants to try to bring her out of the induced coma. She said sometimes the way the brain is shaped could indicate a severe brain bleed when there isn't one. It's something fairly new in the field, and not all radiologists are aware of this possible discrepancy in what they see on the MRI. They've ordered another ultrasound, but they're not sure when they'll do it."

I sit up. "That's great news. Maybe it really isn't as bad as they think?"

"Maybe," my brother shrugs. "Who the fuck knows which one is right? All I know is that my mother is unconscious and my niece is—"

He doesn't finish. Donovan abruptly stands.

"I'm starving, man, let's go grab some breakfast downstairs," he says.

Donovan is going to tell him that we found Frank Anderson's grave.

I sit by my mom's side and lightly run my fingers across the back of her hand. I close my eyes and pray for my mom and Grace.

How can life be turned upside down so quickly? There is such a fine line between being blessed beyond belief and wanting to die from the pain of having both your mother and child ripped from your arms simultaneously. The difference is a mere sliver in time.

I grasp my mother's hand and plead with her.

"Mama? Please don't leave me. I don't think I can survive with both you and Grace gone." When I say Grace's name, my voice crumbles and cracks. "Mama, I'm so worried she's already gone. Do you know? Could you tell when Caterina was gone?"

Her eyelids don't even twitch. Her breathing remains steady, her chest moving up and down rhythmically. The covers are folded neatly down from her light blue men's pajamas. I wonder who dressed her and where these pajamas come from. The tubes protruding from her mouth and nostrils send a wave of panic through me. The machines beside her whir and beep steadily.

An image of my mother facedown at Caterina's fresh grave, digging her nails into the dirt and wailing, shoots into my mind. How has she survived this long? How did she ever live a normal life after she was widowed the same week her daughter was murdered? Right then, I pray to the Virgin Mary to give me even a smidgen of the strength that my mother has inside her. She's been strong for so long. And I know why. For us. For me and Marco and Dante. I'm sure there were many nights she lay awake wanting to die. She doesn't have to be strong anymore.

I've begged her to stay with me, but then I remember my grandparents.

AFTER MY GRANDPA had a stroke, my grandmother held his hand and begged him not to leave her. I was twelve and so happy to see him get out of the hospital. He later told us the story about how he was in a beautiful green field and heard my grandmother's voice calling to him. A man in a black suit told my grandfather he could stay with him in the field or he could return to my grandmother. But if he returned, the man warned, he would be in a lot of pain and have a difficult life.

My grandfather returned and told us this story and the choice he made. However, it didn't take long until the man in the black suit's warning came true. My grandfather became a different man than the one we had all known, suffering in pain from physical maladies and eventually from Alzheimer's until he passed away ten years later.

I THINK OF my grandfather being called back by my grandmother and how we all felt like even though he was still alive, he was so different we essentially lost him years before he actually passed. Is that the life I wish on my mother, for my own selfish good?

I grasp her hand in mine, tears dripping on our tangled fingers.

"Mama, never mind. I was being selfish by begging you to stay. If you have to go, I'll try to understand. If you have to go and if Grace is there, too, please tell her I love her and will never ever forget her. Please tell her that for me, Mama—if you have to, go. You don't have to be strong anymore."

A movement out of the corner of my eye makes me jerk my head around.

Donovan is standing in the doorway, motionless, holding a cup of coffee. I see Marco's form in the hall talking to someone else. He sounds agitated. Donovan must have told him that Frank Anderson is dead.

Instead of saying anything, Donovan lifts the cup to his lips and drinks, meeting my eyes over the rim. His eyes are hard.

IN THE CAR, Donovan pulls away when I reach for his hand.

"You've given up?" He bites out the words. "I heard you talking to your mom. You've given up on both of them?"

"No!" I nearly shout the word, and it surprises both of us. "No, I haven't given up, but I'm also trying to face the facts, Donovan. You and I both know the odds after forty-eight hours . . ."

"Fuck the odds," he says, punching the steering wheel. "Our daughter is not a goddamn statistic, Ella. She can't be."

But we both know he's wrong. Anyone can be a statistic. No one is exempt.

We are not special, privileged people. Just because we have seen evil firsthand does not give us some special protection against it. Just because my family has been torn apart by a child killer once before in our history does not grant us immunity from that now.

Nobody gets a free pass in this life.

Chapter 29

It is nearly three o'clock when we take the exit for my grandmother's house.

Grace has been gone for forty-eight hours. I watch the numbers 3-0-0 on the car's digital clock come and go.

Visiting the volunteer center for Grace an hour ago reinforced the fact that I'm living a nightmare. I've been to volunteer centers for missing kids over the years as a reporter. It is incomprehensible that one has been set up for my own child.

We spent about an hour at the volunteer center, which is basically an empty storefront in a Noe Valley strip mall, just south of downtown San Francisco. I tried to smile and be polite to the row of volunteers sitting in front of phones and printing off fliers to pass out, but I still ended up rushing outside and vomiting up the club sandwich Donovan had bought for me at the hospital. I had been so hungry I'd wolfed it down on the car on the way to the volunteer center, not knowing it was going to come right back up, but there will be lots of food at my grandmother's. I will try again there.

It must be forty degrees warmer here in the East Bay than in San Francisco today. I strip off my jacket and fling it in the backseat. Donovan stares straight ahead, knuckles clutching the steering wheel, jaw set, leaning slightly forward, as if that will get us there faster. Usually a careful driver, he speeds down the freeway, zipping in and out of traffic and gunning it on the straights as if we are late. The speed feels good, as if we are actually doing something to help find Grace, even though part of me feels like the farther we drive into the East Bay suburbs, the more distance we are putting between us and Grace. I know this is irrational—she's not at that beach or anywhere near it. Or is she? I feel so helpless. The police and FBI are working on finding Anderson's son, but I feel as if I should be doing something, as well.

A fresh, earthy scent filters in through our open car windows as we pull into the long winding driveway to my grandmother's house, nestled in rolling hills covered with grapevines.

My grandmother's circle drive is already full of cars by the time we pull in. People have started parking in a small cleared area used for overflow parking.

Most of the cars I recognize, but there is a big black town car that unreasonably makes my stomach clench in fear.

A memory from twenty years ago rushes into my head. It was right after Caterina's kidnapping and the day after my father's death.

MY UNCLE SAL picked up my mother and me at our house. My mother had dark circles under her eyes, but her sleek black hair was pulled back and she had on a pressed navy dress and red lipstick. She usually wore a pinky beige color. I remember staring at the red lipstick for a long time, wondering how she could put it on the day after her husband died while her daughter was still missing. The only other times I had seen her wear lipstick that red was when she and my father went to a fancy wedding or restaurant and Nana came to stay the night and watch us four kids. But on that day, my mother was wearing the lipstick to go to my grandmother's house in the afternoon.

On that day a big black car was pulled up front and center at my grandmother's house when we arrived and two men in black suits stood outside the front door, smoking.

My mother ignored them as we walked inside.

She told us to stay out of the kitchen and put us in front of the TV. But I couldn't help it and peeked inside the kitchen. Three men in black suits sat at the table with my grandmother, mother, and two of my uncles. One of my uncles was talking in a low voice, nearly under his breath, but he seemed angry and was pounding the table.

My mother was listening to what one of the men was saying and nodding her head.

Then one of the men noticed me. All conversation stopped, and everyone turned to look at me.

I held my breath. I waited for my mother to scream at me, but she didn't say anything, only looked at the man.

"Come here, little one." He smiled, showing teeth so white and gleamingly perfect that I couldn't stop staring at his mouth. "It's okay."

The man had a thick accent, sort of like my grandmother's, but harsher.

I looked at my mother, and she gave the slightest nod.

I walked in, tucking my hands behind my dress. These men wore shiny shoes and shirts so white they almost hurt to look at.

I came up to the table before the man and stared at his hands, which were holding a cigarette with gold writing on it. His fingernails were the cleanest I'd ever seen. They looked polished and pink.

He took his hand and put it under my chin, lifting my head so my eyes met his. The first thing I thought was that his hands were girlie. My father's hands were always rough and often stained from his work as a plumber.

"*Come ti chiami?*"

I looked at my mother, and she gave another slight nod.

"Gabriella."

"Ah, Gabriella. *Facia bella*," he said. "Would you like a *sfogliatella*? We brought some for your *nonna*."

"Yes, please."

My grandmother stood up and rushed over to the counter.

"Ella, take these outside in the back with your brothers. I will bring you out some *aranciata* to drink. Go now."

"It's okay, Marcella," the man said to my grandmother. "She is fine."

"*Andiamo!*" My grandmother's tone left no room for argument. The man was nice, but something about the way my mother and grandmother acted around him sent a pulse of both fear and excitement through me. I skipped out into the living room and taunted my brothers with my plate of pastries until they chased me outside. I was less concerned with what my mother and grandmother were doing with that man and more interested in how they knew him. I knew he was there to bring Caterina back home, so I was glad he was there, but I couldn't figure out who he was. Was he the president? I didn't think so. He didn't look like the guy on TV. But he was somebody important, though. I could tell by the way everyone acted around him. I had never heard anyone call my grandmother by her first name. *Marcella.* I said the name to myself as I skipped around outside in my grandmother's garden. She wasn't just Nana. She was *Marcella.* I let the name roll around my tongue until it sounded even more foreign and strange than I had first thought.

The men left shortly after, but my mother and grandmother and uncles stayed in the kitchen drinking wine and talking until late in the night, while I had fallen asleep in front of *The Dukes of Hazzard.*

Chapter 30

Seeing this black car in my grandmother's driveway brought back a memory I didn't even know I had. So much of my childhood is lost in the tangled web of memory that I've tried to block out.

"What the hell?" Donovan looks at me and gestures to the cars and the two men in suits standing sentry out front.

"Let me handle this." We park. Even from afar I can see the telltale bulge of guns under their black blazers. Bodyguards. What I didn't know as a child became so clear now. At the front door, I walk past the two men, ignoring them as my mother had once so long ago.

I'm channeling my mother as I pull back my shoulders and enter the house. *I am a Giovanni and I will act like one.*

With Donovan following me, scowling, I stride through the living room, past the cluster of children playing video games and straight into the kitchen, where the three men in suits wait with my grandmother. Instead of my uncles, my two brothers sit opposite the men at the big wooden table. Two seats are left.

The man from my memory has silver hair now, swept back elegantly, and seems short to me now, instead of towering. But he is still exceedingly good looking even though he must be in his seventies. As I walk in, he rises and sticks out his hand. "Gabriella." This time I meet him as an equal, holding my hand out and shaking his firmly.

I cock my head and raise an eyebrow, waiting for him to introduce himself.

"I am Vincenzo Santangelo."

The name makes my throat dry. The Saint. I've heard about him at Sunday dinners at my grandmother's house. That's who this man was years ago? The adults always shush us away when his name is brought up. My cousins and I used to play *La Cosa Nostra* in Nana's garden, the boys using their hands pointed like guns and the girls joining right along, even though my cousin Lorenzo said that girls couldn't be in the Mafia.

"Your father was my childhood friend at Sacred Heart," he says. "We lost touch over the years, went into different directions with our businesses. When your sister disappeared, he called me. Sadly, he passed before we were able to reconnect."

Nana makes the sign of the cross at the word "passed" and mumbles something in Italian. My father died three days after my sister was taken. The doctor said it was a heart attack. But I now know better. I was the one who found him when my mother sent me down to the basement to fetch him for dinner. The basement smelled like alcohol, and there were shards of glass and spilled booze everywhere. His head was at an odd angle. Now, as an adult, flashing back to that day, I think he had drunk too much and fallen down the stairs, breaking his neck. When I didn't come to my mother's calls, she rushed down the stairs and found us there. We stayed there, curled up against my father's body, until my aunt Lucia found us the next morning.

Even so, Mr. Big Shot didn't find Caterina in time and has never hunted down her killer. My eyes narrow at him. I don't care if he's movie star handsome. I don't care if he's The Saint.

"What makes you think you can find my daughter? You've had thirty years to find Caterina's killer, yet I'm the one who just found his grave."

"Gabriella." My grandmother's voice holds a stern warning. I don't care. I'm not going to waste my time on some thug who dresses in Armani and acts like he's going to swoop in and rescue my daughter and our family.

Vincenzo Santangelo waits for a minute, then meets my eyes.

"With all due respect. Your father asked me to bring your sister home safe. I failed. You are right. I have to live with that until the end of eternity. But I was never tasked with finding her killer. If you or your mother had only once turned to me and asked me, shared with me your need for revenge, it would have been a different scenario."

For a split second, I am angry. Why didn't my mother turn to him? And now I can't ask her. As if reading my mind, The Saint says, "I'm very sorry about your mother's injury. She is an extraordinary woman. I pray that she heals quickly. Meanwhile, I would like to station some of my friends at and near the hospital to make sure she is safe. With your permission?"

I nod my assent and The Saint jerks his head at one of his men, who grabs a cell phone and walks into the living room. "I will make sure whoever hurt her never touches another woman again."

He says it in such a low voice that I stare at him. Extraordinary woman? Does this guy have a thing for my *mom*?

"We aren't seeking revenge," my brother Marco says. "That is not how our family operates."

Marco is a lawyer. After being called a "Wop" and "Dago" in elementary school, he has spent his life trying to distance himself from any Italian thug mentality. His way of dealing with it was to become a star football player, earning the respect of everyone in the school. He is a wine connoisseur and enjoys eating his gourmet meals in his fancy house in the suburbs, where he is lord of his own fiefdom. He also takes being a "gentleman" to a fine art, refusing to curse and making every gesture chivalrous. But despite all his efforts to do so, he can't change his DNA. Because just like me, I know he would kill to protect his family.

"We are a God-fearing family," my grandmother says, her chin wobbling. She wipes her palms on her dress. Her cheeks are flushed.

"I know, Marcella," The Saint says. There it is again. *Marcella.* The only person I know who dares to call my grandmother by her name. Now that I'm an adult, this suddenly seems a bit disrespectful. I can tell by the crease between Marco's brows that he thinks the same thing.

Dante angrily pushes back his chair a few inches, the scraping sound overly loud. He scowls and is about to speak when Marco gives him a look.

Dante's way of dealing with discrimination against Italians was to throw punches. My uncle Dominic channeled that, and Dante became a boxer. Once he became homecoming king, he didn't need to fight to prove his worth anymore. He still boxes occasionally, but I think nowadays he's more worried about marring his good looks than anything else. A few years ago, when I began training at the Oakland dojo, I talked him into doing so, as well. He's taken it a bit further than me, though, and now claims he can kill someone with his bare hands. I believe him. Unlike Marco, Dante has no problem seeking revenge. In fact, I'm pretty sure he'll insist on it. And that's good. I need one ally in this room.

I wait until the room settles down. It is as silent as death before I speak.

"We don't know who took Grace. We thought we did, but as I said, that man is dead."

My grandmother makes the sign of the cross. My brothers exchange looks.

"Whoever has my daughter, I want him found. And I want him dead."

At my words, The Saint meets my eyes and nods solemnly.

"I want revenge," I say, not meeting Marco's eyes. "But more than that, I want my daughter home safe." I don't drop my gaze from The Saint's. "If you can do that, bring her safe to me, I will be in your debt for life."

My grandmother gasps. I'm afraid to look over at Donovan. But I mean every word I say. Vincenzo Santangelo waits for me to look up at him, then gives me a very slight nod, appraising me.

Something my mother told me long ago comes back. If anyone grants you a favor, whether it's your kindergarten best friend or the pope himself, you are obligated to that person. The bigger the favor, the bigger the obligation. This may apply double to the man before me. I don't care.

"You owe me no debt," Vincenzo Santangelo says. "My offer of help is to repay a debt I owe your father. I will help you find your daughter and bring her home safe, and my debt to your family will be paid."

He starts to stand, but I hold out my palm. "I'm not done."

At my words, he sinks back into his chair.

Now I stand.

"I value and appreciate your offer of help, but I need to make one thing clear. Grace is my daughter, so everything that is done in your investigation into her disappearance needs to be run by me. I'm in charge of this search. I want in on every move. Every step."

I lean down, putting my palms flat on the table and meeting Vincenzo Santangelo's eyes. Out of the corner of my eye I see my grandmother slowly shaking her head and making the sign of the cross again.

"If there is a valid lead on her whereabouts, I want to be the first one to know. I want to be the first phone call you make. Before the police, before your men, before your family. If you are home asleep in bed, I want to know before you tell your wife. If you get information, I am the first one you call."

I don't blink as I stare into Vincenzo Santangelo's eyes. He meets my stare with eyes that widen in something that might be a mixture of amusement and respect.

"You are your mother's daughter," he says and stands so we are at equal height. For a second, I question why he didn't call me my *father's daughter,* since he is a traditional Italian man, but I let it go. He still hasn't addressed my demands, so I hand him my phone.

"Put your cell number in here and I will set up a special ringtone just for you. I will answer any time, day or night. If we can agree that I'm the first one to know anything, then I'm ready to get started."

He takes my phone and sits back down, adding in his number.

I sink into my chair and dare a glance at Donovan. He's chewing on his inner cheek. I can't tell if he's furious or nervous, and right now it doesn't matter. Marco is dramatically sighing and shaking his head. Only Dante is looking at me. His eyes narrow, and a small glint of light comes from them. He knows. He knows how I feel. He gives me the slightest nod.

When it comes to finding Grace, I'm going to do whatever it takes at whatever cost.

Vincenzo Santangelo hands my phone back and gives a slow nod, his chin nearly reaching his chest as he watches me.

"Let's do this," I say.

We spend the next hour filling the men in on everything we know about Grace's disappearance.

"Donovan thinks we need to check out this reporter at the weekly," I say. "I'll let him fill you in."

Donovan clears his throat for a second, and everyone looks his way. "This kid called and told Gabriella about Frank Anderson's grave. The FBI has been looking for Anderson for years, and some kid finds his grave and knows his alias? It doesn't make sense. We need to find out more about him. His name's Michael Dillman."

Dillman didn't have a card when I asked for one. Didn't have a reporter's notebook, either.

Then something he said comes back: "*. . . you got to be careful nowadays. You never know who is okay and who is a creep. Sometimes the nicest guys end up being sickos and nobody who knows them even knew it.*"

And I told him about being freaked out when we went to Ocean Beach. If I'm wrong about him, I might even have led him to where he could find Grace.

In the back of my mind, I remember him staring at me at the press conference and then, later, not meeting my eyes. One thing

I know about killers is that they often like to show up at funerals and vigils and press conferences about their victims because they get some sick thrill out of it.

"What do you think, Ella?" Donovan asks.

"Do it."

Throughout our conversation, The Saint's friend, who is never introduced, makes a series of phone calls, speaking quietly in Italian. I raise an eyebrow when he makes the first call.

Vincenzo Santangelo sees it and says, "Sam the Goat is good at getting the ball rolling, as they say."

I don't ask why they call him Sam the Goat. I don't care, but I suspect it has to do with his goofy-looking goatee.

When Vincenzo Santangelo stands to leave, he grasps both of my hands in his and leans down to speak quietly in my ear. "I can't guarantee anything except that we will do everything in my power to find her. And if we do find her kidnapper, if you like, he will no longer be your problem."

"I'll let you know," I say.

Chapter 31

As Donovan and I make our way through the deep sand on Ocean Beach to the crowd gathered near the shore, he reaches out and grabs my hand. Flickering candlelight distorts the hazy images of dozens of people holding candles. A low blanket of gray clouds obscures the night sky, making the darkness deep and impenetrable, but across the sand, faces glow almost eerily above candles. Nothing about this seems real.

My breath catches as I spot Lopez snapping photos, crouching in the sand, the flash going off sporadically. He's not here as my friend. He's here as a journalist. He's covering this for our newspaper. Seeing him on assignment at my daughter's vigil is a dose of reality I don't want.

Grace has been gone for more than fifty-three hours.

TV reporters hover at the periphery of the crowd, and I feel a mixture of hatred and gratefulness toward them. The more media coverage, the more likely that news of Grace's disappearance will spread and the greater the chance that somebody who knows or saw something will come forward.

Then I spot Kellogg, and Nicole, and some other reporters I know. That Dillman kid isn't here. I can't figure out if that is good or bad. I know that while my paper probably sent Lopez and one reporter to cover the vigil for the paper, the rest of them are here to support our family. I swallow back some tears that threaten to overwhelm me.

Nobody has noticed our slow trek across the sand yet, so I look on the vigil as an outsider would, watching people standing in clusters, speaking in low tones. A few hold signs, but I can't read them from here. People hug and dab their eyes with white tissues, which glow in the candlelight. In the darkness I don't see anyone from my family, but I know they are here.

"Thank you for coming tonight," a man with a thick Irish accent says. Father Liam. He is wearing jeans and a blazer over his priest collar. Under his bushy head of hair, his twinkling eyes meet mine and he winks. He was waiting for us to begin. I'm glad he didn't look at me with sorrow, or I would have crumbled.

"I am Father Liam Allegro from St. Joan of Arc Church in Oakland, and Grace's parents, Sean Donovan and Gabriella Giovanni, have asked me to lead us in prayer. If you would please, let's form a circle and take the hand of the person beside you as we pray. I ask that we begin by bowing our heads."

By now, Donovan and I are at the crowd. To my left, a middle-aged woman in a puffy coat smiles at me as she takes my hand. To my right, I reach out and hold hands with a young woman with thick black eye makeup.

"Father, we thank you for all these people gathered here in support of bringing home little Grace safe to us."

As he is praying, I notice something moving down by the shore, where the waves are licking the sand. It's a person, but it is hard to tell anything more in the deep darkness of the beach.

I crane my neck a bit, but I'm pinned between puffy coat woman and makeup girl. I debate abruptly letting go of their hands and running over there. I cut a glance at Donovan, but his eyes are closed as he prays.

People are chiming in "amen" when—this time for sure—something moves in the darkness by the shore. This time, Donovan sees it, too. He draws back out of the circle, and I quickly follow.

Father Liam leads people in the singing of "Amazing Grace" as I squint in the darkness, following Donovan's figure in the dark. A cold chill starts at my scalp and makes it way down my body, settling in my stomach. The ocean breeze carries something oddly familiar. It's just a trace, but I think it is a man's cologne. I can't quite place it.

Ahead of me, Donovan stops and swears. I sprint to where he is.

"He's gone."

People have started to notice us, heads turn out from the prayer circle, and suddenly Lopez is at my side. He has a huge Maglite and is shining it on the sand. There are footprints in the wet sand that lead to the water.

"Jesus Christ." Lopez shines the light on some long marks along the sand at the same time the sound of a motor carries across the waves. "He had a boat. Goddamn it."

Donovan yells and grabs his phone, and within moments, police are everywhere, with large spotlights shining on the waves crashing into the shore, but there is no sign of a boat. Within fifteen minutes, a helicopter with a searchlight is hovering above the water. My brothers and sisters-in-law are there, all of us hugging and holding hands. But it is too late.

Whoever it was is long gone.

Chapter 32

Friday

AFTER WE RETURNED home from the vigil last night, I slept the sleep of the dead. It all finally caught up to me. I honestly didn't think I could sleep with my daughter missing and in a monster's hands, yet one second I was watching the eleven o'clock news in the living room, and the next, Donovan is handing me a cup of coffee and I'm wondering why I'm sleeping on the couch.

I'm disoriented for a second, but then the harsh, cold reality of my life sets in. Grace. Despair fills my chest, my throat, my mouth.

This afternoon, Grace will have been gone three whole days.

A feeling of helplessness settles on me. I thought Frank Anderson had taken her, but he's dead. Now I feel like we are starting over, but without any leads. This entire time we've been searching for the wrong man. What about that weekly reporter? Why wasn't he at the vigil last night if he's now covering Grace's disappearance?

I dial the number for the weekly and am connected to the newsroom.

"Editor."

"Hi, I was wondering if I could speak to Michael Dillman." I stare at my coffee cup, wondering if it's going to make me barf to drink it.

"He's not in right now, can I take a message?"

I hesitate. He's not going to help me unless I lay it all out.

"My name is Gabriella Giovanni. My daughter, Grace, has been kidnapped."

I can hear his sharp intake of breath and shuffling of papers. But I'm not calling to give him a quote.

"I was wondering why he wasn't at my daughter's vigil last night."

The editor clears his throat. "You know, we probably should have sent someone else out there, but Dillman was supposed to cover that. He called in yesterday morning and said he was going to be late coming in to work because he was following a lead in connection with your daughter's kidnapping. I haven't heard from him since. Frankly, I'm a little worried."

I catch my breath. "Did he say what the lead was?"

"Sorry, he didn't. Now I wish I would've asked. He's usually a reliable kid, but he didn't show up in the newsroom later. I called him a few times to see if he was going to cover the vigil, and he never returned any of my calls. If you need to speak to somebody, however, you can talk to me."

He thinks I'm calling to give Dillman a story or a scoop.

"No, but thank you." I hang up, my heart thumping wildly.

My face feels ice cold and numb. What if Michael Dillman

took Grace? I'm the one who told him that we liked to go to Ocean Beach.

When Donovan comes inside from smoking, I tell him what I've learned.

"Goddamn it." He grabs his phone and steps outside, lighting another cigarette as he dials Agent West and fills him in. I stand outside in the cold morning air in the long T-shirt I slept in, shivering and listening to his conversation.

Finally, he disconnects and takes a long drag of his cigarette, eyes narrowed before he speaks.

"They're heading to Michael Dillman's San Francisco apartment as we speak—with a warrant."

"Can we go?"

He shakes his head. "West was already tracking him down. Was over at Dillman's place last night. He wasn't there. The landlady said she hasn't seen him since yesterday morning. West will call if he shows up or they find him, okay?" Donovan says, leaning down and kissing my forehead.

I nod, holding my stomach, which is cramping.

"Get dressed," Donovan says. "Let's go visit Father Liam."

He knows I'm barely hanging on. I'm sunk deep in despair and ready to give up on finding Grace.

At this moment, the only thing keeping me from a swan dive off the Golden Gate is the possibility that Grace is alive. Now I know why the parents of missing children have that dead look in their eyes. They are shadows. Flimsy shadows stuck between worlds, only sticking around on this earth on the slightest, most gossamer chance that their son or daughter will come home to them.

As soon as we get on the freeway entrance to the Bay Bridge,

Donovan guns the motor, downshifting and swerving in and out of cars as if his very life depends on getting us to Oakland quickly.

He says nothing, keeping his eyes straight ahead on the road. I don't think he slept at all. When I woke, the entire kitchen was spotless and organized. All the debris left from having a house full of family and police had disappeared.

We exit at Lakeshore Boulevard and take the curve toward Lake Merritt and St. Joan of Arc Church. A black car that has been behind us since San Francisco takes the exit, as well. Donovan has watched it in the rearview mirror the entire time.

"The Saint's men," I say, even though I don't know for sure.

Donovan passes the rectory of the church and parks a ways past it on the lake side of the road. The black car pulls over about ten car lengths behind us, parking near the front of the church. We cross the road, and when we get near the black car, a man in a black jacket and sunglasses gives us a slight nod. The Goat.

Father Liam answers the door to the rectory without his usual smile and twinkling eyes.

"Oh, Gabriella." He wraps me in a big hug, and I gulp back tears.

He releases me and clasps Donovan in a bear hug, slapping his back.

"Thanks so much for being at the vigil last night," I say. "I'm so sorry we didn't get a chance to talk." I stare at my feet.

"Of course. But what else can I do?" he says when he pulls back from Donovan's hug and searches our faces.

"Can we pray?" I ask. "Just the three of us?"

We stand in the hallway near a giant life-sized oil painting of St. Michael the Archangel. We clutch hands as Father Liam prays for Grace to return home safely.

The words coming from Father Liam's become distorted and faint. I stare at the oil painting across from me. St. Michael the Archangel stands, majestic, with a halo around him and massive golden wings protruding from his shoulder blades. In one hand he holds a sword aloft, at ready. In the other, the shiny scales of justice dangle from his fingers. His sandaled foot presses down on Satan's head, which lifts up above bare shoulders bulging with rippling muscles between his deep black wings. Flames lick at the ground where Satan lies, bested by goodness and justice.

It takes me a few seconds to realize that Father Liam is done praying and that Donovan is staring at me with a look that I don't like.

Father Liam must not notice, because he shoos us up the stairs, saying, "Let's go up to the sitting room and have some coffee and brainstorm what the parishioners can do to help."

Upstairs, Father Liam sinks into his blue armchair by the fireplace, crosses one leg over the other, and grabs a small notepad and pen.

"We can organize a phone campaign," he says. "Have volunteers pass out fliers. We can take up a second collection at every mass to put toward the reward fund."

He sits, listing ideas.

After a few minutes, I scoot forward from my spot on the love seat next to Donovan. I stare off to my left at the sparkling crystal glasses and brilliant colors of the alcohol on the sidebar.

I take a deep breath.

"Can I share something with you? This is going to sound crazy, maybe," I say, closing my eyes for a second. When I open them, both Donovan and Father Liam are watching. It takes me a few more seconds to get the courage to speak, and there is silence as the men wait.

Finally, Father Liam's smile gives me the courage to speak.

"Before I had Grace and I was in Baja California and left in that boat to die, I had something happen. Something that sort of seemed miraculous at the time but that I'm now worried was prophetic. I don't know how it could have been anything else."

I sneak a glance at Donovan out of the corner of my eye. It is the first time he's ever heard this. For some reason I never told anyone about the whale. Not Donovan. Not my mother. Not Father Liam. For some reason I blocked that whole encounter and dream out of my memory for the past few years.

Now I continue on with the story of the whale coming up to my boat and how I was filled with serenity about dying. And about how I later remembered the folktale I'd heard about what to do when you see a whale—go to sleep and remember your dreams. And how I forgot all of this until just before the police officer called to tell me Grace was taken. I tell them about how I dreamed something bad happened to a little girl.

When I'm done, I clamp my lips together and wait.

Donovan shifts uneasily and darts a glance at Father Liam. Donovan gives a barely perceptible shake of his head and runs his fingers through his hair, making it spiky and sticking up.

Father Liam clears his throat.

"That's quite a story," he says, lifting one eyebrow and recrossing his legs.

"What do you think it means?" I ask. "Do you think I dreamed my daughter's face—and her fate—before she was born? Do you think it was possible I dreamed her kidnapping, too? How can that even be possible?"

Donovan is staring at the fireplace and working on chewing

his inner cheek. Father Liam doesn't quite give me the answer I want.

"Stranger things have happened," he says.

"Do you think it's possible?"

"I've found that nearly anything is possible," he says. "Like the soldier who stayed to talk to me after mass Sunday. Last year, he was on a plane that crashed in South America, you might have heard about it, a military transport plane went down in the jungle. Everyone on board, all sixty-seven people, died except him. He not only lived, he walked away without anything more than a scratch or two. And lived for three days alone in the jungle until rescuers arrived. By all logic, he should be dead and yet showed up to church for the first time in his life last week saying he had been spared for a reason. What that reason is? I couldn't tell him. That is his own journey of discovery. And the same goes for you. Whether in your particular case it is possible or not is a question you need to ask yourself. But that is for another day. I think you have bigger fish to fry right now, my dear."

I'm not sure what I expected, but the harsh reality of his words—couched in love—still sinks in: Whether I dreamed it or not doesn't matter. The answer to that won't help me find Grace.

Chapter 33

WHEN WE LEAVE the rectory, the black car is gone.

On the walk to Donovan's car, I call the hospital. Aunt Lucia answers the phone. My mother is the same. They haven't decided whether to take her out of the induced coma. If only I had warned *her* about the beach and my dream.

Instead of starting his car, Donovan clears his throat, staring at the stretch of road before us. "Any reason you didn't tell me about the whale and the dream?" His voice is low.

"I didn't think it was important," I say.

"You are claiming to have prophetic dreams and you don't think that's important enough to share with me?" At his words, my cheeks feel hot and my pulse races. "I thought we were years past this shit, Gabriella. I thought we had learned how to talk to one another and share our lives. I thought that years of therapy might have helped you overcome this tendency to keep shit that involves me to yourself."

"What does it matter? It was just a dream." I'm starting to get angry. Why is he acting like this?

"It's not the goddamn dream that I'm talking about. It's you thinking you had a dream predicting the kidnapping of our daughter. In all honestly, it makes me wonder whether I need to take you in for a psych eval."

For a few seconds I'm speechless, wide-eyed, and my mouth hangs open. He's never spoken to me this way before. My hand clutches the door handle. I turn and face him. I wait until his eyes meet mine.

My fury and grief combine, and I lash out at the person I love, the man beside me.

"You're the one who told me I didn't have to take the day off work to be with Grace and my mom. You're the one who said she'd be fine. Maybe all of this is your fault. I wish I'd never met you." Without waiting for his reaction, I'm out of the car and running toward Lake Merritt, blinded by my tears. I hear the screech of rubber on pavement as he leaves.

I swipe at my tears, which are brief and replaced by white-hot blinding fury as I head away from the church toward downtown Oakland. I don't make eye contact with the people I pass as I race-walk down the paved lakeshore path: a man break-dancing on the grass with his ghetto blaster blaring. A mother in spandex pushing a jogging stroller. An elderly man breaking bits of bread off for the dozens of geese flocking to him.

Instead, I chant an angry monologue in my head.

Fuck you, Donovan. It's your fault Grace was taken. I wanted to take off work and stay with her, but I was worried you'd think I was overreacting. It's your fault that I'd almost rather kill myself now than feel this pain another day. You promised me that what happened to Caterina wouldn't happen to Grace. You were wrong.

Even as I say this, I know how ridiculous it is. And I don't care.

Nobody warned me what it was like to be a mother—the emotional roller coaster that begins the minute you find out you are pregnant. The emotional whiplash that plummets you into anxiety and worry when you have spotting during your pregnancy or when your baby has croup and a high fever and is struggling to breathe in the middle of the night and you are certain she is dying. And then the soaring emotional highs the first time your child belly laughs or the first time she says she loves you. Nobody warns you about these highs and lows. And if anyone had told me that motherhood leads to this—your heart ripped to shreds while you are willing to beg the devil to take your soul in exchange for the safety of your child—if I had been magically given a glimpse of my life right now by the Ghost of the Future, I would've said, "Fuck that."

BY THE TIME I make it around the lake to the boat launch, where the gondolas are lined up, bobbing in the waves, all my anger is gone. Instead I feel like collapsing in a heap on the grass and never getting up. But then a surge of anxiety blazes through me. I left my phone in Donovan's car. Someone could be calling to tell me they found Grace, and here I am storming along the shores of Lake Merritt, stewing in my own foul and bitter emotions.

I look around me both ways. I don't know what to do. Do I race back to the church and ask Father Liam to call Donovan, or do I go into the boathouse and see if I can use their phone and then pray Donovan's not too angry to pick up?

I'm suddenly pissed at The Saint. He had his goon follow us to the church and then bail? What kind of protection is that? If he had followed us, he'd have been here right now and I wouldn't be stranded at Lake Merritt because of my temper tantrum.

I stand frozen in indecision and get the creepy-crawly feeling that I'm being watched. I jerk my head around and then see him in the parking lot of the boat launch. Donovan.

He's parked facing my way, and he's leaning over the steering wheel with both arms folded on it. He holds up one hand. It holds my phone. I wilt in relief. I can't read the look on his face from here, but I run to the car, to the driver's side door. His window is down and I crouch beside it.

Before I can say a word, he reaches through it and grabs my hand. "I'm sorry," he says.

"Me, too," I say and lean in to hug him, feeling his breath on mine.

"It's just the—"

"—stress," I finish for him. "I know."

"It's too much," he says in a ragged voice, breathing into my hair. And then I realize he is weeping. I hold him as he cries, while I stand awkwardly stooped half in and half out of the car window, clutching him around his shoulders like he is a lifeline that I don't ever want to let go.

Chapter 34

Saturday

Grace has been gone four days.

I wake, blurry-eyed, and empty two pills into my palm, swallowing them down with some water. I close my eyes so I'll go back to sleep.

Last night, for the first time since she was taken, I slept in bed. By myself. I don't know if Donovan stayed up manning the phones or smoking or what.

Around midnight, I finally gave in and took the little sleeping pills that my brother slipped me at my grandmother's. All I wanted was oblivion. Scrunching my eyes closed, I hope the pills kick in as quickly this morning as they did last night.

Around noon, Donovan comes and gently wakes me. I feel groggy and resentful that he woke me. I want to go back into the land of darkness where I don't feel or think or even dream. I roll over onto my stomach and close my eyes.

"Let's go visit your mother," Donovan says, rubbing my back. "Officer Craig is here to watch the phones for a few hours."

He leaves. It takes enormous effort to finally convince myself to get out of bed. I sluggishly pull on the same wrinkled dress I wore the day before and slip on some ballet flats. I brush my teeth but not my hair.

Driving to the hospital, I'm numb, but Donovan is scowling and shaking his head, mumbling under his breath. He catches me watching and gives a wry half smile. "Sorry, I'm just so pissed at myself for taking everything out on you yesterday."

I reach over and weave my fingers through his hand on the steering wheel.

"I've got an idea," I say. "Let's make it a rule that anything we say right now doesn't count. Whatever we say, we automatically forget and forgive, okay?"

He nods and smirks. "Thanks for that. But that is a Get Out of Jail Free card I probably shouldn't have. If I allow myself to say anything in the heat of my anger and worry about Grace, then I'll never forgive myself, even if you do. Grace needs to come back to us being as close to the parents she left as we can be."

I nod, but inside I'm thinking, *That's impossible.*

I'll never, ever, be the same after this.

IN THE HOSPITAL, Donovan comes and goes, but I sit for three hours holding my mother's hand and reading her the newspaper cover to cover. *The New York Times.* I haven't touched a local paper since Grace was taken.

Donovan periodically checks in on us. He's often on the phone in the hall. He periodically gives me updates. There are no leads. There is nothing new.

Three o'clock comes and goes. Three. Zero. Zero.

For the first few hours I feel like barfing, as if I have a hangover. Toward dinnertime, my stomach settles, and I force myself to eat a sandwich Donovan brings up from the hospital cafeteria. It tastes like cardboard, but I manage to swallow it and keep it down.

At dusk, Donovan drives us home. I take two more pills and fall back into bed without taking off my dress.

Chapter 35

Sunday

TODAY IS EASTER.

Tomorrow marks the sixth day of Grace being gone. On the sixth day of my sister's disappearance, some off-road bikers found Caterina's body. But Grace is not Caterina. I remind myself, even though I woke from nightmares all night long with the two faces interchanged.

The sun is brilliant coming over the Oakland Hills. All traces of normal early-morning San Francisco fog have disappeared. It is as if the whole world is rejoicing.

It doesn't seem like the nightmare I'm living could exist in a world this beautiful.

But it does.

I try not to think too much about the Easter basket, stuffed animals, and candy I have hidden on a high shelf in my bedroom closet. This year the Easter bunny will come a few days late for Grace, I tell myself.

Standing in front of my vanity mirror, I apply black eyeliner with a steady hand, making the line curve into a slight cat's eye at the corners. Now my hand is shaking, so it takes me a few tries. The eye makeup is my insurance. Its main job is to keep me from crying at Easter mass this morning.

I can't bear to walk past Grace's room, where her little pink dress hangs in her closet, along with the matching sunbonnet and white Mary Janes that we picked out last month for her Easter outfit.

She wanted her outfit to match mine. She can wear it when she comes home. I'll put my pink dress on and we'll walk to mass, no matter what day of the week it is, and have our own Easter celebration.

In the bathroom, I take the mascara wand and, with trembling hands, apply strokes of black to my eyelashes. When I'm done, I stare in the mirror at my hollow eyes. I am a dead woman walking this earth. I yank and pull and tug at the brush, jerking it through my hair until the dark tresses gleam and stray hairs coat the bathroom sink.

My petal-pink linen shift is crisp and cool, and I try not to wrinkle it as I sit on the bed and slip on some nude slingback sandals. At the last second, I grab a shimmery, floaty, pink-and-ivory scarf for my bare shoulders.

Donovan waits for me in the living room, pacing in his dark suit. He does not meet my eyes as I take his offered hand and we close the door to our deathly quiet condo behind us.

It is only when I take the first step into St. Joan of Arc Church that I collapse.

The scent of incense, the sight of Jesus hanging on the cross, and the ethereal voices of the choir overcome me. I slump to my knees, stopping the river of worshippers trying to get in the double doors behind me.

Instead of yanking me up by the arm as he would a child, Donovan kneels beside me and takes me in his arms, gently wiping the tears that streak down my face.

Later, in the church bathroom, I stare at the dark rivulets trailing down my cheeks and debate whether to walk around for the rest of my life marked by this black kohl trail of grief.

FROM THE FRONT of my grandmother's stone cottage, I can hear the squeals and giggles of all my nieces and nephews racing around the backyard looking for bright-colored Easter eggs. It stops me in my tracks.

Donovan has my elbow. "Do you think we should . . ." He looks back toward his car parked in the empty lot among a dozen other vehicles. I close my eyes for a second. I could leave. We could flee back to the city, and nobody would be any wiser. In fact, they would all understand. But the thought of sitting in that empty apartment waiting for a call is more than I can bear.

And when I woke this morning feeling hungover from the sleeping pills again, I vowed not to take anymore.

Right now, an officer sits at our house, manning the phones. Sergeant Jackson promised that the officer has orders to call us immediately if there is any news.

I open my eyes and rest my head on Donovan's chest for a second.

"I need my family."

Inside the darker living room, I blink to adjust my vision and see my brothers sitting around the TV, watching golf.

Marco and Dante unfold themselves from the couch and come over to greet us with kisses on our cheeks. They seem happier than they should be on a holiday when my daughter should be beside me and is instead missing and maybe dead. I pull back with irritation and head toward Donovan, who is shaking hands with my uncles, insisting they don't rise. They exchange words in low voices before we head to the kitchen.

Marco takes my elbow and leads me into one of the bedrooms.

"The Saint and his men are out following leads today. I saw Santangelo at the cathedral this morning. He said he will be in touch if anything comes up. Now, go see Nana, she has something to tell you." He says this with a smile I don't understand. How can he smile on the worst Easter of my life?

It's only when I see my grandmother and cousins and sisters-in-law busy cooking and stirring in the kitchen that I realize I'm empty-handed. They all give me a smile I don't understand. Like my brothers, they are brimming with some sort of happiness, when all I feel is deep, dark despair. I try to smile back but want to scream instead.

"Nana, I forgot to bring something."

"Shhhh, *mia cara,* come here," she says and presses me close to her soft body. She pulls back and hands me a basket of rolls, loads Donovan up with three bottles of wine, and nudges us toward the patio with a wink. "Go. There is somebody here to see you."

For a split second I think they have found Grace and brought her here to surprise me. That would explain all this secretive happiness and smiles. But as soon as I walk out the French doors, I see who it is and nearly drop the basket of rolls.

My mother.

Without taking my eyes off her, I drop the basket on a table and rush to her. She looks so small sitting in a cushioned chair.

Before I know it, I'm kneeling at her feet, my head buried in her lap, and she runs her fingers through my hair. Finally, I look up.

"I don't understand... the last time I saw you..."

"I woke last night. They did an MRI. The bleeding is gone. Like a miracle. In time for Easter. The doctor came in especially this morning on his day off to release me so I could be here today. To surprise you."

"Are you sure it's okay you are home? It seems so sudden." I squeeze her hand tightly.

"At first the doctor didn't want to release me, but Marco somehow talked him into it as long as we hired a nurse to sit with me for the next few days." She looks over her shoulder, and there are Marco and Dante and my nana and sisters-in-law, all grinning. In the corner I see a young woman I don't know sitting on a chair nearby. She smiles. "They said the brain bleed wasn't as bad as they thought," my mother says. "It was only a grade one. Besides, I promised if anything seemed off I would call nine-one-one."

"Are you sure it's safe? I mean, I'm so happy you're here, but..." *Yesterday I thought you might die.*

When I look back at my mother, a shadow seems to flit across her face.

She releases my hand, and for the first time, I take her in. She looks as polished as ever, embodying *la bella figura* like Jackie O. Her black hair is swept back in a sleek ponytail, and her white slacks and navy blue blazer make her look like she's about to go out on a yacht.

But the look in her eyes says it all. I stare into her black eyes, so like Caterina's and Grace's. Eyes whose black depths well with pools of emotion, guilt, and sorrow. It does me in. Burying my face in her shoulder, I can barely hold back the tears. I will not cry. I need to be strong for Grace. I need to be strong for my mother. The last thing she needs is me blubbering snot and tears all over her shoulder. Finally, she pulls away a few inches. That's when I notice the three small black stitches still there on her forehead, marring her beautiful face.

"That bastard." I gingerly reach up, my hand hovering over the wound. "I will kill him for hurting you and taking Grace." My words are barely audible, said under my breath. I am a killer, and I won't fight it any longer.

"I will kill him first," my mother says, just as quietly.

AROUND 3:00 P.M. my grandmother gathers up the troops. Time to bring out the food.

I glance at the clock, with the little hand on the three and the big hand on the twelve. I will never, ever look at three o'clock the same way again. Grace has been gone exactly five days. My aunts and cousins and sisters-in-law stream in waves out of the kitchen, bearing huge platters of food: slices of ham, giant bowls of mashed potatoes, trays of fruits and vegetables. Plates of deviled eggs and green salads. An entire small table quickly fills with Easter pastries. More bottles of wine and Pellegrino are brought out.

Like he has the past few years, my oldest brother, Marco, says grace. Dante whistles shrilly to get everyone's attention. The children drop their kickballs and jump ropes and race to the cobblestone patio. We gather under the vines draped upon the grape arbor and hold hands in a giant circle. I stand between Donovan and my mother.

Marco makes the sign of the cross. "In the name of the father, the son, and the holy spirit. Amen."

Everyone murmurs in unison.

"Thank you, dear God, for all the blessings in our lives. We thank you for bringing Nana Maria home safe." I squeeze my mother's hand as he says this. "We thank you for our health and our family and our friends and neighbors and coworkers. We thank you for all the blessings you have bestowed on us. Today we open our hearts to you, Lord, and plead with you, we call on you and the Virgin Mary and all angels and saints to hear our prayer. We pray Lord that you bring Grace home to us."

His voice cracks on Grace's name, and Donovan squeezes my hand tightly on one side, while my mother's nails dig into my palm on the other. "We ask that you send your angels down to watch her and protect her and give her strength until we find her. Keep her safe and comfort her as she . . ."

I can't take any more. I fling my mother and Donovan's hands aside and rush into the house. I collapse on the floor in a bedroom and gulp for air, but nothing is there. My throat has closed and I can't breathe. My eyes feel like they are about to pop out of my head. There is a buzzing sound in my ears that drowns out everything else. It is only when I feel a hand on my back that I realize Donovan and my mother are there. I see their mouths move, but I can't make out what they are saying.

My mom starts crying, and it does me in. The last time I saw her cry like this, this weeping and wailing, was when she was lying on Caterina's grave. She is not a woman who cries. When we found my father dead in the basement, she didn't cry. She curled up with his dead body overnight, but her eyes were dry.

At Caterina's funeral mass inside the church, she wore dark

sunglasses, but I don't think she cried. She only cried that one time when she thought she was alone at the grave, but I was there crouched behind an angel headstone, spying on her. Horrified at what I was witnessing. I was supposed to have been taking a walk around the cemetery with my brothers, but I had slipped away and run back to my sister's grave.

Donovan has slipped out, missing this astonishing display of grief.

My mother is down on her hands and knees beside me on the carpeted floor, wailing, pulling her hair out of its bun. My grandmother is beside her, shrieking in Italian, mumbling about the *malocchio* and the Virgin Mary and the saints and angels and the devil.

I stand there, petrified, watching them.

It's like those Italian funerals I've seen in films where the women dressed in black weep and gnash their teeth as the casket is lowered into the ground. Except this is the spare bedroom in my grandmother's suburban California home, the bedroom we called the "Shell Room" as kids. We fought to sleep here in this room instead of in the red room down the hall. The red room sort of scared us. It had a red-and-black embroidered bedspread and red lampshades on the nightstand lamps.

Instead, we kids argued over who would sleep in the Shell Room during our sleepovers. We liked all the shell decorations. The base of the lamp made of seashells. The little creatures sitting on the dresser made of seashells glued together. I remember playing with them as a little girl—very, very carefully, so they wouldn't break. The pictures of the beach above the bed and the palest pink bedspread covered in a seashell pattern.

In this 1960s-decorated bedroom in suburban America, my

grandmother and mother wail like peasants in the old country, cursing the evil spirits that took Grace.

It is like the entire world has stopped as I sit, stunned, watching my mother and grandmother. A small stab of fear courses through me, seeing my mother tugging at her black hair near the stitches. What if she starts bleeding on the brain again? But I push that thought aside.

I want to join them, I want to weep and wail and tear at my clothes and yank at my hair, but I'm immobile with fear. I sit back against a dresser, my chest heaving, watching in amazement. My eyes are dry. I cannot cry. If a knife was to my throat, I don't think I could squeeze out a drop. Instead, a holy terror fills every cavity in my body. A fear that makes my entire body tingle.

While my mother and grandmother continue their litany of praying and cursing, I close my eyes, leaning back against the dresser, and pray one thing over and over. *Let Grace be alive. Let Grace be alive.*

LATER, WHEN WE emerge from the bedroom, nobody even glances our way, although I'm sure the keening could be heard the next valley over. Instead, when we come out, my sister-in-law hands me a dishtowel and tells me to start drying dishes.

Everyone is trying as hard as they can to act normal. For our sake or for the children's? I don't know, but I'm okay with it. If anyone else around me broke down, I'd be done for.

After the dishes are dried, my nana takes my hand, clucks in my ear, and takes me aside to a corner in the den.

"How is *mia ragazza*?" she asks.

I give a shrug, and she hugs me tighter. She presses her lips together and nods. "Be strong, *mia cara*. You are your mother's daughter. You cannot give up. I know she is out there. She is like her mama and her nana. She is strong. She is a survivor. Just like you and your mother."

She pulls away and is about to leave when I call her back.

"Nana? Can I talk to you?"

My grandmother has always been my confidante. I have always found comfort in running my worries by her. She sits down in a gold and burgundy upholstered chair and holds my hand as I tell her about my dream.

"Do you think I'm crazy?" I ask when I'm done. Although Donovan later apologized, his comment about a psych eval has been bothering me.

"No, *mia cara*." Her eyes are sparkling, and I can't stop staring at them. "You are *benedetta*."

Blessed.

"We always have some in our family, like my aunt Paola, she was *benedetta* and *veggente*—could see things. Things that had not happened yet. When someone in the family died, there would be a *battere* on her headboard."

"A *battere*?" I don't know this Italian word.

My grandmother's forehead crinkles as she tries to think of the English word. "Yes, a ticktickticka," she says, standing and making her way over to the doorway. There she makes her tiny hand into a fist and bangs on the wooden door frame to the den.

"A knock?"

"Yes. Knock, knock, knock."

"Really?" I feel strangely better. I'm not crazy.

"And my cousin Paciono, he always saw the dead in our photographs. In our pictures, he could see others, spirits. I never could see them, but my younger brother, Albert, sometimes could. Many in our *famiglia* are like this."

I hug her for a long time. When I draw back, she smiles at me.

"To see, to be *veggente,* it is a gift, *mia cara.* A *benedizione.*"

A blessing.

It sure doesn't feel like a blessing to me right now. It feels like a curse.

Someone calls my grandmother and she turns away.

Thank God for my grandmother. She thinks I'm blessed and that the women in our family are survivors. A small lump rises in my throat. At least one female member of our family wasn't a survivor. Caterina.

Survivor. Is that what I am? I sure as hell don't feel like one.

AROUND SIX, THERE is a knock on the door, then one of the kids brings in a giant pot of flowers, and then there is another and another. Three kids file in with the potted flowered plants.

"It's for you, *Nonna Maria,*" they chime in excitedly. At the end of the line, little four-year-old Lucia is carrying a card. She hands it to my mother, and we all wait.

My mother's hands are trembling as she opens the card. A small pink flush spreads across her cheeks as she reads, and then she tucks the card into a big pocket on her cardigan.

"Well, Christ's sakes, Ma, who's it from?" Dante asks, scowling.

"Vincenzo," she says and quickly turns away. "He is wishing me good health now that I'm out of the hospital."

Marco gives me a look and I raise an eyebrow. It hasn't gone unnoticed that my mother has suddenly taken to calling The Saint by his first name.

The sun is setting when we finally leave. The hugs are extra long, and even the uncles' eyes are glistening as they kiss my cheeks.

The door closes behind us, and the twilight is before us.

I made it through Easter without Grace.

In the car, I turn to Donovan.

He gives me a haunted look.

"I want to die," I say, searching his eyes.

He lights a cigarette and nods before turning the key in the ignition.

Chapter 36

I'VE MISSED A call from The Saint. It looks like he called when we were hugging and saying our good-byes.

I realize it at the same moment that Donovan tells me he missed a call from Noah West at the FBI. We both dial our phones at the same time as he pulls onto the entrance to the freeway.

"Giovanni." I don't bother with niceties. I see out of the corner of my eye that Donovan is scribbling an address on one of my reporter's notebooks. I lean over.

"I'm texting you a photo," Santangelo says. "The son. Anders Frank. I will also text you an address. Benicia. We are on our way. We will meet you there."

For a split second, I am filled with disappointment. We no longer need to find Anders now that we know his dad is dead, but then the photo comes across my phone and I gasp. I shoot a glance at the address Donovan is writing down.

"Is it 2574 Long Lake Road in Benicia?" I say to The Saint. "FBI just got the same address and are sending in the troops."

"We will be there, but you will not know," The Saint says. "We have some, uh, issues with the FBI right now, and I have to stay out of the limelight. I will still help you. I promise you."

"Okay," I say and disconnect. Issues with the FBI? Not my problem. As long as he still helps me find Grace.

Donovan is still talking to Noah West when I hold up the picture of Anders to show Donovan, who gives me a sideways glance and a furious nod.

Now I see the resemblance. Frank Anderson had a buzz cut and dark, deep-set eyes. His son, Anders Frank, has arctic eyes and a dirty-blond bowl haircut like a little boy. But they both have that same defined Superman jaw.

"Motherfucker," Donovan says after glancing at the picture. "It's him. It's the guy we saw on the beach."

Frank Anderson's son has Grace.

WHEN WE ARRIVE on Long Lake Road, my heart is racing in my throat.

The sun has dipped closer to the horizon, and the neighborhood is bathed in a surreal golden light. Small, bungalows have tidy yards and flowerbeds. We pull up in front of one house, which has a hummingbird feeder hanging from the front porch and two turquoise retro metal chairs set at an angle on the lawn. A white doily curtain in the front window swings shut when I glance over.

Sergeant Jackson and Special Agent West meet our car. Jackson is wearing khakis and a Hawaiian button-down shirt, the first time I haven't seen him in a tie and blazer. He must have come straight from Easter dinner. The SWAT team will arrive in a few minutes, as they had to be scrambled from family celebrations, West says. In the back of my mind, I wonder if some will be drunk or tipsy. We are staging about two blocks away and around the corner from Anders Frank's house.

I glance around to see if I can spot anyone from Santangelo's crew in cars, but I don't see a soul.

Donovan pulls a Kel-Tec P-11 semiautomatic pistol from his glove compartment and hands it to me. It's just like the one he has at home. He's already packing two guns himself—one in his shoulder harness and one strapped to his ankle. Glancing over at the white doily curtains, I quickly tuck the P-11 in my deep jacket pocket. My hands are shaking. I don't trust myself not to accidentally shoot someone besides Frank. God forbid he uses Grace as a hostage. Because she has to still be alive. He has to follow his pattern—keep the victims alive and then kill them on the sixth day.

I'm about to jump out of my skin with nervousness, when my phone rings. It's Lopez.

"Hey, man, just wanted you to know I was thinking of you guys."

"Thanks, C-Lo, but I'm in the middle of something. It might be Grace." I almost weep saying those words.

"Man, I'll let you go, I was calling 'cause I just was out at a slumper you might want to know about."

A dead body in a car.

"It was that kid from the weekly. Throat slit from ear to ear. Been there a day or two."

I can feel the blood drain from my face. "Michael Dillman?"

"Yeah, one from the fire. Seemed like he was a nice kid, so I wanted to let you know. I didn't want to bother you right now, but didn't want you to read it in the paper in case you guys were friends."

"Thanks." I whisper it and hang up.

His editor said he was following a lead about Grace's abduction. He must have found something—something that led to his murder.

Donovan glances over at me with a frown.

"The kid from the weekly who told me about Anderson's grave was murdered."

Before he can respond, a van pulls up and six men in riot gear tumble out.

Seeing them sends a spurt of fear racing through me. I know they are here to save Grace, but I'm so worried something could go wrong. One guy adjusting his belt meets my eyes. He gives a slight nod.

Sergeant Jackson and another man call the men in riot gear over in a circle for a brief meeting. As soon as the circle breaks up, the men disperse in groups of two, and Jackson heads our way.

"We've got some flash bangs and tear gas. We're going in the front and back of the building simultaneously. At the same time, we've got the sheriff's department helicopter on standby right over that ridge. As soon as the signal is given, the helicopter will be over the house with its infrared. Nobody is going to leave that house without us knowing about it."

I press my lips tightly together and nod. I realize that I've grabbed Donovan's hand and am squeezing it so hard that my fingernails are digging into his palm. I let up the pressure, and he gives me a reassuring squeeze.

"I want to be closer," I say, not blinking.

"Can't do that," Jackson says.

"Yes, I can." We stare at each other for a few seconds.

"Okay. Come with me."

The three of us cram into the front seat of his unmarked Ford sedan. I grab Donovan's hand again. It's not as obvious as a detective's unmarked rig—more like the unassuming sedans the FBI rents at the airport when they come to town.

Instead of taking the curve around Long Lake Road where the house apparently sits, Jackson turns at the first road.

"This will take us the back way."

My mouth is dry, and my heart is pounding in my ears. My palms are clammy. I let go of Donovan's hands and wipe them on my jeans. Out of the corner of my eye, I see the muscle in his jaw throbbing like a drum. Every inch of his body is tense. I close my eyes and take a deep breath, saying a quick prayer. *Mother Mary, never have you refused someone who comes to you in prayer. I pray you return my daughter, Grace, to me safely.*

When the car stops, I slowly open my eyes. A few seconds later, a van races past us and skids to a stop by a plain yellow house. Jackson guns the motor and we park behind it, perpendicular, blocking the way as the back doors of the van fly open and four men race into the backyard of the house in a blur. Donovan flies out the door behind them, gun drawn. Jackson shouts, but I don't hear it because I'm right on Donovan's heels, the gun in my pocket thumping against my thigh as I chase him.

There is a deafening boom and glass shattering and crashing and shouting all at once. The bone-rattling thud of a helicopter overhead sends a chill through my body. As I get to the backyard of the house butting up to Frank's house, I only catch the tail end of the tactical team bursting through the door of the yellow house. Donovan holds up a hand to stop me, and we wait in the back of the yard, catching our breath. The adrenaline is shooting through me, and I feel like my knees are going to collapse. At the same time I can barely stop myself from rushing into that house.

I hear shouting inside, but it doesn't sound frantic, only routine. The three of us wait for what seems like an eternity but can only be a few seconds. Then I can make out one word—"Clear"—shouted a few times from inside the house. The helicopter hovers for a few seconds, then zips off.

Jackson is at our side and shakes his head at us. "No hits from the infrared."

As he says this, the men pile out the back door. The first guy out shakes his head emphatically. No.

Nobody rushes out with Grace in his arms. Nobody says a word. The helicopter has left. The men look down at their feet instead of meeting my eyes. The man who shook his head is now before us and I stop breathing, preparing for the worst.

"Grace?" It comes out in a hoarse whisper.

"Sorry, ma'am. No sign of her."

Grace isn't here. But neither is her body.

Relief and disappointment surge through me.

I start to push past the men. "Let me see inside the house." I'm hoping to find some sign of her. Some stray strand of hair. A handprint on a window. A message scrawled in the dust. Anything. Any little sign that she was here. And alive.

A few of the men in tactical gear move to stop me, but after seeing something over my shoulder, they step back and let me through.

I step into the back door and am in a small kitchen. The sink and counters are empty. The room smells faintly of bleach and pine scent. Not even a coffeepot rests on the scratched and stained green Formica countertop. Using my sleeve so I don't leave fingerprints, I pull open the refrigerator door. It is empty and scrubbed clean.

But still I search the rest of the house.

Two bedrooms. Each has twin beds, neatly made with threadbare bedspreads. One set brown. One gold. The closets are empty. The bathroom is cleared out, its counter coated with a thin layer of dust. Nobody has lived here for a long time.

In the living room, a man is crouched near the front door,

dusting the doorknob for fingerprints. A detective I vaguely recognize is beside him. They both nod as I enter the room.

"Did he leave any fingerprints anywhere?"

The man crouched with gloves on shakes his head slowly. "I think whoever lived here last was a neat freak. Everything is scrubbed clean."

"We'll keep looking," the detective says. "We've only begun to process the house."

If Anders Frank lived here, he was meticulous about clearing out all personal effects when he left and wiping down all surfaces. He's the one who killed those women. He was sending me a message. Just what is it, though?

Casting one last glance around the living room, bare except for a couch, coffee table, and ancient TV, I'm pretty sure about two things—Anders Frank knew we would find this home, and he's not planning on ever coming back.

"CAN I LOOK in the garage?" I ask Sergeant Jackson.

He meets eyes with another cop and there is a slight shrug.

"Hold on." He shuffles off around the corner.

A loud crack echoes down the alley. I hear some voices, and a few seconds later, he returns.

"Be my guest."

Donovan gives me a look and we round the corner to the entrance to the garage.

The lock on the door is broken, and a tactical team member with a battering ram stands nearby. When we approach, another two men in camouflage come out from the open doorway and nod at us.

"It's clear. Go on ahead."

The men move off to the side.

Donovan gestures for me to go first.

With a trembling hand, I push the door with its chipped and peeling green paint.

Enough light from a band of windows on either side of the garage shows it is empty. There isn't even a candy wrapper or scrap of trash on the floor. I step across the concrete floor dotted with dark blobs from oil stains.

Light filters in from the windows to the west, casting long beams of light that illuminate long shafts of swirling dust. I stare. I catch the faint whiff of something, some type of cleanser that smells familiar, but I'm not sure what it is.

"Ready?" Donovan stands in the open doorway, a dark silhouette, one foot out the door, one in. He's ready to leave.

I shake my head no.

There is something here that is nagging at me, but I'm not sure what I'm supposed to see. But I know I'm missing something.

I turn slowly in a circle, looking in all directions, then up at the ceiling and down at the floor. What is it?

Then I recognize the smell—glass cleaner. That's when I see it. All eight of the windows—four on each side—are coated in dust. Except one. It is sparkling clean. Gleaming. Light shines through brighter than the others. A golden beam of sunlight stands out from the other columns of dust.

I look at the floor of the garage where the beam lands, but it is bare. Drawn closer, mesmerized by this anomaly, I take a step. Slowly. Then another. Until I'm right in front of the window.

Why is this one window clean? Why would someone clean one window only? The wooden wall underneath the window is dirty, but I think I can make out something there.

Rushing over to the garage door opener on the wall beside the small door, I punch it, and it opens with a loud screech. Donovan and the police pop in the open garage door.

The screechy door grumbles and opens, filling the dark garage space with even more light.

I'm crouched underneath the window. I was right. In small black writing, smaller than someone would normally write, there are tiny letters printed.

"Your iniquities have separated her from you. She will not hear you. Repent at the city of souls and then go where the three points will lead you."

The first part is a paraphrase of the fourth Bible verse Frank Anderson sent me. Somehow Anders knows all the e-mails his father sent me. What is he trying to say? The fourth message is about Grace. But it's also a clue.

Finding the message sends a thrill of hope laced with fear through me. He wouldn't do all this if there wasn't a chance of saving Grace, would he?

But in the deepest depths of my heart, I know he would. All the other Bible verses were only found after the murders. He might want me to think there is hope when there isn't. I know that for some reason he would fuck with me just for his own sick pleasure.

AFTER THE CRIME scene technicians push into the garage to look at the writing, we leave.

As we head home, my face is scrunched and my hands clenched as I mull the message over and over and over again until I think I'm going to scream.

What does it mean? The three points. It's a location. But where?

I'm mulling it over when Donovan stops and grabs a coffee in

Berkeley. I wait in the car. He hands me an iced latte, something I would usually savor. I reach for it automatically and tug on the straw, sipping it. Before I know it, the latte is gone and I'm sucking air.

The sun is dipping lower on the horizon behind the Golden Gate Bridge, turning the San Francisco skyline into a landscape of dark, looming towers.

My stomach does a small somersault. The rush of caffeine on an empty stomach, along with all the stop-and-go traffic on the Bay Bridge, has made me feel barfy. *Don't vomit.*

I keep going over what the tiny message said. "Your iniquities have separated her from you. She will not hear you. Repent at the city of souls and then go where the three points will lead you."

We are nearly at our exit to the Embarcadero when I burst out.

"Holy Cross Cemetery in Colma."

He yanks the steering wheel and our tires yelp as we pull into the through lane.

"I don't know what he means by the three points," I say, "but I remember my mother telling me that not only is Colma called the City of the Dead, it's also called the City of Souls."

Donovan doesn't answer, just moves his head up and down and grits his teeth. His knuckles are turning white on the steering wheel.

"Do you think we need to call someone else to meet us at the cemetery?" I say.

"You mean, like a cop?" His voice is bitter.

"Donovan?" He glances at me out of the corner of his eye but doesn't answer. "Are you okay?" He knows what I mean. He knows that I'm not asking an inane question. We are both in the exact same spot. Hell. We don't need to acknowledge that. It is as present as the night falling around us.

"I'm a cop. I'm a detective. I'm the one people are supposed to call for help. I'm not supposed to call anyone else. *I'm* a detective," he says. "I used to think I was a pretty good one."

"You're a fucking brilliant detective," I say, my voice breaking.

"So why can't I find our daughter?" He bites off the last two words and swallows hard.

I reach over and grab his hand, holding it tightly. I don't know how to answer him.

Traffic comes to a stop on the freeway in front of us and he has to put both hands on the steering wheel. I want to scream. In the last few days, anything that has kept me from going quickly where I need and want to go has felt like a physical barrier to me saving Grace. It's crazy and not true, but I feel like I need to be barreling forward at warp speed or I will lose her. And the one time I tried to quell that despair-filled anxiety by obliterating my thoughts with sleeping pills, I was nearly comatose. There is no normal.

There will never be normal again.

We both know this in the bottoms of our hearts. But we are here together. For now, we have each other. In the back of my mind, a statistic jumps into my mind: Eighty percent of couples separate after the death of a child.

Even thinking this makes my stomach heave. *She's not dead. She's not dead. She's not dead.* I would know.

I scoot closer to him, sitting on the edge of my seat. I reach over and lace my fingers through his on the steering wheel. *Don't barf. Don't barf. Don't barf.* We both stare straight ahead, our faces lit up by the brake lights in front of us.

Chapter 37

When we finally get to Colma, night has fallen and the fog has crept in, low on the ground. The only light comes from orange streetlights that cast feeble glowing light into the cemetery. The gate to the Holy Cross Cemetery is open, but a sign says the cemetery closes at midnight.

As I open the car door, a fishy, briny smell greets me even though we are inland. I stuff the pockets of my trench coat with my gun, a small flashlight, and my cell phone.

Donovan grabs my hand and pulls me along with him to the entrance to the cemetery. My feet are on fire from wearing these high-heeled Easter sandals all day. I've been ignoring them as we have gone from one place to another, but when Donovan turns to me at the front gate, he sees me wince.

We both look down and see tiny bits of blood seeping out the sides of my sandals. I had thought it felt squishy to walk. At the same time, a wave of nausea strikes me and I hold my stomach. I feel bile rise in my throat, and I swallow it down.

Donovan notices.

"You okay?"

I shake my head. He hands me his keys. "Wait in the car. I'll go check out the grave. I don't expect to see a damn thing. There's not another car parked around here for miles. I'll be right back. Rest here for a minute. I promise I won't be long."

"No way." But I'm still so nauseous that any movement seems like torture.

He takes out his gun and checks the chamber. "Please don't argue with me. Besides, I need you to wait here. I doubt he's in the cemetery with Grace. If he is, there is no way he's getting over the twelve-foot-high metal fence with her. This is the only way in and out. I need you to stay here and guard this entrance."

What he says makes sense. I still have the P-11 in my jacket pocket. Its weight on my leg is reassuring. And the chance to sit back, put my sore feet up, and not move until my stomach settles does sound appealing.

"I'm not sure you should go alone," I say. "Maybe we should call nine-one-one?"

His eyes narrow. "Ella, I'm a cop. I am nine-one-one. I have two guns. I am a trained law enforcement officer. If anything, I'm putting an innocent civilian in danger by having you come in with me. In fact, I should make you get in the car and lock the doors to keep you safe."

"Okay, I didn't mean to insult you," I say, a little irritated. "I just worry. Will you call me when you get to Anderson's grave?"

"It's not that far. Less than a five-minute walk."

"Will you call?" My voice is pleading.

"Yes." He takes out his phone and holds it in his hand. "I'll call."

I sit sideways in the passenger seat so my legs stick out as I pry the bloody sandals off my feet and wince at the pain. I dig in my pocket and take out the gun, laying it on the driver's seat. I rummage in my bag for something to stop the bleeding from blisters erupting across my toes, on my ankles, and on the bottom of my feet.

All the while, I keep listening for any sound from the cemetery. Any voices. Anything. For a second, I reach for the gun as a car goes by on the road, but I relax when it doesn't pull into the parking lot. I look in the glove compartment and see a roll of silver duct tape. Carefully, I rip off strips of the tape and loosely wrap my feet in them, not taking my eyes off the entry to the cemetery.

Donovan should call any second. My feet are taped and my stomach feels much better. If he doesn't call me in two minutes, I'm going in there if he likes it or not.

Chapter 38

The night is warm, so I keep the passenger door open and lean my head back on the seat. I look at the time on the phone. One more minute and I'm going in.

Gunshots fill the night. At the same time, my cell phone rings and I scramble to grab the gun, my phone, and get out of the car all at the same time.

"Got . . . me." Donovan's voice is feeble, weak through the phone line. A tingly chill of horror streaks down my body, and my face feels ice cold.

"Where are you?" I'm in front of the car, peering frantically into the dark cemetery. Even before he answers, I'm running toward the entrance to the graveyard.

He doesn't answer.

"Sean!" I'm shrieking. "Sean. Answer me, Sean? Does he have Grace?"

"No." He gasps the word out. Disappointment floods me, along with sheer terror. Donovan has been shot.

"I'm coming, but first I'm going to hang up and call nine-one-one. Can you wait that long?"

I know I'm asking if he's going to die. If I can hang up and still talk to him ever again.

"Yes."

I click off and dial 911.

"Officer down. Gunshot. Holy Cross Cemetery in Colma. Detective Sean Donovan with Rosarito P.D. A police officer has been shot and might bleed to death. Send a helicopter now. NOW!"

"Ma'am, could we get your name?"

"Holy Cross Cemetery in Colma. Police officer shot. Get a helicopter in the air. This is a police officer's life you are fucking with. Do you have all of this? Are you sending help?"

"Yes, ma'am, Holy Cross Cemetery in Colma. Officer down. Emergency responders are on their way. What is your name? Are there other injuries?"

I'm about to hang up when I remember something I hear on the police scanner frequently. Dispatchers sometimes won't send in EMTs or paramedics to a shooting until the danger is gone, the shooter is gone, and the scene is clear.

"Scene is clear. Safe for emergency personnel. The shooter has fled."

I hang up. I don't have time for niceties. Most gunshot victims die from bleeding to death. There is about a ten-minute window to get a wound sewn up if the bleeding is profuse. I have no idea if the shooter is still around or where Donovan has been shot, but I'm not taking any chances.

I'm punching Donovan's number. His phone rings. He doesn't pick up. *Oh my God. Oh my God. Oh my God.* I'm chanting and running, I'm racing through the grass of the cemetery, which feels cold and wet on my nearly bare duct-tape-wrapped feet. Inside my jacket pocket, the gun slaps against my thigh. I continue my chant mumble. "Answer, answer, Donovan, answer. Please answer the phone. Please pick up. Please pick up. Please pick up."

I know the grave is in the middle of the cemetery, so every once in a while I glance to both sides, making sure I'm not getting too close to one fence or the other. I keep running and pleading with him to answer. It feels like hours, but I know it hasn't even been a minute I've been running. The cemetery gets darker as I get farther away from the parking lot. Low-hanging clouds reflect orangish city lights, but the deeper I get into the cemetery, the more the ground is covered by low, roiling fog clouds. Little puffs of clouds that dissipate as I run through them. At eye level, I can still sort of see, and I'm pleading for Donovan to pick up when out of the corner of my eye I see a whitish blur at the top of the cemetery fence. It stops me dead in my tracks. Someone is scaling the fence.

"Stop." I scream the word as the figure drops to the ground on the other side. At my voice, the person stops and stands there, an eerie figure in the fog, staring at me. For a few seconds, we both freeze—me, holding the phone in my hand, which has gone to voice mail for the millionth time; the figure, standing with legs spread, facing me, arms extended toward me. Light from a distant streetlight briefly reflects off what he is holding in his hand. A gun. Pointed at me. The figure is slight, not much taller than me, and seems lithe and willowy, almost feminine. Anders. My gun is in my pocket. He will shoot me before I can draw it. My heart is pounding.

We stand there silently for a second until he says in his nasally voice, "You have until dawn to find your daughter. Come alone. If you bring the cops, I kill her and then myself. If you don't make it in time, she dies. When the sun comes up, she dies."

He lowers the gun and sprints away, disappearing into the night.

I nearly collapse in relief. Grace is still alive. Just then I hear a groan.

"Donovan?"

I scramble toward the noise, tripping over a small headstone and falling flat on my face, but I turn my head to listen. He's close.

"Donovan?" My voice is ragged as I scramble to my feet.

Then I see him. He's pulled himself up to a sitting position and is leaning against a big headstone with an angel statue on top of it. He is holding his side.

I kneel and put my face close to his. I lower him to the ground at the same time I'm clawing and ripping at my dress, tearing strips off. "It's okay. It's okay. Help is on the way. Hang in there. Grace is alive." I want to give him reason to hang on. My words are one long sob. I have him flat on his back now, and I press the torn fabric of my dress around him, removing his hand that is staunching the blood. It comes away dark and sticky. I work my way under his back, then tie the scrap of dress as tight as I can. The blood doesn't immediately seep through, which is a good sign.

I grab his hand. He squeezes it lightly and makes a grumbling sound. He must be weak from loss of blood?

"So stupid of me. I didn't think he'd be here."

"You didn't know," I say, rubbing my thumb across his palm. "Hang in there. Help is on the way."

Even as I say that, I hear sirens in the distance at the same time

I hear the deafening clatter of helicopter blades. "It's okay. They're almost here."

Then, as if from the heavens, a spotlight illuminates us and sends my hair whirling in front of my eyes from the churn of the blades. Looking up, I try to move my hair to see, but then the helicopter is gone, heading toward the parking lot.

As soon as it sounds like the helicopter lands, I stand and shout. "Over here. Over here. This way. Over here. Over here."

As soon as I see a white-shirted man across the foggy graveyard and see that he sees me, I kneel back down with Donovan.

"It's okay, baby. Help is here."

"Ella, he said dawn."

"I know. I know. Don't worry about that right now. Let's get you help first." I squeeze his hand.

"The three points. The navy. Call West." The words seem to cost him tremendous effort, and this sends a volley of panic through me. Please don't let this be his last words. Dear God, please don't let him die.

I glance at Anderson's grave marker. Something is different. In front of the grave are some fresh flowers. *How sweet of his son,* I think bitterly. And there is something else. Next to the United States flag is a new flag. This one says United States Navy.

Of course, Frank Anderson was a navy man.

All at once, people with flashlights surround me. I'm actually picked up and moved out of the way, and then there are four people huddling around Donovan. The first thing they do is shoot questions at him rapid fire.

"Do you have any allergies? Are you on any medication? Where does it hurt? Does this hurt? Are you feeling warm? Do you feel sleepy?"

He is mumbling answers, but at least he is responding. I know they ask the last two questions to gauge whether he is going into shock.

I stand back, watching, clutching my arms around my waist, hugging myself, shivering with fear, not cold.

Within seconds, he's on a gurney and they are running back toward the parking lot. I follow as close as I can. They have some huge pad on his side, and one of the EMTs is running alongside the gurney, holding the pad. Once Donovan is loaded into the helicopter, they hook him up to an IV and EKG. They also press an oxygen mask to his face. His eyes meet mine above it as I peer in, trying to get a glimpse of his face between all the bodies hovering around.

A man warns me I need to move, they are going to close the doors.

Donovan lifts up his oxygen mask and leans a little toward me.

"Excuse me, can I say good-bye? I'll be quick. I promise," I say to the man in front of me, leaning into the helicopter.

"No," the man says without blinking an eye.

"Go. Go get Grace," Donovan says hoarsely as they close the door. I see the paramedics pressing him back down as he tries to get up. "Go!"

"But I can't leave you, Sean." I'm sobbing now.

"Go. Get Grace." He is begging me. I close my eyes for a second and then nod. I have time to duck out of the way before the helicopter blades start up and the helicopter rises into the air and swoops away. I will do as he asks. For our daughter. If his last wish is for me to try to save Grace even if it means I will never see him again, I will live with that. Because I understand. I get it. Because just like me, he loves Grace more than life itself.

But that doesn't stop my heart from breaking a little as the helicopter disappears into the night. I peel out of the parking lot and have blended into traffic when three squad cars come flying past me, heading toward the cemetery.

I point the Saab toward the one place where the three points meet.

Chapter 39

EVERY TIME I'VE gone over the Bible verses and the message on the garage wall, my mind has spiraled into a vortex of despair.

When Donovan repeated "three points," though, something clicked. What if the "three" refers to the three women Anders Frank killed?

He killed all three women, or at least left all three bodies, in particular locations on purpose. As I race onto the Bay Bridge, I reach behind me for Donovan's map book. If I look at all three points on the map, I'll find what lies in the middle of the bay smack in the middle of those bodies. I already know, but am just going to confirm it. Yep, I was right.

The Phantom Fleet, the ship graveyard.

I hold the map page up to the orange glow made by city lights reflecting off the cloud cover. Yes. I'm right. With my finger, I touch each spot along the bay where a body was found. If you make a circle of the three bodies, directly in the center is the Phantom Fleet. Where the three points meet.

The navy flag on his grave was the other tip-off. His son left the flag for us to see. He's hiding on an old navy ship.

Anders lured us to the cemetery to find the clue, but also to take Donovan out. He let me live. He wants me to find him at the Phantom Fleet. Alone. For a split second, doubt floods me. What if Grace is dead and he's luring me to the ship graveyard to kill me, too? I can't think that way. She has to be alive.

She's on one of those ships. But which one? He's been keeping her there, hidden, on one of the abandoned ships. Some of the articles I printed out about the fleet said some ships were surprisingly intact, with beds and linens and even canned food still onboard. They had to be at the ready in case they were commissioned for service. It wasn't just a ship graveyard; it was also a holding bay.

That would explain the boat we'd seen that appeared and disappeared—once from Roe Island and once on Ocean Beach. Just like the Channel 5 TV photographer explained about his high school friends, Anders Frank could pull the inflatable boat onboard so nobody would be any wiser.

So how to find which ship? And how to get to it?

The Saint.

I punch in the number on my cell just as I exit the Caldecott Tunnel leading under the hills connecting Oakland to the greater East Bay.

"Santangelo."

"I need a boat . . ." I scan the map for what looks like a place to launch a boat. There is a small roadway leading down to the slough. "At Suisun Slough. I need it there in thirty minutes. Can you help me?"

"It will be done. My men will meet you there in fifteen minutes."

I breathe a sigh of relief. Thank God. I swerve around slower cars, punching the gas pedal and peering into the darkness ahead. I'm about to hang up when The Saint clears his throat.

"But there is a problem," he says.

"What?" I'm impatient. I don't care what he has to say as long as he gets me a boat to the dock.

"Sam the Goat, he is under some heat. My men can give you the boat, but then they must leave to take care of some other business. I'm sorry. It is my fault. I didn't realize when we set out to help you we would be crossing paths with some old FBI friends. But no matter. It is a minor issue. It will be resolved soon. Is this a problem for you?"

"Nope. I just need the boat." Cars in front of me are bunching up, so I slip into the emergency lane against the median and zip by, leaving an angry chorus of honking horns in my wake.

"I can come," Santangelo says. "Alone. If you need my assistance, I will be there. I promised."

I don't need him. "No. That's okay. I'm bringing in the feds after I hang up with you."

"Is that wise? You know I can be . . . more discreet than the FBI," he says.

Navigating a tricky curve, I take in his words. For a second I'm torn. He means we can kill Anders Frank and get away with it if it is just the two of us. If the FBI is brought into it, that's not going to be possible.

I notice that my knuckles are turning white from clutching the steering wheel.

As much as I can imagine myself looking down at Frank's cold, dead body, right now I'm more concerned with getting Grace back safe than seeking revenge. Before me, the cars clear as the 680 freeway heading north opens up into more lanes, and I floor it.

"Thank you," I say softly. "I need to focus on getting my daughter back safe. I'll deal with the man who took her later. That's when I may need your help."

"You have my word. I am at your service."

I don't answer, only gently disconnect the call.

There is more to do, more people to call. I call Marco and tell him that Donovan has been shot and is heading to San Francisco General.

"Please go be with him. And call me if . . . anything changes."

"Slow down. He's been shot? Where are you? What the hell?" says Marco, the brother who tries to never curse.

"I'm going to get Grace." I hang up before he can answer.

I'm now crossing the Benicia-Martinez Bridge. I can see the Phantom Fleet to my right, below me. It looks as eerie as ever, maybe more so in the low fog hovering on the water. I'll be at the slough in a moment, but I still don't know how I'm going to figure out which ship they are on. I vaguely remember a list of the ship names. I go over every so-called clue Anders Frank has left me. The Bible verses he's left—the same ones his father e-mailed to me.

I wrack my brains again, thinking of commonalities in the women. Nothing clicks.

I'm so close, but I'm petrified I'm not going to find her in time.

As soon as I hang up with Marco, I dial Agent Noah West.

Before I can leave a message, I lose cell service as I dip into the hills north of the bridge. I keep hitting redial. As my car dips down to the slough and out of the hills, I finally get West's voice mail.

"I know where he has Grace. The Phantom Fleet in Suisun Bay. He's holed up on one of the ships. He knows we're coming for him.

He said if I bring cops, Grace dies." I take a breath. "As soon as I figure out which ship she's on, I'll call you so you can send some backup. Maybe have your men meet at the entry to Suisun Slough. That's where I'm going to launch my boat. But make sure they are covert. He sees backup, Grace is dead."

AT THE WEEDY entrance to the slough, a black Escalade is the only vehicle on the dirt road. My lights briefly illuminate the front seat, and it appears empty.

Down near the water, I see dark figures moving. The cherries of their cigarettes glow in the night and bounce around, showing the men's movement. I tuck my gun, a small flashlight, and my phone in my trench coat pocket and walk down in my bare, duct-taped-wrapped feet.

At the water, I stop. Both men nod. It's hard to make out their features in the dim light coming from the orangish light reflecting off the clouds above.

"Want us to start the motor?" one man asks. "It's an electric trolling motor."

"Are there oars?" I lean over the boat and peer inside.

"Yes, but you are going to have to use the motor to get most of the way out there," the same man says. "It is quiet. Purrs like a kitten. You can kill the engine—like this." He takes my hand and has my fingers feel the switch in the semidarkness. "See?"

"Okay. Then show me how to start it."

The noise of the electric motor seems extraordinarily loud, but I know it's my paranoia that makes me think that, since we can still speak in low voices near it.

Stepping into the brackish water, I put one foot in, gain my balance, and put the other in. Once I'm sitting, they push me off.

I point the boat toward the ship graveyard, navigating through some reedy plants. I glance back once in time to see the taillights of the Escalade disappear up the dirt road.

Now that I'm alone, I notice the smell of the marsh—a combination of wet dog and dead body smell. I pat my pockets to make sure I still feel the flashlight, gun, and phone. Taking out the phone, I silence the ringer, pausing over the call button. I dial West again but still get his voice mail.

"I'm heading out to the fleet in a small rubber boat." I'm not sure what else to say, so I hang up. All I know is that I need to find Grace soon. If it means searching all seventy-five ships one by one, I will do it. If only I have enough time. Dawn is only hours away.

He's going to kill her on the sixth day. Just like it was for Caterina and those three college women.

A small splash startles me, and I realize a river otter is floating on its back, staring at me in the dark. After the chill settles off my spine, I smile. "I'm going to take you as a sign of good luck," I say.

The otter just watches me, floating on its back and using its paws to try to crack some type of shellfish on its belly. He floats off as thicker fog rolls in.

The fog is a blessing. Even if Anders Frank is looking out for me, he won't be able to see me until I'm right up against the fleet.

After a few minutes, I'm near the first row of ships. I blow right past. They are too close to the Coast Guard station and the shore. Too risky for him to hide out there. I'll try the second row of anchored ships out. As I round the last ship, I see the blinking red and green lights of a boat coming near. Shit.

I glance at my phone. No calls. Did Noah West get my message and warn the Coast Guard I'd be out? I lunge back and kill my motor, drifting along, ducking. A huge spotlight from the patrol boat shines on the sides of the ghost ships, traveling the length of the one near me and then seemingly shining on my tiny inflatable boat. I'm caught. My only hope is to get them on my side. I reach for my phone to dial Noah West so he can explain what I'm doing. I have the phone in my hand, ready to dial, when I hear voices carrying faintly across the water. I freeze, but I can't make out what they are saying.

I lie down in the bottom of the boat and wait for them to discover me. The boat is filled with about an inch of water. I hold the phone on my chest so it won't get wet. After a few seconds of silence, I peek my head up.

The patrol boat is gone.

Peering into the night, I try to see the patrol boat's lights again through a haze of fog that is rolling in, but the lights have disappeared. How did they not see me?

Instead of risking the noise of the motor again, I take the paddles down from the sides and begin to skate across the water, slowly but surely, the only sound the muffled dipping of the oars into the water.

I'm not too surprised that the muscles in my upper arm burn after only a moment of exertion. Even though I'm in the best shape of my life from the last few years of martial arts, I've been slacking for the past year and haven't made it to the dojo in months. I've been too busy juggling mommyhood with being a reporter.

The first ship I come across is suddenly so close I nearly run into it. Risking a bit of light, I shine my small flashlight up and see that it is called the *Gettysburg*. Clicking the light off, I round the nose of the ship and see that right beside it is a smaller ship, called *Iris*. It's not a navy ship, so I paddle on. The next ship is called the *Santa Ynez*. It definitely looks like a navy ship. How do I know which ones to search, though? I'll look around more. Without stopping, I paddle on and see the next one is called the *Comet*. The *Comet* isn't a navy ship, either.

I shine my flashlight up on the other ships in this row. The SS *Green Mountain State*—what state is that?—the USS *Iowa*, the SS *Cape Jacob*, the *Merrimack*, the *Adventurer*, the *Kansas City*. None of them have names that mean anything.

How am I ever going to find which one Grace is on? I list all the names in my head over and over.

I'm about to paddle on to the next row of ships, which feels miles away even though I know it can't possibly be that far, when something jars me and my arms stop their stroke in midair.

Santa Ynez.

In a flash, I remember reading about Saint Agnes in Sunday school.

Thank God for Rosa Inez Martinez, who was in my Sunday school class. I was always jealous of her because she lived in the biggest house in our neighborhood and always had the best and most expensive toys. The ones I always wanted but never received. She was also a know-it-all. On the Sunday we studied about the saints, we passed around prayer cards with different saints on them. Someone commented on how cute the lamb was that Saint Agnes was holding. The teacher went on to tell us something about how we should pray to Saint Agnes for our future husbands.

I ignored most of the lecture until Little Miss Know-It-All beside me raised her hand, like she always did. I quickly tucked the drawing I was doodling into my Bible and looked like I was paying attention when the teacher called on Rosa Inez.

Rosa Inez Martinez told the class that in Mexico, Saint Agnes was called "Saint Inez."

I think I rolled my eyes at the time, but now I would kiss her on both cheeks if I ever saw her again. Thank you, Rosa Inez Martinez. I'm sure she's an aerospace engineer at NASA or something now.

Agnes was the name of Ander Frank's first victim, on Roe Island. Agnes Clark.

Saint Agnes—or Saint Inez—is the patron saint of young girls. "Inez" is also spelled "Ynez." Frank Anderson is holed up on the *Santa Ynez*. With my daughter.

Chapter 40

DRIFTING IN THE low tendrils of fog, I peer up at the huge gray hulk of a ship before me. It rises up and nearly blots out the night sky. As the water sloshes my small boat into the side of the behemoth vessel, I put my palm out against it and feel the cold steel hull. There has to be some way to get onboard.

I miss Donovan so much. He would know how to get onboard. My stomach sinks imagining him at the hospital, maybe in surgery, maybe worse. But I can't worry about him right now. I can't help him. The only thing I can do is help Grace right now.

I paddle around the bulkhead of the ship, examining the gray body that seems to go on forever. If I'm right and Anders Frank is on board this ship with Grace, he has to have had some way to get her up that didn't involve scaling the huge chains hanging down the pointy front of the ship, where they dip into the water. It isn't until I paddle between the ship and the *Comet* beside it that I see it tucked into the shadows—a small rope hanging down the side of the ship into the water.

My small boat sloshes against the big ship as a wave rolls in.

The hulk of the *Comet* is about ten feet away, so I feel like I'm in a small canyon.

Instead of a brisk, crisp, salty ocean smell, a musty, rotten smell rises up out of the water of the bay. A light breeze carries with it the rotten cabbage smell of the refineries in the distance. If I squint, I can see the smokestacks rise like birthday candles in the darkness, flames periodically spurting out the tops.

I need to try West again. I prop the oars on the sides of the boat and fish for the phone in my pocket, looking down. Sheltering the light from my phone with one hand, I am dialing West when I notice the *Comet* is veering my way. Small ripples of waves have sent it careering toward me.

I'm right in the middle of two massive hunks of metal, and there is nothing stopping them from crushing me between them. I scramble to grab an oar to try to push the boat away. As I do, my phone slips from my hand into a small puddle of water in the bottom of my boat. The blue light is on for a second, and then it grows black. Fuck. Kneeling so I don't capsize, I hold the oar toward the smaller vessel, the *Comet*. The wood touches steel, and for a few seconds, the oar bends slightly under my weight and then releases. The prow of the boat has stopped on its own right beside me. A whoosh of air escapes me. So close. If I'd been a few feet farther down between the boats, I would've been crushed between the two masses, which are only separated by a few feet from buoys hanging over the smaller boat's deck.

If I lean one way and then the other, I can touch the *Santa Ynez* with one hand and the tip of the *Comet* with the other. Then another wave arrives, rolling the smaller ship gently away from me.

For a second I look back the way I came. Without the phone, I have no way to tell Noah West—or anyone else—where I am.

Should I head back to the shore and wait for West and his men? But I'm not certain he got my message. What if he didn't and I'd just be wasting time? Valuable time before dawn?

When I see a small light on the water—the patrol boat back at the Coast Guard station—it gives me a plan. The Channel 5 cameraman said the patrol boat makes rounds every thirty minutes. That gives me thirty minutes to find out if Anders is on this boat. Thirty minutes to sneak up on him before there is outside help.

I'll leave my little inflatable boat in the open as a signal to either West's men or the Coast Guard patrol boat. This will give me enough time to find Anders and surprise him and get Grace. I'm too afraid to cross him and not come alone. Plus coming alone is my only advantage. He thinks if I come alone, he can take me. He does not understand the extent of my desire to seek revenge on him for taking my daughter. My only advantage is him underestimating me.

Rather than wait for the *Comet* to come back on another wave, I get close enough to grab the small rope hanging off the side of the massive ship. There is no way he scaled the ship's side with this rope. Climbing up the anchor chains would be easier. So what is this rope for? I tug on it and it gives slightly, so I yank it with all my might. It gives so much that I fall back into my boat, feet up in the air, as a small rope ladder with wooden planks skitters down the side of the ship and comes to rest near the water.

My heart is pounding, and I'm certain the noise woke the dead that must haunt this graveyard. I hold my breath, peering up at the top of the ship, waiting for a head to appear overhead, looking down at me.

After a few seconds, when a giant spotlight and bullets haven't hailed down on me, I paddle closer to the ship and grab hold of the ladder. With my other hand, I reassuringly pat the gun in one trench coat pocket and the small flashlight in the other. Grabbing a rope that is tied to one of the boat's handles, I quickly knot it around the bottom of the ladder.

Peering up, the deck of the ship seems impossibly high, but thinking about Grace being up there somewhere sends an adrenaline rush through my limbs and I am seven rungs up before I even realize it.

Don't look down. My hands are cold and trembling as they clutch the rope ladder. I can feel the skin on my palms chafing and chapping on the rough rope as I continue up. The parts of my body that got wet in the bottom of the boat now feel icy cold as I climb in a breeze that is streaming in from the open ocean a few miles away.

About halfway up, my arms burn from the exertion, and I have to take a break. Looking around, I see I'm above the boat beside me and can see across its deck. No movement. Taking a deep breath, I continue on. Every once in a while I look up, expecting to see a head looking down on me, cutting the rope ladder loose, sending me plunging to my death below. But the night remains empty above me.

Finally, still riding the rush of adrenaline, my head pops above the deck. I freeze, slowly turning my head in both directions. At first I don't see it in the darkness, but then a gust of wind blows a flap up, revealing what lies beneath. It's an inflatable boat like mine, loosely covered with a tarp.

He's here.

Grace is somewhere nearby. A rush of fear and excitement and hope surges through me, making me want to leap onboard and rush to her, but I know I need to be careful. I need to move with caution and think things through. I need to think like a chess master, plotting my strategy, luring my opponent out of hiding. This time, the stakes are the highest they've ever been. My daughter. My heart walking around outside my body. I think about that invisible cord they say connects a mother and child. She's here. And she's alive. I know it.

Anders has lured me here for a reason. He obviously thinks he is smarter than me and that I am no threat. That I'm a victim.

Well, I'm no victim, Anders Frank.

With my arms trembling from fatigue and my muscles on fire, I pull myself up onto the edge of the ship and swing my legs over, landing with a soft thud on the deck.

Digging into the deep pocket of my trench coat, I slowly take out my gun. I hold it loosely at first, crouching and listening intently for any sound in the night.

I'm coming for you, Anders Frank.

This will be the last time you ever make the mistake of underestimating me.

Chapter 41

THE NIGHT IS SILENT.

I listen for any noise that might indicate Anders is around, but also signs that West and his men have found this ship. Nothing. The only sound is a seagull squawk and the distant sound of water flapping against the anchored ships.

I've come onboard at the front of the ship, a somewhat wide-open space with giant metal chains looped here and there and odd thimble-shaped protrusions as big as barrels sprouting up here and there in no seemingly logical way.

At the very front of the ship, a small gangplank-like bridge three stories up in the air connects two structures, one that must be the bridge and pilothouse, and another room, octagon shaped, with windows on nearly all sides. The captain's quarters? Toward the middle of the ship, there is a one-story area with doors and windows.

Thinking about what the Channel 5 cameraman said, about how there are some rooms with beds perfectly preserved on some of the ships, I decide to search the main deck first. A door nearby appears to lead to the bulk of the ship.

Gripping my gun in one hand and my flashlight in the other, I creep toward the door. I tug gently on the handle. It won't budge. With my fingers, I carefully feel the outline of the door. It is sealed shut. It hasn't been opened for ages. I head toward the center of the ship. Another door greets me, about twenty feet down.

I run my fingers around the edges of this one. It is not sealed. It has been opened recently. I wrap my fingers around the handle and turn, holding my breath and counting to ten so that if someone is watching the doorknob from inside, it will be difficult to tell it is moving.

When I've turned it a full rotation, I stop, holding it, and count to ten again. Then, taking the gun in my other hand, I crouch to my knees and crack the door. I open it only wide enough for the nose of the gun and one eye to peer into the darkness. It is so dark inside that I realize I'm a sitting duck if someone is there and sees the crack of light I'm letting into the dark room. If someone is there, he's biding his time and already knows I'm here, so I throw open the door, casting a door-shaped glow of faint light into the room. It is just a small hallway with stairs leading up and down. I point my tiny flashlight in both directions. Which way to go? The walls of the passageway are painted white and are lined with thick pipes and electrical boxes, also painted white. Oblong doors, about a foot off the floor, cut into the wall of the passageway every ten feet. All the oblong doors have big red wheels that open and close them, making them waterproof. I head toward a small staircase to my right. At the foot of the staircase, I wait, listening. After a few seconds of hearing nothing, I mount the stairs and enter a rectangular room.

The beam of my tiny flashlight reveals it's a mess hall. But what looks like an executive one, for the officers alone, with only a few long tables with flat bowls and utensils still scattered on them, as if a group of sailors just got up from a meal. The wallpaper is peeling, revealing green mold and streaks of red. Dim moonlight filters in from several porthole-type windows. Green chairs with bases bolted directly into the floor are coated with dirt and rust, and the floor is the same.

For a second I think I hear a small, soft sound from one of the windows, but after I freeze and strain to hear, the only noise is a gust of wind.

I leave and head back down the stairs. Moving faster now and keeping the tiny light trained ahead of me, I head down the passageway, stepping carefully through oblong doorways, the hairs on my arms standing up as I imagine the light, now bouncing around the white-painted walls, shining on Anders Frank's face. At the end of the passageway, another flight of stairs leads up.

At the top of the stairs is another oblong door, but this one is sealed. I stick my flashlight between my teeth and turn the red wheel with both hands. My arms strain with the effort, but finally the wheel stops and I push. The door opens with a tiny whoosh and reveals a smaller passageway lined with doors and a few portholes. Through the portholes, the black sky seems a bit lighter. I'm running out of time. Dawn is growing closer.

Realizing this, adrenaline shoots through me, making me feel panicky. I need to find Grace now. Find her and get back to check on Donovan. I wish I could call and find out how Donovan is. But I can't think of that. I have to focus on finding Grace. At the end of the hall is a sign that glows orange in my flashlight: ESCAPE SCUTTLE. DO NOT BLOCK.

I pause, listening for any noise. When I hear nothing, I crack the closest door, the first door to my left, flinging it open and pointing the beam of the flashlight inside. It is a tiny room with a small sink and curvy green dentist chair bolted into the ground.

Leaving the door wide open, I rush to open the next door, my flashlight darting around the room, looking for gleaming eyes that show life. Looking for Grace.

But this room is also empty. The wires and cables in the ceiling are exposed. Maps line each wood-paneled wall, and several tables back up into benches built into the walls. This time the chairs bolted into the floor are red. This must be a game room. One table, which is tipped sideways off its stand, is marked for chess, checkers, and backgammon. These rooms are all surface level, with open portholes that have exposed them to the weather and corrosion.

I rush out of that room and push open the next door, until I've glanced in all twelve. Nearly tripping, I race down a set of metal stairs at the end of the passageway that must lead to the deck below.

On this floor, the first door opens up into a giant dorm area. This deck is much more protected. There is little dirt or rust; just some dust. The dozens of yellow metal bunk beds set closely together still contain rumpled white sheets, as if a sailor only recently arose from them to start his day. A chill travels up my back and across my scalp. How many ghosts of former sailors haunt this vessel? I make the sign of the cross, and this time, I gently close the door behind me.

At the end of the hall is another door, leading up three metal steps to a smaller hallway. The first door reveals a private bedroom. Officer's quarters? This room looks untouched. Giant windows let in moonlight. But I still use my flashlight to scan it. Lamps built into the tables and nightstands seem new, although they are not. The bed, a couch, a line of dressers, a vanity in front of a large mirror are attached to the walls, while a chair in front of the vanity and a small coffee table with dusty magazines is bolted to the floor. A small doorway shows a tiny bathroom. This floor must contain officers' quarters.

Realizing this, I hold my breath. If Frank is on this ship, he's probably nearby. If he lives on this ship or is staying here, he's most likely in one of these luxury suites.

I strain to hear anything in the silence but only hear the distant creak of the ship pulling at the chains that hold it to the ship next door as the waves pull them slightly apart. I can almost feel him. My fingers tingle. Grace is close. I am close.

A search of the other officers' quarters is futile until I throw open the door at the farthest end of the hallway. My heart races when the beam of my flashlight shines on two couches made into beds, each with sleeping bags spread upon them. A small counter holds bottles of water and boxes of crackers and cans of soup. I rush over and lay my hands flat on the sleeping bags, first one, then the other. The heat still radiates slightly from the down filling. They were here. I stop myself from screaming her name.

Shining the flashlight around the room, I see chess pieces set up on a small table marked with a chessboard. Only three pieces remain on the board. A black king, a white pawn, and a white queen. Frank, Grace, and me. I study the board. He left this for me to find. The white queen is in the center of the board, while the black king and white pawn are on one end.

If this chessboard were a ship and we were the pieces, I'm in the middle, and Frank and Grace are at the very front of the ship. The captain's quarters. The pilot and bridge.

I race into the hall and up the metal stairs, not worrying about the noise. It's only when I fling the door open to the fresh air that I take a minute to think. I jerk my head around. There. Up high is a room with windows on nearly all sides. It is connected to the bridge by a small walkway. That has to be the captain's quarters.

I swivel my head in both directions. That's when I see it. Off to the right is a small winding metal staircase. It has a chain across it. That is where I need to go to get to the captain's quarters. That is where he is waiting for me. I stare at the black windows.

A cloud passes over the full moon and the night grows even darker, but as it passes and the moonlight streams back down, I see something shadowy pass in front of the windows. Something even darker than the dark. He's there.

Chapter 42

THE FOG HAS crawled its way up the sides of the ship from the water below. A billowing stream of it floats across the deck at eye level between the captain's quarters and me. It will help conceal my stealthy trek to the stairway. I'm pretty sure that spiral staircase is the only way up to the captain's quarters. It was designed to keep the captain safe. Who knows when some rogue sailor would go crazy after months at sea and decide it would be a good idea to kill the captain of the ship?

I creep through the fog at a crouch, keeping one eye on the windows of the captain's quarters to see if there is movement or light. I'm not sure, but as I grow closer it seems like there might be a faint pinprick of light darting around inside. Then I see it for sure. A dancing sphere of light bouncing around the dark room. I blink, trying to focus, but don't see it again.

He wants me to know he is there.

My heart is screaming for Grace. It takes all my willpower to stop myself from running blindly up the stairs and crashing through that door with my gun drawn. It can't be that easy. He knows I'm coming. He's been waiting for me.

At the foot of the stairs, I peer up. From where I am, I can't see the windows, which means he can't see me. I hear the slightest thud and freeze, blood racing to my temples. Is he hurting her? Again, it takes everything I have not to rush up the stairs. Instead, I hunch over, crouching until my head grows level with the metal platform that leads to the bridge.

The captain's quarters are across that platform, on the opposite side. But traversing that gangplank-like pathway makes me a sitting duck. I'm not sure I have a choice, though.

I hug the walls of the bridge and peer into the dusty window. In the dim moonlight, I can see the room is empty. I glance at the eastern horizon. Good God, the sky is getting lighter. There is a slight tinge of color in the distance. Dawn is coming.

My heart throbs in my ears. I'm running out of time. I can't go inside the captain's quarters. He wants me to go. That's why he let me see the light. It's a trap and I know it. If I'm dead, I won't be able to save Grace. He wants us both dead.

I need to lure him out of the captain's quarters before he hurts Grace. He shot Donovan, so I know he has a gun. Thinking of Donovan sends another wave of panic through my chest. *Get Grace.* He told me to get our daughter.

I'm counting on Anders Frank underestimating me. My only choice is to show myself. I have to do it. As the light rises on the horizon even more, I know I'm running out of time.

Where is West and his men? With a sinking feeling I realize he might never have received my voice messages. Right now I could sure use a sheriff's helicopter with a tactical team landing on the ship's deck.

But I'm also scared to death of that happening. What if the troops storm the ship and Frank panics and hurts Grace?

My advantage, what Anders Frank may not realize, is that I'm willing to die so my daughter doesn't. This is what I have to use to my advantage.

I take a deep breath and walk to the edge of the gangplank, eyes straight ahead on the captain's quarters.

"I'm here. Is this what you want?" The wind takes my words and swirls them away, but I know he can hear me. I can almost feel him listening to me across the way. "I'm here now, playing your game. Just like you wanted. Now, give me my daughter."

I wait, holding my breath, bracing myself for the shock of a bullet or, worse, the sound of a blast coming from across the way where he is. But there is nothing but silence.

I'm staring at the bank of windows in the captain's quarters, searching for any movement in the darkness. I'm waiting and watching, when a small white face appears in the lower corner of a window. I gasp and scream her name, "Grace!" I'm already two steps forward when I see the look on her face and her small pink mouth forms a big O. She has her palm on the glass window as she mouths, *No* and looks behind me with terror.

For a second that seems to spin off into eternity, I take in my daughter's face. During this warped time, I am so filled with both terror and joy that I can't move. I know I should run or duck or sidestep whatever Grace sees behind me, but for a split second, just like on that beach, my limbs are frozen with fear. But I instantly shake it off. Not this time. Looking at Grace's little face in the window, I'm filled with a burst of adrenaline and hope. My daughter is alive. I have everything in the world to live for. This time I won't let my fear take over.

Chapter 43

KEEPING MY EYES on Grace, I fling myself to the side and down, but not before I feel searing pain in my shoulder. The white pain cripples me for a second, bringing me to my knees.

"Don't try to run," Frank's nasally voice hisses behind me. "I'm not done with you yet."

I try to roll away from him, but he takes his forearm and loops it around my head, pressing against my neck. My shoulder screams in pain at the same time I struggle to breathe against the pressure he has against my throat. With his arm around my windpipe and his knee in my back, he pats down the pockets of my trench coat and feels the gun. Then the weight of his hand and the gun is gone.

I gasp for air as he removes his arm from my neck and yanks me to my feet. The hilt of a knife is pressed against my throat. Then I see her. Grace stands at the other edge of the gangplank in a dirty white dress and bare feet.

"Mama?" Her lower lip is trembling.

"Grace. You have to listen to me very carefully. Go back into that room and go in the bathroom and lock the door until I . . . until a policeman comes to get you. Go now."

She looks at me uncertainly but takes one step backward, eyeing the knife that Frank now holds to my throat. "Mama? Are you hurt?"

I don't think the stab wound in my shoulder went very deep, or I'd feel dizzy from blood loss. And the white-hot pain has disappeared. "No. You need to go back inside right now."

Grace looks at me and her face scrunches up. "Mama, I don't want to go back in there. I want to be with you."

"That's right, Grace," Frank says with his head resting on my shoulder, slightly rotating the hilt of the knife against my throat. "Come on over here and see your mama. I told you she would come, didn't I? Come see her now." As he says this, I smell that cologne smell I caught on the beach during the vigil and now know why I recognized it. It was how he smelled the first time I saw him on the beach when he approached Grace. Now it is mixed with an unwashed sour smell.

Grace takes three steps forward, coming onto the gangplank, drawing closer.

He leans down and whispers in my ear, "Tell her to come over here and I won't slit your throat in front of your daughter."

"No, Grace. Go back now." I keep my voice firm and confident with authority so she will do as I say.

He holds the hilt of the knife tighter against my windpipe, making it hard to breathe.

"Grace," he says in a low growl, "you know what will happen to your mother if you do what she says instead of what I say, right? We talked about this already, didn't we?"

Grace nods. Tears drip down her face. She takes another step toward us.

"He's lying, Grace." It's hard to talk. "You know that nobody messes with a Giovanni. He knows better than to hurt me. He knows he will pay." My words, more a threat to him than a message to Grace, are raspy from the pressure on my throat. "No matter what happens here, you need to go hide in that bathroom. Your papa and uncles and Nana would want you to do this. You know I'm telling the truth."

Where is Agent West? I move my head, casting a glance to the side. Is he even coming? What if he never got my messages?

"You expecting someone?"

"Maybe."

"You're lying." He digs his knee into my back again.

"Go, Grace, now. Do as Mama says. Go lock yourself inside there. Whatever you do, don't open the door to this man. Promise? Promise?"

She looks uncertain. "Mama, I *have* to come so he doesn't hurt you. He said." She takes another step toward us.

Panic floods me. I'm losing her. "Grace, *e` un uomo cattivo. Lui mente. Scappa via subito!!*" He is a bad man. He lies. Run away now!

"Speak fucking English," he says, kneeing me hard in my kidney so I gasp.

But Grace understands. She nods, tears streaking her face, and steps backward until her back hits the building. Then she turns and runs. "Good girl." Every muscle in my body relaxes. Even if I die right now, Noah West will find Grace. She won't open the door to Frank. As soon as I relax, my shoulder begins to throb in pain, some type of weird delayed reaction.

"It doesn't matter. She will die anyway. I will leave her here to starve," Frank says.

"Let my daughter go. I'll do anything you want if you just let her off this ship. You can kill me and escape. Just spare her life."

"There is no bargaining," he says. I feel his breath near my ear. He has his body pressed up against me, and it sends a shudder of revulsion through me. "You can beg. It won't do you any good. That defeats the whole purpose."

"What purpose?"

"Your death."

"Why?" I don't care why. I just need to stall him until West and his men arrive or I figure out a way to get out of this situation.

"I got in touch with my dad again after my first kill," Frank says, his voice a sour whisper by my ear. "It was sort of an accident. I didn't really mean for her to die. After my mom died, I was drinking a lot. I'd picked this woman up at a bar just for sex. Nothing else. But she didn't want to have sex, and we argued over it when I tried to unbutton her blouse. I pushed her, and she fell and hit her head. I panicked and dumped her body in the Delta in a sea bag with rocks, probably somewhere in the water below right now. And that's when I realized, that's when I finally understood my father and his needs and desires. I was just like him. I had never wanted to admit it, but after my first kill, I realized he couldn't help it.

"Later, when I found him, he told me everything about his life." Anders shifts, and I wonder if I can use my heel to take out his knees. If only he loosens the grip on the knife hilt a little bit. "He told me what he did to your sister. He said it was her fault. She tempted him. He'd never touched a kid before. He had to kill her so he didn't get caught. She would've told on him for sure."

A wave of dizziness seizes me at his words. *Pull it together, Giovanni, keep him talking.*

"I confessed to my dad what I'd done—killing that girl—and he absolved me. He told me we couldn't help it. It was in our blood. He told me all about how he denied that side of himself until that day he was driving down the road and saw your sister out in front of your house alone. It was like a message for him. He knew when he took her that there was no going back. He tried to deny it. He came home a week later and tried to pretend that nothing was going on, but my mom was onto him, he said, so he had to leave."

His words send sour acid flooding my stomach. He just randomly picked my sister off our street and ruined all of our lives. On a whim. By a fluke because he happened to be driving down our road and saw her alone. Because I fucking had to brush my teeth before I went outside that day.

I try to focus on Frank's words. Now that he's started, he is on a roll.

"You ruined my life, so I wanted to return the favor. I work for the college system, and it wasn't easy finding a girl named Agnes. I called the bodies in to the Rosarito police station so your cop boyfriend would find them and see the Bible verses. I wanted you to know they were for you and you alone."

"How have I ruined your life?" My voice verges on hysterics as I look at the lightening sky, praying for the sound of helicopter blades to carry across the water.

"My father is dead because of you."

"That's absurd." I nearly spit the words out. "As much as I wish I had killed him, his blood is not on my hands."

"My father stopped being my dad the day he took your sister. After that, he could never go back. He could never again contain his impulses, his needs. It ruined my life. I was only four years old. Up until then my life was perfect. I don't have a lot of memories of my dad, since he left when I was so young, and I blame you for that, too, but I do remember that he took one whole week off work during the summer to build me a swing set in the backyard. He was my dad, all mine, until your sister came along." His breath with its foul stench is hot on my neck now. "He left and I never saw him again until three years ago. I spent a year with him trying to make up for lost time before he died. I blame you. I blame your sister for leading him astray in the first place."

I clench my fists in fury.

"Fuck you. My sister was an innocent little girl playing jump rope in our front yard when your father, a fucking perverted monster, took her and then left her dead like so much garbage. Your father is rotting in hell right now."

I close my eyes for a few seconds. I need to keep him talking until West and his men arrive. The first small shimmer of light is rising on the horizon to our right. He must notice the slight turn of my head, because he sneers in my ear.

"As soon as the sun arises on the horizon, I'm slitting your throat. You will be my blood sacrifice."

I need to keep him talking while I figure out how to escape. Right now, with the hilt of the knife pressed against my throat and his body pressed against my back, I am unable to get into any position to fight back.

"How did you find your father? The police and FBI have been looking for him for years."

"It wasn't easy," he said, shifting from one foot to the other. The grip on the knife hilt does not lessen, but I don't feel his body pressed as closely against mine as it was. I keep my eyes on the windows of the captain's quarters. *Focus on escaping and getting Grace.*

"My uncle finally told me. He'd been afraid to tell me when my mom was alive. She didn't want me to even know my dad was still alive.

"The first time I saw him he showed me the e-mails he sent you. He said you were the reason he was living in a dump, living like a dog, hiding out from the FBI under a fake name. Because of you. He was fine for a while, but then he came home one day and his lady told him some FBI-looking dude had been snooping around. He had to quit his job. He had to get a fake ID. He had to go into hiding. When I saw him, he was really sick, he had tuberculosis and couldn't even fucking go to the hospital for treatment because of you. He couldn't get a Social Security number, so he couldn't work and couldn't get health insurance."

"None of that is my fault." If I can only get him to back up a little, I can maneuver and use my heel to kick his groin or foot or calf.

"I'll tell you what *is* your fault," he says, drawing back a little bit from me—but not enough—and spitting on the gangplank. "After my whole life wishing I had a dad, I finally found him but only got to be with him one year because of you. He didn't need to die. People can live with TB if they get meds. He said he'd rather die than risk exposure and go back to prison. So he did. He died. He didn't have to die. If you hadn't brought in the FBI and turned up the heat on him, he could've lived the rest of his life in peace."

"You are talking nonsense," I say, shooting a glance to my side. I don't think anybody is coming to help. I'm on my own. I need to make a plan.

At that moment, the very tip of the sun breaks the horizon.

"Better say your prayers. Your seconds are numbered now," he says in his nasally voice, which has suddenly become wobbly.

Is he afraid to kill me in cold blood like this? Remembering the women he strangled, I doubt it.

"Killing you will not only help me seek revenge for my father, it will help me fulfill my need. Because that is what killing has become. A need. You understand that, don't you? You may not realize it, but you are just like me. You got a taste. You know what I mean."

"I'm not like you." *I'm a loving mother. I'm a normal, functioning member of society. I'm a good person.* "You are the spawn of the devil and a pervert."

"I'm not a pervert."

"Grace is five years old," I say, spittle flying out with the force of my words.

"I'm not like him. I didn't touch her."

Relief overcomes me so much that I sag until he catches me and jerks me to a standing position. My shoulder is now howling in pain. At the same time, my insides are filled with acidlike fury. Grace might have escaped this family's perversions, but Caterina didn't. I fight back images of his father with my sister. I can't go there. Not right now.

"You should've recognized me that day on the beach," he says. "You should've known what I was."

Not *who* he was. *What* he was. A killer.

He's right. I dismissed my intuition as paranoia. I ignored that warning that sang through my blood. Never again. Time is running out. It's now or never.

Chapter 44

ANDERS FRANK WRAPS his arm around my neck. I don't feel the pressure of the knife anymore, and there is some space between us. Now is my chance. I lift my foot and shove my heel into his crotch at the same time my opposite elbow arches back into his gut. He releases his hold on my neck, but before I can turn, he punches me in the lower back. I double over in pain and fly forward as the knife goes skittering off the gangplank, landing with an echoing, metallic ring on the deck below. I land on my stomach on the gangplank, one leg over the side underneath the lowest rail. I slip, and for a second, I'm half on and half off the cold steel. I could easily slide under this rail, which is two feet off the gangplank.

For a few seconds I eye the deck of the ship about three stories below. If I land right on my feet with my knees bent, I might not break my legs and will be able to run away before he can make it down there. If I land wrong? A whole different story. But I'm not leaving without Grace. I roll over to the middle of the cold metal gangplank, seeing between slit eyelids that Frank is pointing a gun at me. I keep my eyes closed and give a loud groan. For two reasons. To give myself time to stall and think of a plan to disarm him. I am like the mama bird that pretends she has a broken wing to draw the predator away from her babies in the nest.

From under my eyelashes I watch his reaction.

"Not yet. The sun isn't up yet," he says.

Then he mutters under his breath. "She couldn't have lost that much blood."

He paces, holding the gun now as I watch him through the slits of my eyelids. The gun hangs down by his side. Every once in a while he lifts it and points it toward me. As he speaks, he takes his other hand and rubs his palm on his jeans, a nervous habit I remember from the beach. The way he holds the gun—loosely in one hand—gives me hope. He's an amateur. That's probably why Donovan is alive right now. A one-handed shot can veer off target very easily.

"Before you die, you are going to see your little girl die. Actually, I don't care if you die at all. Maybe it is better you live with the pain of her death. An eye for an eye. Your kid for my dad."

I moan, so low I worry he can't hear, but hoping that he will think that it would be louder if I was faking it. I barely hear it, but I tense slightly when he lifts the gun toward me. He's going to shoot me. Now? After all this?

"Get the fuck up."

The gunshot is deafening, but I'm not hit. I felt the whiz of the gun a few feet away. He's trying to scare me, but he's blown it. Now Noah West and his crew will know exactly where we are.

He realizes this. "Shit! All bets are off, lady. We've got about ten minutes before the patrol boat makes its way over here to investigate. I have one last thing I want you to see before you die. Get up."

It takes all my willpower to stay flat on my back. Unless he comes closer, I'll lose this entire game. So I keep my eyes slitted and wait and watch.

"Ah, hell," he says, leaning over. At the last moment, he reaches for me with the gun still in one hand. I think he's going to shoot me for real this time, but he reaches down and grasps both of my shoulders. I gasp in pain when he touches my wounded shoulder. At the same time, I rear my head up with every ounce of my being and head butt him, our foreheads smacking so hard for a second that I see stars. But he receives the worst of it, and he groans and rolls off me onto his side on the metal gangplank. The gun lies beside him.

I have an instant raging headache, but I manage to crawl onto all fours and scramble for the gun. I grab it at the same time he does. His hands are gripping mine, his fingernails digging into my skin, drawing blood, but I yank myself away and am up on my feet, pointing the gun at him before he can roll over.

"Don't fucking move."

He looks up at me and starts to laugh, but I also notice he doesn't budge an inch.

"You won't shoot me."

"Try me." I grit the words out, and his eyes narrow. "You already said I'm a killer just like you."

But unlike him, I know how to hold and shoot a gun like a motherfucker. I stand with my legs spread apart, my right hand gripping the gun as high as possible under the trigger guard to prevent slippage and recoil. My left hand is wrapped around the other side of the weapon at a forty-five-degree angle, filling in the gap on that side of the grip. The gun is in line with my elbows, straight ahead, and both my thumbs are pointed toward my target—Frank.

I'm feeling dizzy. Between the head butt and blood loss from my shoulder, I'm not sure how long I can hold him at gunpoint. I need to keep him talking and distracted, because West's men have to be here soon. I only have one more question for him.

"Why did you kill Michael Dillman?"

His face scrunches in confusion for a second, and then recognition sets in. "You mean that kid at the weekly? He called me. Thought we should meet. So I met him."

Oh, Michael. He was trying to get a scoop and help find Grace.

Then I hear a sound behind me.

"Mama?"

Grace.

Without thinking, I react on instinct and glance back. That is the break he was waiting for. With one swift slide and kick, he has swept my feet out from under me, and I land on my back. The gun goes tumbling off the edge of the gangplank. He's on top of me now and pulls me up, my shoulder screaming in pain.

Once we are standing, he grabs me from behind, grasping my neck, choking me.

I jam my heel in a stomp kick on the top of his foot where it meets the leg. The crunching sound of the bones in his foot breaking combines with his scream, and he instinctively releases me from his chokehold. At the same time, I elbow him with the opposite arm, making contact with something hard. Hopefully, his ribs this time.

I turn, and my punch to his gut connects. The force sends him prone, then into a slide on the slippery deck, where he plunges off the edge of the gangplank, slipping under the bottom rail. He manages to grasp the edge with the fingertips of one hand. I lean over the lowest rail to brace myself, then I reach down, grabbing his forearm, my nails digging into his flesh. I have hold of his arm with both hands and am pulling on it. It is pure instinct. So is what I say: "Give me your other hand."

His other hand is flailing wildly, trying to reach the rail, which is too high. My hand is only a few inches from his. My body is braced on the lower rail so his weight can't pull me down with him.

"Reach up."

But he shakes his head. His arctic blue eyes bore into me. There is nothing human I can see in them.

"You'll let me drop," he says.

For a split second the temptation is nearly too strong to resist. He's right. I have sworn to kill him. I can tell by the look in his eyes he knows this. If I pull him up, he's still going to go after me. If I let him go, Grace and I have a chance to escape.

As a woman holding the fate of the man who kidnapped her child, I want vengeance. As a mother, I want mercy.

"No, I won't let go," I say firmly. "Give me your other hand. Let me help you up."

He looks at me with a smirk in his bestial eyes. Then his fingernails slide down my arm, drawing blood in long rivulets as they go, until his fingertips graze my own and he is free-falling. For a second, it is as if time is suspended. His arms paddle wildly in the air as he tries to right himself and fall feet first, but he doesn't have time. For a split second he meets my eyes, and I whisper, unsure if he can even hear me.

"You're wrong. I'm not like you."

And then there is a sickening thud as his skull hits the metal deck below.

At nearly the same time, I see a dozen heads pop up on the

sides of the ship, and within seconds, bodies hurdle over the edge. Noah West's team is here. West rushes to Frank's body, checks his pulse, looks up at me, and slowly nods.

I turn and am already running toward the captain's quarters when I see Grace's little face in the window. I freeze, staring at her. She was watching. There is something in her eyes I never saw in Caterina's eyes. A fierceness of will. My daughter is a survivor. Not that it is Caterina's fault that she died. But when I look at Grace, I sense a strength in her that makes me look at her in wonder. She is not a victim. No matter what happened during those six days, she will be okay.

And then she puts her palm up on the window and smiles.

That smile nearly sends me to my knees. But I race toward her, smiling and crying all at once.

"Donovan? There's somebody here who wants to speak to you."

"Hi, Daddy." Even though Grace is holding West's phone, I can hear Donovan sharply inhale at the same time a sob escapes from his mouth.

I listen to her with my eyes closed, my fingers wrapped around her tiny hand.

"I miss you, Daddy. I want to go home."

We wait on the gangplank for them to bring a tarp to cover Frank's body before we go down to the deck, where a helicopter is waiting to rush us to San Francisco General. They will check Grace out, look at my shoulder, and let us see Donovan. He's recovering from surgery. The round missed all his vital organs. They said he's doing great.

"Mama, look."

I turn just as the sun peeks over the horizon, bathing the sky in pinks and oranges. Grace is in front of me and I hold her shoulders, trying not to hold on too tightly even though I want to pick her up and bury my face in her curls and never let her go again.

But instead, we stand, Grace and I, facing the sunrise as the wind blows my hair back from my face in a stream, making the sides of my trench coat flap back behind me like wings.

Chapter 45

An emergency room doctor put eight stitches in my left shoulder. Marco pulled some strings and got Grace in Donovan's room, though I don't know how he did it. The nurse is going to set up a cot between the two of them, but I would've slept on the floor. There is no way I'm not being with my family tonight.

Her pediatrician came to visit her here. He says she's doing pretty good and that it will be okay for her to stay in Donovan's room overnight for observation. They had initially put her on an IV, saying she was dehydrated and malnourished from her ordeal, but she wasn't on one for long.

Every once in a while, she grows quiet and distant, withdrawing inside herself. I try not to let her see the anguish I feel. Instead, I hold her hand and tell her I love her and make silly jokes until she comes back to me, her eyes focusing on me again and a smile playing at the corners of her lips. We've kept the darkness at bay for now. And I am still in awe of the look I saw in her eyes on board that ship. She's a survivor.

One day, I know I will ask her to tell me what it was like during those six days. For now, I'm just going to concentrate on celebrating that she is alive.

The hospital room is filled with family. My mother, brothers, sisters-in-law, cousins, aunts, and uncles. Most people brought something to eat. My aunt Lena brought a huge pan of lasagna and paper plates. Everyone is laughing and crying and shouting and eating.

It is just like a Sunday at Nana's, except we are all jam-packed in a small hospital room.

The Saint is here, too. He has his henchmen stationed outside the hospital room, even though I told him it wasn't necessary. He's talking to my mom, and she's laughing and blushing, which makes me do a double take. Her boyfriend died a few years ago, and she hasn't dated since. I watch them for a few seconds until Donovan catches my eye and winks. Then he shrugs. I shrug, too.

L'amore vince sempre. Love conquers all.

When the bottle of wine and Dixie cups get passed my way, I take a big slug. Why not? It's a celebration. A celebration of life. I scoot over to Donovan's bedside. A circle of more than a dozen cousins surrounds Grace's bed, and she is laughing and having too much fun for her mother to intrude. Besides, I don't want anything to quell the sweet music of her laughter.

But not everyone is enjoying the festivities. An exasperated nurse has just checked Donovan's vitals and is making huffing noises that I suspect has nothing to do with his monitors.

"Would you like some lasagna?" I ask.

"No, thank you." Her voice is clipped.

"I'm sorry for the noise and commotion. We're Italian," I say, as if that is enough.

She purses her lips together and squeezes out of the room.

My grandmother is sitting in a chair near the window. I make my way through the crowd and kneel beside her. "I love you, Nana."

She pats my hand resting on the chair. She juts her chin toward where my mother sits with Vincenzo Santangelo. "I never let her date a Santangelo in high school," my grandmother says, and her chin bobs up and down, as if she is agreeing with herself. "And believe me, this one, he tried. He never gave up, did he?" she asks, looking at Vincenzo Santangelo and my mother, heads close together, laughing. "I think maybe she is old enough now to decide on her own."

I laugh. "I think so, too, Nana."

After leaning down and kissing my grandmother on her cheek, I go sit on the edge of Donovan's bed and hold his hand as he speaks to my uncle Dominic about the San Francisco Giants, of all things. But better than talking about the past week of our lives, I suppose.

A newspaper is sitting on the bedside table. It's my paper, the *Bay Herald*. Working at the paper seems like another life after what has happened. I pick up the paper and flip through it. Nicole wrote about the murder of the weekly reporter kid, Michael Dillman. Lopez found a picture he must have taken of the kid at the fire. The house with flames coming out the windows looms in the background spectacularly, and in the forefront stands Michael Dillman, his brow furrowed. He looks intense. He looks determined. He looks like a true journalist.

I tuck the page into my bag. I will go visit his family. I will tell them what he did and how he helped me find my daughter. I will both lie and tell the truth. I will lie and say he was just offered a job at our newspaper. And I will tell the truth—that he was a real journalist.

Watching my family crammed in this small room, laughing and eating and talking, I'm filled with hope and love and gratefulness. I refill my Dixie cup, make the sign of the cross, and sip my wine.

Chapter 46

DONOVAN AND I stand with our arms wrapped around each other, watching Grace race up and down the beach with her new dog, Dylan.

Dylan is a German shepherd K9 who retired after his leg was injured in Iraq. I've already taught Grace the commands to order him to attack if anyone ever bothers her.

Other than that, we have tried not to change our life too much.

Grace is back at kindergarten.

Today, we are at the beach gauging Grace's reaction to the place where she was abducted. She is having so much fun with Dylan that I relax. I can feel Donovan do the same. Her belly laugh rides on the wind, across the sandy beach, back to us, making Donovan squeeze my hand.

He lets go of my hand for a second and stands behind me, putting his arms around my waist and his chin on my shoulder as we watch the sun sink lower on the horizon.

"Grace, it's almost time," Donovan calls, and she stops, standing still, her tiny body facing west. She keeps her hand on Dylan's fur, stroking him absentmindedly, staring at the sun.

Donovan presses something into my hand. I glance down. It's the black velvet box. He pops it open, and the ring inside sparkles with the last rays of the setting sun.

"Look, Mama and Papa!" Grace shouts.

As the sun dips into the water, we see it, the green flash.

At that moment, I know. I'm ready. I know my answer with every fiber of my being. With Donovan's arms wrapped around me and his breath in my ear, I whisper one word:

"Yes."

Acknowledgments

A giant thank you to my readers. Every day, I'm grateful that people want to read my books.

Thanks to the members of my stellar writing group, Supergroup, for their keen feedback, constant inspiration, and steadfast friendship: Kate Schultz, Jana Otto, Sarah Hanley, Kaethe Schwehn, Sean Beggs, and Coralee Grebe.

I'm grateful to Sam Bohrman, who is on maternity leave from the Back Room Writers, and is one of my most trusted early readers. Thank you also to Sam's father, Brian Tschida, for his neurological expertise. Thanks to the rest of the Back Room writers for answering obscure questions I throw out, in particular my *paesana*, Cristina Pippa, and her father, Nino Pippa, for answering some questions about Italian traditions, and to Bruce Campbell for martial arts information. Also big thanks to Frida Tosi for helping me make sure my Italian was correct. If it's not, it's because I didn't ask her about that particular part.

Thank you to Pat and Gary at Once Upon a Crime for their

support and encouragement. They will be greatly missed in this mystery community.

I'm so grateful for all the support, enthusiasm, and encouragement from my *paesanos*: Emily Goehner, Mimi Ryan, Taloo Carrillo, Liz and Doug Cronk, Kari Isaacson, Vickie Johnson, Rebecca Peterson, Terry Welch, John T. Bychowski, Mikki Ashe, David Chilimidos, Anissa Kennedy, and Dan Koopmans.

A special thanks to Beverly Belcamino for her donation to an organization dear to my heart, The National Center for Missing & Exploited Children.

Thanks to Minneapolis Police Sergeant Bob Dale for police procedural questions.

Lots of love and thanks to so many members of this mystery tribe. I won't be able to name everyone, but some off the top of my head are Dan and Kate Malmon, Jon and Ruth Jordan, Erin Mitchell, Dru Ann Love, Kristopher Zgorski, BOLO books, Elise Cooper, Quinton Skinner, Jeremy Nelson, and Wilson Webb at Minnesota Monthly. Thanks to valuable early readers and reviewers, including Dick Barbuto and John Kurtze.

Thank you to the fine people at HarperCollins, including my editor, Emily Krump; publicists Maria Silva and Danielle Bartlett; the super savvy Dana Trombley; and Judy G., who copyedited this book so carefully.

Thank you to my agent, Stacey Glick.

And as always, a big thank you to my husband and two fierce daughters, who are my everything.

About the Author

KRISTI BELCAMINO is a writer, photographer, and artist. In her former life as a newspaper crime reporter in California, she flew over Big Sur in an F/A-18 jet with the Blue Angels, raced a Dodge Viper at Laguna Seca, watched autopsies, and interviewed serial killers. She is now a journalist based in Minneapolis, and the Gabriella Giovanni mysteries are her first books. Friend Kristi at www.facebook.com/kristibelcaminowriter or follow her on Twitter @KristiBelcamino.

www.facebook.com/kristibelcaminowriter
www.witnessimpulse.com
@KristiBelcamino

Discover great authors, exclusive offers, and more at hc.com.